"I want you to marry me."

Kieran recoiled as she spoke. There was no other word for it. He even took a step backward, as if she'd hit him.

"Marry you?"

"Yes. You don't need to look so stunned. That's frequently what people do in situations like this."

"But—" He undid the top button of his shirt, as though he suddenly wasn't able to get enough air into his lungs. "Those people have relationships. They know each other well, have a history, have plans for a future. They're usually in—"

"In love." Her voice cracked, and she tightened her throat to avoid breaking down. "I know. It's awkward. I wish being in love were a requirement for making babies, but apparently it isn't. Apparently even people who have an utterly meaningless one-night encounter can still end up pregnant."

Dear Reader,

If you're human, it's impossible to escape being labeled. From the moment the nurses tape your name on your hospital bassinet, you've got one—and as life goes on, you'll accumulate more and more. Good child, bad child, smart one, lazy one. Coward, prom king, egghead, jock.

The problem is that labels never fit quite right. Jocks read books; eggheads run marathons. The "good child" stumbles, and the "bad child" helps him up. Each individual is an ever-changing kaleidoscope of often-contradictory traits.

For the sons of Anderson McClintock, an arrogant millionaire with an explosive temper, five ex-wives and a Shenandoah Valley town he called his own, the labels came early in life. And they've been almost impossible to shake. Kieran, the Saint. Bryce, the Sinner. And Tyler, the Stranger. Bryce and Tyler got out early, wanting only to escape the eccentric little town of Heyday, their tangled heritage and the smothering labels. Only St. Kieran remained to befriend his difficult father, and to become the struggling town's official hero.

But sooner or later something always comes along and knocks the halo off the hero. For Kieran, that something is Claire Strickland. Claire may be the only person in Heyday who knows the truth about Kieran—the only person who knows there's a little bit of sinner in the heart of every saint. Welcome to Heyday—and to the heroes who unexpectedly find love, forgiveness and family here. I hope you enjoy your stay!

Warmly,

Kathleen O'Brien

P.S. I love to hear from readers! Write me at P.O. Box 947633, Maitland, FL, 32794-7633. Or visit my Web site at KathleenOBrien.net.

The Saint
Kathleen O'Brien

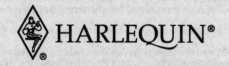

HARLEQUIN®

TORONTO • NEW YORK • LONDON
AMSTERDAM • PARIS • SYDNEY • HAMBURG
STOCKHOLM • ATHENS • TOKYO • MILAN • MADRID
PRAGUE • WARSAW • BUDAPEST • AUCKLAND

ISBN 0-373-71231-6

THE SAINT

Books by Kathleen O'Brien

HARLEQUIN SUPERROMANCE

HARLEQUIN SINGLE TITLE

Don't miss any of our special offers. Write to us at the
following address for information on our newest releases.

Harlequin Reader Service
U.S.: 3010 Walden Ave., P.O. Box 1325, Buffalo, NY 14269
Canadian: P.O. Box 609, Fort Erie, Ont. L2A 5X3

CHAPTER ONE

CLAIRE HAD ALREADY WARNED Steve six times that he was going to be late, so she bit back the seventh as she heard him come shuffling down the stairs, yawning and scratching his bare chest.

"Morning," she said, stifling an answering yawn herself. She hated football practice mornings. Five-thirty was just too darn early for human beings to be awake, much less bashing each other around on the football field. The sky outside her kitchen window was still black. She couldn't even see the apple tree, which was no more than ten feet away.

"Mmlng," Steve mumbled pleasantly as he entered the kitchen, squinting against the bright overhead light. She wasn't sure he'd had any sleep at all last night. She'd heard him still up at three, talking on the telephone to Michelle, his new girlfriend. He'd sounded so stupid and sweet she hadn't had the heart to break it up.

But he'd pay for it today. He wasn't naturally an early riser. Left to his own devices, like most teenagers, he'd sleep till midafternoon. She yawned again. Once, back when they were kids, they had both loved to sleep late. But she hadn't had that luxury in years. Not since their mother died.

As Steve slouched into the kitchen, she pulled out his chair, which he promptly used to stash his heavy backpack. He always ate standing up. Even very sleepy seventeen-year-old boys were too full of energy to sit. She felt sorry for his teachers.

"The pancakes are getting cold." That was really the seventh warning, of course, but it sounded better than "damn it, Steve, step on it, for heaven's sake," which was what she wanted to say.

Or did she? Setting a glass of milk on the table, she took a deep breath and tried to find her perspective. Maybe she was just nagging because she was exhausted and resented getting up an hour early to see him off to football practice.

Or maybe she was a little bitter because he still walked and talked and slept like a kid, while she could hardly remember what that kind of freedom felt like.

But that wasn't fair. Allowing Steve to finish out a normal childhood had been her choice. And besides, she didn't care if he was late for football practice, anyhow. In fact, if he got booted off the team altogether, it would suit her just fine.

That, however, was about as likely as snow in July. The Heyday High School Fighting Zebras were one win away from the state championship, and Coach McClintock would never risk losing his star quarterback now. Steve could probably show up late, doze off during push-ups and make paper airplanes out of the playbook without causing his coach to bat an eye.

And the little rascal knew it, too. She watched him pull a grungy T-shirt over his head, his curly brown hair emerging from the neckline even more tousled than before, if that was possible. Aware of her disapproving scrutiny, he grinned and ran his fingers through it.

"Sorry, officer," he said. "I didn't know the hair police would be here. I left my comb upstairs."

He was waking up, she saw. And, as usual, waking up sassy. He was so damn cute, that was his problem. She reached out and yanked the curl that dangled farthest down his broad forehead.

"Ouch," he said. But he didn't mean it.

Standing close to him like this, she realized he was wearing a ton of cologne. He smelled as if he'd bathed in the stuff. It seemed odd, given that he was headed out to run around in the mud, until she remembered that Michelle sometimes stopped by the football field to sneak in a few quick kisses before practice.

"The pancakes," she repeated slowly, as if he didn't speak good English, "are getting cold."

"Yum." Steve grabbed the top one off the stack and, holding it in his big fist, munched on it as if it were a piece of dry toast. "I love cold pancakes."

She turned back to the stove, hiding her smile. He probably did. He loved everything. He'd probably eat the box the pancake mix had come in, which was a good thing, because she hadn't ever learned to cook very well.

"So did you finish your English paper?"

The silence that followed her question was ominous. She could hear Steve chewing earnestly, and when she looked, he was studying the front page of the newspaper as if he held a doctorate in foreign affairs.

"Oh, Steve, no. *No.* Don't tell me you didn't write your paper. You promised that if I let you stay out—"

"I wrote it." He gave her a look. "I did. I wrote

it." He grabbed another pancake. "I just didn't print it. I'm out of ink."

She managed, once again, to hold back her exasperated response. She had to be careful. She didn't want to become the enemy here. The two of them had always been close, even before their mother died. After the accident, they'd become even closer, a tight team, as if they understood it was just the two of them now, two of them against the whole world.

Lately, though, Steve had seemed to be pulling back. Rebelling, even—just a little. He spent more time at football practice than he did at home. Coach Kieran McClintock seemed to have become his new hero, the one he confided in. Which was fine with Claire, really it was.

Except that she wished football didn't take so much of his time. He was going to need a scholarship to get into college. Coach McClintock seemed to think he could get one for football, but was that realistic? Coming from a tiny nowhere-town like Heyday?

"Claire? Don't give me that look. It's okay about the English paper. Mrs. Keene said all the football players could turn it in on Monday. Full credit."

"She gave an extension to the football players? Just the football players?" Claire knew how unpopular that would be with the other teachers…and perhaps the other students, as well. If the principal heard about it…

"Well, yeah. She knows we've been practicing every minute." He gaped at his watch in open-mouthed horror. "Oh my God, look how late it is!"

Too bad he hadn't joined the drama club instead, she thought. He could have used some pointers about overacting.

"Steve. I'm serious. You can't let her give special deals to the players. If you can't get your work done on time, you shouldn't be playing football in the first place."

He groaned as he hoisted his backpack over his broad shoulder. "God, don't start. We do this every morning. It's like Chinese water torture. I told Coach you're on me about this every friggin' day, like grass on dirt."

"Oh, you did, did you?"

That stung, and she couldn't help reacting. She wondered what other domestic complaints he shared with Kieran McClintock. The stingy allowance, which was all she could afford. The crummy dinners, which were all she could manage. The nagging, the criticizing, the clinging. "And what did he say?"

Steve paused. "Well," he said slowly. "He said he felt really sorry for me. He said it must be tough to have such a nasty old shrew in the house."

Like a fool, she fell for it. "What? That takes a lot of—"

She was so tense she hardly noticed the sparkle in Steve's hazel eyes.

"Yeah," he went on, gathering steam. "He said, boy, your sister sure is an ugly old bag, isn't she? I don't know how you stand it. He said the night he took you out on a date he almost couldn't eat, just looking at your ugly mug across the table."

"Steve." She sighed. He was joking, of course. He had been ribbing her about that dinner for days. "He didn't take me out on a date. We just went to dinner and—"

"Yeah, right. And I guess you haven't had a huge crush on him since you were about fifteen years old, either."

"Don't be ridiculous." But it was pointless to deny it. When she'd been fifteen, and Steve was ten, he'd found her diary. Kieran's name had been on every page, surrounded by hearts and exclamation points. And always the same plaintive question, *Why won't he notice me?*

Steve had made himself insufferable for weeks, swanning around, his hand to his forehead like Sarah Bernhardt, wailing, "Why won't he notice me?" It hadn't stopped until Claire had found an F on a math test under his bed and threatened to tell their mother.

"That was ages ago," she explained calmly. "Besides, all the girls in Heyday have crushes on Kieran McClintock when they're fifteen. It's in the bylaws, I think."

Steve arched one eyebrow, but, because he had matured a tiny bit since he was ten, he let it go. Claire was relieved. She didn't quite know yet herself what was going on between her and Kieran. She wasn't ready to discuss it with anyone else, even Steve.

"So what about the astronomy test? Are you ready for that at least? Did you study?"

"Yeah." He wolfed down one last pancake. "Sorta."

"Stevie." She folded her arms and blocked the doorway. The astronomy test wasn't until Monday, but... She suddenly dreaded being alone. When Steve was here, she didn't have time to brood, but when he left, the house always seemed dark and lonely.

"I'm late, Claire."

"Can you still name the seven important moons of Saturn?"

He cocked his head and grinned. "No, but I can

still name the Seven Psycho Dwarfs of the Eerie Alternate Universe. Mopey, Sleazy, Frumpy, Weepy, Queazy and Dork.''

''Great.'' That list was from seventh grade. ''Unfortunately, I don't think anyone is going to be asking you those on a test. And besides, that's only six.''

He put his hands under her arms and lifted her up, moving her away from the door. ''Oh, yeah?'' He kissed her on the cheek and yanked open the door before she could stop him. ''I guess I forgot to mention Bitchy.''

She laughed as she watched him go. ''Stevie,'' she said one more time.

He paused by the door of his ratty old Mustang, which he'd bought and restored with money from mowing lawns. God knew she couldn't have afforded to buy him one.

He looked like the Cheshire cat in the darkness. All she could see was his smile. But it was a very cute smile. It made her smile just to see it.

''What?''

She hesitated. They never told each other to drive carefully. It was a strange but deeply entrenched superstition between them. They'd never known their father very well—he left the family before Steve was even born. Then, three years ago their mother had been struck by a drunk driver who drove his car up onto the sidewalk. So now it was the just two of them. And they never said ''drive carefully.'' It was simply understood.

''Nothing,'' she said. ''I just love you, dork.''

FORTY-FIVE MINUTES LATER, she should have been on her way to work, but she was making a detour to the high-school football field. She had found a new ink cartridge and printed Steve's term paper out. She wanted him to have it when he got to English.

Half a mile from the field, traffic ground to a halt—something that almost never happened in the little town of Heyday, which had a population of somewhere between five and six thousand, depending on whether the local college was in session.

But Poplar Hill was a narrow, two-lane, tree-lined road, and the high-school rush hour had just begun. She growled under her breath and then yawned again. God, she was so tired she didn't even have the energy to be properly annoyed.

Drumming the steering wheel, she craned her neck, but she couldn't see anything. She didn't have time for this. She hadn't had a spare minute in the past three years. College and work, handling the house and raising her little brother... At only twenty-two, she was so tired she felt about fifty.

She couldn't be late today. She was in her first year of teaching seventh grade at Heyday Middle School, and she had a faculty meeting in fifteen minutes. She wasn't a football player, so she was expected to be on time and fully prepared.

Darn it, she should never have printed out Steve's paper. All the parenting books, which she'd devoured in secret as soon as she'd realized she was going to have to take over the job, said you should let your kids suffer the consequences of their own mistakes.

But Steve was such a good kid, really. And hadn't he suffered enough already? No one should be an orphan at fourteen.

So maybe she overindulged him. Or maybe not. Oh, heck, she didn't have a clue what was right. Maybe even real parents struggled to find the proper balance.

She eyed the area, wondering where she might be able to wriggle her car into a U-turn. The ground was soggy on the easements from last night's pre-winter rain, and the pines were still dripping wet.

It always rained in Heyday in November. Probably someone had skidded on the slick pavement and kissed fenders with the car in front of them.

But why such a snarl-up? A few people—parents, high-schoolers, even teachers—had exited their cars and were walking forward to see if they could get a look at the problem. Claire didn't have time for gawking. She rolled down her window. Maybe she could persuade the guy in front to inch his car forward so she could get free.

Oh, good. It was Doug Metzler from the bank. He'd be eager to help her. He knew that if she lost her new job she wouldn't be able to pay the mortgage—and his bank held the note.

"Doug," she called. "Do you mind moving up a little? I can't get out."

The balding, middle-aged man whipped around as if she'd shot him. He stared at her, a strange, blank expression on his normally pleasant face.

"Claire!" He put both hands up toward his cheeks, and they froze there. "Oh my God." He began looking around, as if he needed help. "Oh my God."

She had time for only a couple of half thoughts. Was Doug drunk? Crazy? Had she caught him doing something he shouldn't be doing? But even in those confused fractions of seconds, her subconscious must have registered something more sinister, because instinctively she began to climb out of her car.

"What's the matter, Doug?"

The man didn't speak. She'd just barely set both

feet on the soggy ground when Officer Bill Johnson appeared.

"Claire," the policeman said. His face was gray, and, unless she was imagining it, his voice shook. "Claire, don't go up there."

She tilted her head, confused. "I wasn't going to," she said. "Why? What's going on?"

Out of the corner of her eye, she could see that Doug Metzler was still frozen in place. A few others had joined him. They were all staring at Claire. Something sick and liquid began to boil in her stomach, like the beginnings of an internal earthquake.

"What's going on?" She gripped the door, suddenly aware that her hands were shaking just like Officer Johnson's voice. She stood on tiptoe, trying to see over the line of cars. Was that a blue flashing light? Was that larger vehicle an ambulance?

She looked back at the young policeman. *"What's going on?"*

"It's Steve," Officer Johnson said, and this time his voice did break. "Claire. It's…it's Steve."

No. *No.* That was ridiculous. This had nothing to do with Steve. Steve was at football practice, tossing that little brown ball high into the blue morning air for some other teenage boy to catch. Yes, Steve was safe at football practice, boyish and muddy and sweaty.

And happy. Steve was always happy.

She shook her head. "No," she said.

"Yes," the policeman said. "You see he… Steve…"

Claire felt her mind going limp, balking like a child, refusing to be led to whatever terrible place he was trying to take her. Bill Johnson was so young, she thought. Just a kid. What did he know? He was no more than four years older than Steve himself.

He tried again. "It… Steve must have been going very… It was an accident, a terrible accident."

She frowned. Look at him, he was close to tears. He looked so distressed, so completely undone. She wondered if she should put her arm around him. But she discovered to her horror that she couldn't move her arm. How odd. It was like sleepwalking. She couldn't feel any part of her body.

And when she spoke, her voice sounded strange. Hollow and slow, like something recorded at the wrong speed. "What do you mean an accident? What do you mean it's Steve?"

"I guess it was just too dark." Officer Johnson's face was suddenly running with tears that gleamed in the rising sun. "I guess he was going too fast. I'm sorry, Claire. I'm so sorry. I guess he hit a tree."

"Hit a—"

But the legs she couldn't feel decided right then to fold up under her like wet paper. She slid down, still holding on to the open car door. The muddy ground was cool and dark as she met it.

She lost track of time, just a little, like a clock with an unreliable battery. When her heart began to tick again, she was surprised to hear Kieran McClintock's voice, very close to her.

"Claire," he said. "Claire, are you all right?"

She realized she was in his arms. She looked up at him.

"He said Steve had an accident," she whispered, as if she needed to keep the news a secret. As if making the information public would make it true. "Can you take me to him? I'm not sure I can walk, but I have to get there. Steve needs me."

Kieran's face worried her. Anguish was written all over his handsome features, turning his clear blue eyes to hot, shadowed volcano beds. Turning his rugged jaw to jagged steel, his full, wide mouth to a razor line of bloodless white.

"Claire, sweetheart, Steve never made it to practice. He had an accident."

Strange, she thought, that a mouth so fierce, so twisted with pain, could speak in such gentle tones. His arms tightened around her. "It was very bad. He didn't make it, Claire. He's gone."

"Gone?"

He shut his eyes, and it was a relief not to have to look into their tortured depths.

"Yes, he said. "I'm so sorry, Claire. Steve's dead."

Dead…

Not playing football, not laughing, not running, not even breathing.

Dead.

She shut her eyes, too, as the knife blade of the word sank deep into her chest. She felt her heart's blood gush everywhere, she tasted the metallic hot ice of the cruel steel, and then, thank God, the terrible black universe began to disappear again.

My little brother is dead.

She wasn't sure whether she spoke that sentence or merely thought it. But she heard herself say the next one.

And you killed him.

CHAPTER TWO

Two years later

KIERAN MCCLINTOCK RUBBED the stinging red spot just above his swim trunks where the latest water balloon had landed and wondered if his reflexes might be getting a little slow. That made eight hits already, and it wasn't even noon. He couldn't seem to duck, dodge or jump out of the way fast enough.

The darn things hurt, too. High-school boys really threw some heat these days. He scowled at the one who had just nailed him in the gut.

"Ingrate," he called as the boy chuckled and scooted away.

"Golly, Coach, I'll bet that smarts." Suddenly a female voice purred in his ear, and a soft female hand rested over his. "Need any help with that?"

"Hi, Linda." Kieran didn't need to look up to know whose hand it was. No one but Linda Tremel would dream of rubbing the football coach's wet, naked stomach in public. He moved her fingers away. "Thanks, but I'll live."

Linda pouted, but otherwise she took the rejection in stride. She was quite used to being rejected by Kieran—she was his neighbor. Since her divorce, she'd been programmed to bait her hooks automatically whenever she saw any man. She didn't really expect him to bite.

She adjusted her large straw sun hat to a prettier angle and surveyed the chaos in front of them, where Heyday High's annual Junior-Senior Send-off was in full swing. About a hundred students and their families were slip-sliding on water toys, hobbling in three-legged races and gnawing on cold fried chicken legs and deviled eggs.

She sighed and fanned herself with her paper napkin. Summer had come in swinging this year. The temperature was already in the nineties.

"I'd take off my cover-up, but I'm not sure these hormonal young boys could control themselves," she said. "It's bad enough that you've got every female under fifty salivating over your six-pack, stud. Think you should toss a shirt on and put them out of their misery?"

Kieran didn't respond. Linda always talked like that. In fact, she never talked about anything but sex. Kieran suspected that might mean she wasn't really all that interested in it. Protesting too much, as they said.

Besides, he saw a couple of his best players huddled over by the ice chest, and he could imagine what they were plotting. The next water balloon was probably going to be filled with Gatorade. He could only hope they had one of the other teachers in mind for this one.

All the faculty, right up to the principal, were here today. Even the school volunteers had showed up— like Linda. The Send-off was the highlight of the school year. Each May, just before the start of final exams, the junior class hosted a water party for the outgoing seniors. It had been a Heyday tradition for at least fifty years.

Heyday was big on tradition. Kieran's father, who had, until his death less than two months ago, owned most of Heyday, had always said that tradition was what the little town had instead of culture, prominence, wealth or wisdom.

"So, I hear you've got another superstar coming along next season, Coach. You know the one." Linda tilted her head. "What's his name? Nice muscles. Bedroom eyes."

"Bedroom eyes?" Kieran looked at her. "I have no idea who you're talking about, but you'd better watch it, Linda. These boys are underage."

"Well, he does have sexy eyes." She grinned from under the wide brim of her hat. "I can't help noticing, can I? Oh, what is his name? The boy everyone is saying could be the new Steve Strickland. Eddie-something."

"Eddie Mackey?" Kieran wondered where Linda had heard about Eddie. "He's good, but he's not on the team yet. He's not sure he wants to play."

"Oh, you can talk him into it. You can talk anybody into anything. Steve Strickland didn't want to play at first, either, and look how good he turned out to be."

Kieran tossed his empty Gatorade bottle into the recycling bin. "Of course Steve wanted to play," he said. He hoped he didn't sound defensive. "Where did you hear that he didn't want to play?"

"I don't remember..." Linda chewed on her lower lip. "Oh, that's right. It was his sister who didn't want him to play. That's what I heard. They say Claire hated the idea of Steve playing football. I never understood why. Was she afraid he'd get hurt or something?"

That was stupid, even for Linda. Instantly, she realized her mistake and drew in a deep breath. "I mean—you know. In a game. Like getting tackled or something. Naturally, no one could have imagined he'd end up—"

"No." Kieran popped open another drink and downed half of it in one gulp. It really was hot out here. "No one could have imagined that."

"Where is she now, do you know?"

Kieran squinted into the sunlight, trying to see if the people barbecuing hot dogs needed any help. "Who?"

"Claire. Do you know if she's still in Richmond?"

"No."

Linda flicked him with her napkin. "Be specific," she said. "Do you mean no, she's not in Richmond, or no, you don't know?"

"No, I don't know."

"You haven't seen her since—"

"No."

"Do you think she's still angry? Do you think she still blames you for—"

"I don't know."

"I'll bet she doesn't." Linda unbuttoned her top two buttons, exposing as much cleavage as possible, and began fanning herself again. "I mean, how could she? It didn't make any sense to start with. I mean, you didn't force the kid to drive seventy miles an hour down Poplar Hill, did you?"

"No, I didn't."

According to Claire, though, that was just a cop-out. He had put too much pressure on the players, she'd said, her voice filled with tears and fury. He had expected them to do the impossible, and, because they had loved him, they'd tried to deliver.

At least that's what she told him the night she called and asked him not to come to the funeral.

"See? You didn't have a thing to do with it. Claire Strickland just went a little crazy, that's all. She wasn't thinking straight, and she needed someone to blame."

Kieran did not want to have this conversation. Especially not with Linda Tremel, who didn't have an ounce of imagination. She could never understand how, when Kieran had held Claire in his arms and told her Steve was dead, it had been like holding a ghost. She had seemed completely empty, as insubstantial as smoke. He had thought, for a minute, that she might just float away forever.

He scanned the crowd, desperately seeking a savior. But being with Linda Tremel was like acquiring leprosy—even your best friends wouldn't venture near enough to save you.

Finally he caught Principal Winston Vogler's eye. The elderly man was too softhearted to resist a plea for help. Kieran felt a little guilty as Winston came over, smiling politely at Linda. But only a little.

"Hey there, Ms. Tremel. Howdy, Coach." Principal Vogler patted Kieran on the back and gave Linda a kiss on the cheek. "It's a terrific day for the Send-off, don't you think? The weather always cooperates with Heyday High."

Linda opened another button. Winston was almost seventy years old—he'd been a contemporary of Kieran's father—but he was a male, and that apparently was Linda's only requirement.

"Well," she drawled, borrowing Kieran's Gatorade and rubbing its cool plastic sides against her collarbone, "it's pretty hot."

Kieran couldn't help cringing for her. She hadn't been like this before Austin Tremel divorced her last year. Back when she had first landed Austin, the rich boy from the right side of the tracks who was supposed to make all her dreams come true, she had spent every moment trying to be worthy of him. Trying to remake herself into the perfect lawyer's wife.

It must have hurt pretty bad when he dumped her. She'd spent the past year trying to prove to herself that she was desirable. Austin had a new lover—had probably acquired her long before the divorce—so Linda obviously wasn't going to be happy until she had one, as well. Or two, or three. However many it took to show Austin she didn't miss him.

Winston was watching the three-legged zebra race, which involved bags painted with black and white stripes. "Do you think," he asked suddenly, "that any of these kids even know why they're called the Fighting Zebras at Heyday High?"

"Heck, no," Linda said.

Kieran knew that was probably true. Many of Heyday's younger citizens had no idea that the city got its name because a trainer for a little nomadic circus got drunk one night and left the animal cages unlocked.

They didn't know about the zebras, which, once having escaped, had eluded capture for days, then weeks...and then forever. Long after the monkeys and the lion had been recovered, long after the circus owner had decided to cut his losses and move on, the clever zebras remained at large.

For months, people reported sightings of zebras galloping in the woods, zebras strolling in the park, zebras grazing along the highway. But the two animals danced in and out, taunting their would-be captors, and eventually the fairy tale of freedom caught the public eye.

Newspapers as far away as D.C. wrote stories. "Zebras Have a Heyday," the first story proclaimed. And the little town of Moresville, tired of being "Boresville," saw its chance to reinvent itself. On the Fourth of July, nineteen hundred and three, the mayor had gleefully knocked down his gavel on a five-to-one vote, and Heyday was born.

Every Fourth of July since, the city had sponsored its Ringmaster Parade. Most people didn't ask why. They merely accepted that the city would elect a Ringmaster and Ringmistress, just as they accepted that the Big Top Diner had a roof like a circus tent, and that the bartenders at the Black and White Lounge wore striped tuxedos topped with zebra ears on a headband and springs.

"So." Winston shifted from one foot to the other and was apparently having trouble deciding where to look. Linda Tremel's rather large chest seemed to take up too much of his field of vision. "So, Kieran, what time do you head for Richmond in the morning?"

Oh, hell.

Kieran could feel the curiosity emanating from Linda. But what could he do? If he told the truth, that he was going to spend the weekend in Richmond, she'd be giddy with speculation. If he evaded or lied, it would look suspicious.

And it wasn't suspicious. That he should be heading for a conference in the city where Claire Strickland now lived was a minor coincidence, yes. But Richmond was a big city. Probably two thousand people went there every day without running into Claire Strickland, either deliberately or accidentally. He'd just be number two thousand and one.

"Actually, I'm leaving tonight," he said as blandly as possible. "The conference starts early in the morning."

"You're going to Richmond?" Linda had begun to smile. *"Richmond?"*

"Yes," he said. "I'm speaking at a coaching conference. I'll just be there overnight."

"Are you planning to—"

"No."

She chuckled. "You don't even know what I was going to ask."

"Yes, I do. And the answer is no. It's purely a working trip. I won't be making any social calls while I'm in town."

Winston looked confused. "But you'll have the evening free, Kieran," he said. "You know that time's your own to do whatever you want. Social calls are fine."

Kieran laughed. This was becoming the conversational equivalent of gum on your shoe. "Linda's joking, Win. I don't want to make any social calls."

Linda grinned. "Yes, but if you do—"

"I won't."

"Okay, fine. But if you *do*." She winked at him. "Give her a kiss for me. Anything beyond a kiss, well, then you're on your—"

Kieran groaned and turned away, which meant he was in the perfect position to glimpse the incoming missile just in the nick of time.

He called out the standard warning. "Heads up!"

Winston, who was seasoned in the ways of mischievous high-school boys, sidestepped instantly. Unfortunately, Linda, who wasn't, stood there looking confused.

"What—?" She frowned.

A pop, a splat, a splash. And suddenly her lacy white cover-up was splattered from neck to knee with sticky orange liquid. She looked down, horrified.

Somehow Kieran managed not to laugh. He didn't even smile. He actually tried to feel sympathetic. He didn't allow himself to believe it had been fate, intervening to spare him any more of Linda's lip-licking curiosity.

But it had been a lucky shot, hadn't it?

Principal Vogler, on the other hand, was furious. A courtly man himself, he obviously found pegging a woman with a water balloon to be an outrage. He reached out and snagged the nearest teenage boy, a kid with dark hair and deep blue eyes. "Bedroom" eyes, in fact.

"Come here, young man," Winston bellowed.

He didn't wait for the poor kid to say a word. He dragged him by the collar and forced him to face Linda.

"Ms. Tremel, this is Mr. Eddie Mackey. I believe he has something he'd like to say to you."

THERE MUST BE A LINE from *Hamlet* for a moment like this. Claire studied her sedate navy-and-white spectator pumps and considered the issue. How about the one that said a person could "smile and smile and be a villain?"

It seemed apt enough. Mrs. Gillian Straine, the principal of the Haversham Girls' Academy, never stopped smiling. It was how she wooed the best parents, the best girls, the best alums, the best college recruiters. But after almost two years teaching seventh grade here at HGA, Claire had learned how sharp the steel was that lay behind that smile.

Today the metal was in full, lethal force as Mrs. Straine sat at her huge mahogany desk, in her magnificent wood-paneled office, and read a letter of complaint that had just arrived. The letter stated that Miss Claire Strickland was teaching the girls from texts of questionable morality.

The letter was apparently very long—or else Mrs. Straine was a very slow reader. Claire adjusted her modest navy skirt and tried not to be nervous. But Mrs. Straine's smile was so tight right now her lips had almost disappeared. Not a good sign.

Maybe the better quote was "To be or not to be." To be or not to be *fired*.

Finally Mrs. Straine looked up. "This is very troubling," she said softly. She said everything softly. It forced other people to be perfectly quiet, and to lean in slightly, in a deferential pose, in order to catch her words.

"Is it true, Miss Strickland? You have unilaterally decided to teach *Hamlet* to your seventh graders?"

"Not the entire play," Claire said. "Just some of the famous speeches. It's part of a larger unit on Shakespeare."

Mrs. Straine took off her reading glasses and tapped them against the letter. "It says here you've been telling the children there are such things as ghosts. It says you've told them about fratricide and suicide." She shook her head. "They even accuse you of using the *I* word."

Claire frowned. The *I* word? What on earth was the *I* word? Insanity? Iago? No, that was *Othello*.

Iambic pentameter?

Mrs. Straine closed her eyes, apparently grieved that Claire was forcing her to utter it.

"Incest," she whispered.

Oh, for heaven's sake.

"I didn't call it incest," Claire said. "Shakespeare did. Or rather Hamlet did. It's just a small part of the overall story. You see, Hamlet's mother marries his uncle—"

"I know what happens in *Hamlet,* Miss Strickland."

Claire leaned back in her chair. "Of course you do. I'm sorry." She'd swallowed her pride in this job so often she'd almost gotten used to the bitter taste. "Then of course you know it isn't incest with the same connotations we might have today."

"I don't believe any of that word's connotations are socially acceptable," Mrs. Straine said. She was sitting up so straight her back wasn't touching the chair. "I honestly would have thought you understood that vocabulary like that has no place in an HGA classroom."

Claire tried one more time. "But this is *Hamlet,* Mrs. Straine. This is Shakespeare. *Hamlet* is taught in classrooms all over the world every day, and—"

Mrs. Straine waved her hand. "We do not judge

ourselves by everyone else, Miss Strickland,'' she said. ''At HGA, the standards are far higher.''

Higher than Shakespeare?

''I'm afraid we must insist that our teachers meet those standards. Every teacher, every day.''

So was this it? Was this where Claire would be told to take her copy of *Hamlet* and go home? She realized suddenly that she didn't care very much. Since Steve died, she hadn't cared about much of anything. But she tried to look earnestly concerned. She did have to earn a living, and HGA at least had the virtue of paying well and recruiting bright, well-behaved students.

''However,'' Mrs. Straine went on, ''I don't think we need to overreact. Overall, your performance since coming to HGA has been exemplary. I think it will be adequate merely to place you on probation.''

''Probation?''

Mrs. Straine folded up the letter and placed it in a file marked Strickland, Claire. ''Yes. It should not be construed as punitive. It's merely precautionary. I'll be keeping a close eye on your work. I'll need to see your lesson plans daily, of course. After six months, we'll review the matter and see where we stand.''

Claire understood she'd been dismissed. She stood and nodded—though she drew the line at thanking Mrs. Straine for her tolerance. She looked at the other woman—at her high, tight, extremely sophisticated French braid, her severe Armani suit, her Tiffany-set diamond wedding ring—and she wondered whether there really was no Mr. Straine, as the other teachers sometimes suggested.

It was possible. Claire's own mother had pretended she was a "Mrs.," and she undoubtedly wasn't the only woman who did. Mrs. Straine's reasons would be different, of course. She wouldn't be trying to protect her two illegitimate children. But whatever the reason, living a lie took its toll.

As she left the school, Claire thought how much nicer it would be if she could go home and tell Steve about all this. What fun they'd have parodying Mrs. Straine's Victorian syntax and ridiculous whisper. If Steve were there, this would seem hilarious in no time. They'd laugh away any sting, and then they'd sit around and think up absurd new meanings for the school's initials. She could almost hear him now. Humongous Growling Amazons. Hippos Gathering Acorns. Hot Greasy Aardvarks.

But Steve wasn't there, of course. Her half-furnished apartment would be empty when she finally got home later tonight. She had a meeting after school, which she would go through like a robot. Then she'd stop by the grocery store, and then drive to the apartment.

When she got in, she'd ignore the five or six messages on her machine—it was easier to ignore an invitation than to turn it down, and the result was the same in the end. She'd read a little. And then, as soon as she possibly could, she'd go to sleep.

To sleep. Perchance to dream. Yes, Hamlet knew where the real dangers lay. Claire still dreamed about Steve at least once a week. They were cruel dreams—the kind that woke you up with your heart in your throat. In the dreams, she always drove down Poplar Hill one second too late. Steve always died in her arms while Kieran McClintock stood over them and smiled.

But that night her meeting ran long and it was after ten before she got home. All in all, it had been an exhausting day. Maybe she'd be too tired to dream.

She pulled into the complex parking lot, gathered her books and papers and purse and groceries and made her way to her second-floor apartment.

And, there, on her elegantly lit landing, she came face-to-face with a man she had thought she'd never see again.

The smiling man of her terrible dreams.

CHAPTER THREE

KIERAN WAS SHOCKED by how different Claire looked. How much older.

He hadn't seen her in two years, but still...

Part of it was her hair. She had beautiful hair, a deep, shiny brown. She used to wear it almost to her waist. When she taught, she just whisked it up into a casual twist that always had adorable bits and pieces escaping from it. Now it was cut in a sleek, chin-length bob that fit like a helmet.

And her outfit. It was the pencil-thin uniform of a corporate lady-shark. What had happened to the flowing cotton jumpers and soft pastel T-shirts?

But most of all, it was her face. Even in the worst days of her first grief, she hadn't looked this tight and closed-in. Her brown eyes, round, large and long-lashed, had always reminded him of some gentle woodland creature.

Not any more. Now she just looked tired and strangely distant. She didn't even seem interested enough to be shocked to see him standing on her front porch.

"Kieran," she said. "What are you doing here?"

That was a damn good question, actually. What the hell was he doing here? Back in his hotel room, he'd told himself a thousand times to quit being such a fool, put down his car keys, order room service, raid the minibar, turn on the television, *anything*. But none of it had stopped him.

"I'm in town for a conference."

She shifted her packages so that she could see him better over the groceries, but she kept her fist tightly closed around her keys. She seemed to have no intention of opening that door.

"Not here in Richmond," she said. "I meant *here*. What are you doing *here?*"

"I wanted to say hello." Was that true? Actually, he had no clear idea why he had come. He'd just opened the telephone book, found her name and found himself getting a map from his laptop. "I wanted to see how you were doing."

She shifted again, her keys clinking against a glass bottle, or maybe a can. "I'm doing fine."

No, you're not, he wanted to say. Any fool could tell she was lost. But he didn't have the right to say anything like that. Hell, he didn't even have the right to be standing here.

One date. That was all they'd ever had. One night when he'd sat across from her, eating salmon and salad and some stupid little bonbon dessert, and quietly going wild with wanting her.

One night—compared to Steve's death, for which she had always blamed him. No, he'd say he had pretty damn few rights in this situation.

"I just—" He cleared his throat and began again. "I thought maybe we could talk for a while. Maybe I could take you out for coffee. I haven't eaten dinner yet. I just got into town. Are you hungry?"

She looked at him with those shallow eyes. "We don't really have anything to talk about, Kieran. We don't have anything in common except Steve. And I don't talk about Steve.''

You don't? Oh, Claire…that's not healthy. But of course he didn't say that, either. He just looked at her sober face in the silvery light from the carriage lamp and wished he could go back two years and start over. God, the things he'd do differently!

"It's been two years, Claire. Isn't it time to let old—'' But her face warned him to stop, so he did. "All right, then, how about if I promise we won't talk about Steve?''

Her fingers must have clenched a little. The brown paper bag made a brief crinkling noise. "What topics would be left, then? Politics? The weather?''

"I could tell you about Heyday. It's grown since you left. They've put in a new multiplex movie theater. Stadium seating. Four whole screens. The kids all want jobs there.'' She wasn't interested, but he kept going, determined to hit on something. "The bookstore expanded. And they put in a new traffic light.''

"Did they really. Where?''

Oh, hell. He hesitated just a second too long, as he recognized his mistake. She was smart. She knew what the hesitation meant.

"Where?''

He took a deep breath. "On Poplar Hill.''

"So much for that topic.'' She turned away firmly. "I don't mean to be rude, Kieran. I appreciate the effort you made to come. But I really think it's better if we just say good-night.''

She fumbled with her key, trying to insert it into the lock.

"Claire.'' He touched her shoulder, and she

twitched away quickly. Too quickly. The oranges on the top of her grocery bag began to teeter. She shifted them, reaching out with her other hand to try to balance things, but at that very moment the door swung open, and she lurched forward.

Fruit and fresh vegetables spilled everywhere, and a box of spinach spaghetti hit the landing with enough force to split open. Thin green straws hopped and tumbled crazily, covering the concrete and bouncing down the stairs.

He caught the bag as it fell, just in time to save the sparkling water.

She knelt immediately and began scooping up bits of broccoli. "I'll get it," she said. "It's okay. I've got it."

He crouched beside her. "Let me help."

For a minute he thought she was going to refuse. For a minute, she thought so, too. He could read it in her eyes. But obviously even she could see how impossibly rude that would be. She blinked, brushed her hair out of her eyes and nodded.

"Thanks," she said. She dumped a handful of little green florets into the bag and began scooping up some more.

It took several minutes, but finally they had it all, down to the last strand of green spaghetti. She went in first. She left the door open behind her, so he assumed she wouldn't call the police if he followed her in.

It was a beautiful apartment. Had she just recently moved in? The living room had high ceilings and an elegant coffee-colored molding; a brand-new, thick, champagne-beige carpet; and almost no furniture. One chair with a throw blanket across its arm, one small coffee table and a bookcase with a stereo on top—that was it. No sofa, no lamp, no stack of unopened mail on the foyer table. No tail-wagging puppy, no roommate, no—

No *anything*.

"It's a nice place," he said. "How long have you lived here?"

"A couple of years. Since I left Heyday." She had gone straight to the kitchen. He heard the growling sound of the garbage disposal churning up broccoli—and discouraging any further conversation.

Two years? He stood in the doorway and looked around incredulously. She'd lived in this apartment for two years, and she had yet to hang a picture? She had never bought a television?

He moved through the big, hollow room and entered the kitchen. It looked a little more lived-in. The small breakfast bay had two chairs, and the table was covered in books and papers. He had heard she was still teaching. This must be where she created her lesson plans and did her grading.

He handed her his collection of ruined food and watched as she fed it to the disposal. "Thanks," she said again. But she didn't quite look at him. She didn't quite meet his eyes.

When she was finished, she washed her hands carefully; dried them on a blue towel, which she refolded neatly on its bar; and then turned to him.

"So. You said you were hungry. I'm a terrible cook, but I have a few frozen dinners. Would you like me to heat one up for you?"

"That would be very nice," he said. He wasn't sure what had made her decide to let him stay. Maybe she was too tired to go on arguing with him.

Maybe she'd decided it was easier to feed him and then send him on his way.

Whatever the reason, he wasn't going to give her an opportunity to change her mind. "How about if I set the table?"

She turned and smiled a little. "The table's a terrible mess. Sometimes I eat in the living room. But there's only one chair. I'm not exactly set up for entertaining."

It almost took the years away, that smile. He felt something relax inside. Perhaps the real Claire was still alive inside that uptight iron maiden. He hoped so. He wasn't sure why that mattered so much, but it did.

"No problem," he said. "Just tell me where everything is, and I'll improvise."

She pointed out the cabinets and drawers that held all the flatware and dishes. Then she rummaged a minute in the freezer and emerged holding two red-and-white cartons.

"I've got vegetable lasagna and vegetable lasagna," she said. She raised one eyebrow. "Your choice."

He smiled. "Vegetable lasagna sounds good."

They didn't talk while she put the microwave through its paces. His instincts told him not to rush things. They were doing fine, especially considering how long it had been since they'd seen each other, and how hostile their parting had been. But the truce felt fragile, and he didn't want to test it.

When both boxes were warmed up, she moved to the breakfast table and began stacking papers, preparing to move them to the kitchen counter.

"That's okay," he said, touching the pile of papers. He avoided connecting with her hand. "I've got us set up in here."

She looked up with a quizzical expression. "Where?"

"Come see," he said. He led the way to the living room. He'd put the plates and utensils on the coffee table, but he'd solved the seating problem a little more creatively. While she'd been putting away the few groceries that survived, he had taken the throw and spread it across the carpet like a picnic blanket.

He thought it looked kind of nice. The only light in the room came from three brass sconces at intervals along the cream-colored walls, so it wasn't terribly well illuminated. But it had a pleasant, picnic-under-the-stars feeling, and he hoped she'd go for it.

She hesitated, holding a little plastic tray of vegetable lasagna in each hand. He could feel her internal debate—was this too cozy? Was he trying to get too close?

Finally she held the food out to him. "If I'm going to sit on the floor, I'd better put on something more comfortable. I'll be right back."

And she meant it. When she returned, just a couple of minutes later, she was wearing a yellow cotton sundress, and she had brushed some of the stiffness out of her hair. Now that it was swinging more naturally, and shining in the light from the sconces, he realized that her haircut was actually quite sexy.

In fact, she looked beautiful.

She paused at the stereo. She turned it on—maybe feeling that awkward silences would be more easily covered up if they had some background music. A classical station was playing Chopin, and she made a small face, probably judging it to be too much like "mood" music. She punched a couple of preset buttons and found an oldies station that was playing some nice, low-key rock and roll.

"That okay?"

He nodded. "Sure."

He was already cross-legged on the floor, with his pseudo-food in front of him, and as she dropped down beside him, he caught the scent of her perfume. It was the same perfume she'd always worn. He smiled, strangely relieved. It was as if Claire, the real Claire, was materializing before his eyes.

They each took a bite of their lukewarm lasagna. God, it was awful.

She grimaced. "Maybe if we open a bottle of wine, that would take the edge off this stuff. Someone gave me one as a moving-in present. I'm pretty sure it's still in there."

Two years ago? If the lack of a dining-room table hadn't told him she didn't socialize much, the two-year-old bottle of wine would have.

"Great," he said. He didn't care about the food, but he was definitely in favor of anything that might take the edge off this stilted conversation.

"I'll get it." As she climbed to her feet and headed into the kitchen, he watched her go, pleased to see how soft and feminine her sleeveless dress was, pleased that she still wore yellow, which used to be her favorite color.

Strange that he should remember that. He wasn't usually the least bit interested in women's clothes. Through the years, many of his girlfriends had complained that he simply never noticed, no matter how much money they spent. So why on earth should Claire's wardrobe matter?

Suddenly, he felt a flash of insight. And he finally realized why, in spite of every urging of his own better judgment, he had searched out Claire Strickland's address tonight.

It was purely selfish, really. He needed to assure himself that, all things considered, she was doing okay. That Steve's death had not destroyed her.

He needed to get at least that one small load of guilt off his breaking back.

Kieran didn't know whose fault Steve's death really was—not in any absolute moral, philosophical, religious sense, anyhow. In the eyes of the law, of course, it had been Steve's own fault. He had been speeding.

But *why* was he speeding? Because he didn't want to disappoint Kieran. Because Kieran had made it clear that commitment to their team was the most important thing in the world.

Maybe, as Claire had thrown in his face that night, Steve had died trying to live up to Kieran's impossible expectations.

He couldn't bring Steve back. But perhaps, if he could see that Claire's life hadn't been lost that morning, too, his conscience would let up a little.

He leaned back against the wall, swallowed another bite of cardboard lasagna and waited. Wine was exactly what they needed. Maybe after a couple of glasses he just might find out how deeply under this mound of grief and repression the real Claire Strickland was actually buried.

WHILE KIERAN RINSED the dishes, Claire rested her head against the wall and decided that she definitely shouldn't have opened the wine.

It wasn't that she was drunk. She'd had only a couple of glasses, and, even as out of practice as she was, it would take more than that. No, the problem was that she had begun to feel relaxed. Somewhere during this weird picnic dinner, she had begun to enjoy herself, to enjoy Kieran's company, to enjoy hearing about home and laughing at his stories.

When she reviewed how it had all started, out there on the porch, she wasn't exactly sure how he had managed to insinuate himself into her apartment and turn the whole stilted evening into a living-room picnic, complete with music and liquor and laughter.

But that was Kieran McClintock for you. He was smooth like that. The woman didn't exist who could tell him no when he wanted to hear yes. He was born charming, and he'd just gotten better at it as he got older.

Wait… That wasn't quite right. *She* had put on the music, and *she* had unearthed the booze. Maybe she was putting the blame in the wrong place….

She'd done that before, hadn't she? When she had told Kieran that he killed Steve…that hadn't been completely true. Part of her still blamed him for his part in the accident—and always would. But part of her had finally accepted that there was plenty of blame to go around.

And that's why opening the wine had been such a mistake. She owed him an apology, and it wasn't going to be easy to say what she needed to say. It was two years overdue, and it was going to stick in her throat. Steve's name always did.

And it was definitely going to spoil what had become a rather nice evening. She hadn't had company in so long, she'd forgotten how pleasant it could be.

He came in from the kitchen now, holding an apple, a small knife and a paper plate. He sat down beside her, his back against the wall, too.

He hummed along with the old Beatles song on the radio. He never rushed into small talk. That was one of his most charming traits. He could let a silence rest easy in the room. Of course, when you were the gorgeous Kieran McClintock, beloved heir to the McClintock fortune, which included practically the entire town of Heyday, it probably wasn't difficult to be relaxed and self-confident and let other people do the impressing.

"Kieran, there's something I need to say," she began.

He turned his head and smiled at her. "Okay," he said.

Up close, even by this dim light, she was struck by how blue his eyes were. And how gorgeous. God, she had forgotten how handsome he was. When she'd first left Heyday, she'd drawn horns and evil, arched eyebrows on her mental image of him. Even after she admitted, much later, that he might not be the devil, her memory had been distorted.

Most of all, she'd forgotten his amazing charisma. She'd forgotten that he radiated power and masculinity and charm like a light. That was, of course, why teenage boys, fifteen-year-old girls, spinsters and old men and puppies followed him anywhere. The only people she'd ever met who didn't like Kieran were the men whose girlfriends openly lusted after him.

Suddenly the wine seemed to rise straight to her brain. And, as the warmth from his shoulder pressed into hers, she felt the edgy fingers of sexual tension feather at her spine.

Oh, God. She should have known this would happen.

When she didn't speak, he smiled easily and held out the apple he had been peeling.

"Want dessert? I washed it. It doesn't seem too banged up, though it did do a Slinky down two flights of stairs."

"Sure," she said, though she knew she was just stalling. She didn't want to talk about Steve, not tonight, not to Kieran. She felt all mixed up inside. It was nerve-wracking to hang here like this, caught between the building desire and the lingering bitterness.

He cut off a wedge of the apple and handed it to her. She chewed it slowly. It tasted sweeter than anything she'd had since she left Heyday. In fact, she thought, shutting her eyes, it tasted like Heyday itself. It tasted like her mom's apple pies and candy apples at the Ringmaster Parade. It tasted like green trees and blue skies and sunshine that slanted slowly over long afternoons.

When she opened her eyes, Kieran smiled and handed her another. As she took it, their fingers touched briefly, both of them slick with apple juice, and warm. Something sharply sweet jolted through her. Kieran would taste like Heyday, too, she thought. His lips would taste like home.

Oh, dear God, she still wanted him. But why should that surprise her? She had always wanted him, ever since she was fifteen years old and didn't even understand what wanting meant. Up until that very last, terrible day, she had always felt a little breathless at the sight of him.

And now here they were, after all that had happened, after two whole years apart. Everything had changed between them—and yet, in this most primitive way, nothing had changed at all.

Just then the radio station began playing a love song that had been all the rage five years ago. She knew that song. It was corny and lilting and unabashed in its emotion. She had secretly loved it, but Steve had thought it was hilarious. He had wandered through the house, making up alternate lyrics, each more nauseatingly saccharine than the last.

"Steve made such fun of this song," she said. "I never had the nerve to admit how much I liked it."

Kieran smiled. He didn't even seem to notice that she had finally brought up Steve, although that was probably another example of how smooth he was.

"I bet Steve loved it, too," he said. "Teenage boys do that a lot. They aren't comfortable expressing emotion yet. Eventually they grow out of it."

She looked at him, feeling the sadness come streaking through her. No, she thought, tightening her shoulders to resist the pain. Steve wouldn't grow out of it. Steve would never get the chance to grow up.

Kieran's face tightened, and she knew he could read her thoughts. Or maybe he had just recognized his own insensitive blunder.

He put out his hand and touched her face.

"I'm sorry, Claire," he said. "Oh, hell. I'm so sorry."

She turned away. She looked down at her apple. She'd been holding this piece too long. It was starting to turn brown where her fingers pinched it.

"I think—I think maybe it's time for you to go," she said.

"Claire, don't. Don't close off again—"

But she had to. Didn't he understand that? When she left herself open, open to wanting him, open to remembering Steve, then the pain came charging in, like an enemy rushing a breach in the defenses. She couldn't endure it. It simply hurt too much.

She tried to climb to her feet, but he was so close. It was hard to get leverage without reaching out and touching him.

"Really," she said. "It's late—"

"Claire, talk to me. Please…tell me what you're feeling."

What she was feeling? She got to her feet some-how and stood staring down at him. She tried to find her earlier numb indifference, but it was gone. Some-thing had stolen it. Kieran, with his blue eyes and his sexy smile and his knotted, inextricable ties to Steve, had stolen it, as he had stolen so many things in her life.

"What do you think I'm feeling? I'm hurting. Is that what you wanted me to say? I've lost everyone I ever loved, and it hurts. Is that what you wanted to hear?"

He rose, too, but she shoved away from him and moved toward the radio. She flicked it off just before he reached her.

"No," he said. "I never wanted you to hurt."

"Oh, that's right. What was I thinking? You'd much prefer to hear that everything is fine, that I'm okay and you're forgiven. In fact, that's why you're here, isn't it? That's why you came. So that you can be forgiven, and you can get on with your life."

She was right. She could see it in his face. He didn't deny it. He just stared at her, looking ex-hausted and guilty as hell.

Somehow that drained all the fury right out of her. She went limp. "All right, then, you're forgiven," she said. "And I'm fine. Now please go home. Please."

Her voice cracked, and she felt something warm, like blood, on her cheeks. She reached up and touched the liquid, but it was clear. It was tears—the first she'd cried since Steve's funeral. She tried to choke them back. She didn't want to do this. Not now, not ever. She lifted her chin and swallowed hard, but still they poured down her face.

Kieran stood in front of her, his face dark. "Don't fight it," he said. "It's all right. You need to cry."

He brushed the tears with his fingers. And then, very slowly, he kissed the damp places where they had been. She didn't resist as he pulled her into his arms and bent his head close to hers. She could feel his heart pounding.

He was so strong, she thought. And she was not. Once, she had been...but now she was being helplessly drained by this flood of tears.

So she let herself rest against his chest. Just for a little while, she thought. Just until she borrowed enough strength to stand on her own again.

When he took her chin in his hand and tilted her face up to his, when he bent his head and kissed her, she thought at first it was just another kind of comfort. His lips were tender, moving slowly, as if he hoped he might be able to stroke new life into her.

And it *was* comforting. His kiss was sweet and warm, and she had been right, he did taste of Heyday. He opened her lips gently and breathed the sweet air of home, the pure memory of Steve, of happiness, of innocence, of love, into her mouth.

With a soft groan, she accepted it all, grateful but passive, still helpless to resist or participate.

Somewhere, though, her body had already begun to answer him. A subtle heat in the small of her back. A warm, honeyed liquid trickling through her veins. It must have begun very deep, so deep that she wasn't aware, because by the time it reached her conscious mind, her heart was racing, and she was on fire.

She caught her breath against the piercing pleasure.

Pulling away, she turned her face toward his neck, where she could feel his heart pounding, just as hers was. She moved her mouth against him, until he was wet with her tears, and skin slid easily on skin. His arms jerked and tightened, and the pulse throbbed harder against her lips.

He made a low noise in his throat, more vibration than sound.

"I want you, Claire," he said, turning his face to capture her lips again. His breath was still sweet, but fiery now, an extension of the flames inside her. "I want you so much I can hardly see straight."

"I know," she said. She wrapped her arms around his shoulders. "I know."

His hands moved over her back, down to her hips. He pulled her closer. "I didn't come for this, I swear I didn't." He cupped his hands around her buttocks and tilted her into him. "At least I don't think I did. I honestly don't know. I don't know anything anymore."

"It doesn't matter," she said.

And it didn't. Little frozen bits of her body were melting, and the warm flood was carrying her away.

She might have regrets tomorrow, but tonight she didn't care.

After all she had lost, didn't she deserve this? Didn't Kieran owe her this? Didn't he owe her one night when she didn't have to feel so dreadfully alone?

And tomorrow?

But she shut the question out of her mind. No one should live for tomorrow. It might never come. It might fly away in the gray, speeding hour before dawn. And then it would be too late.

"Please," she whispered, putting her lips against his throat. "Make love to me."

He hesitated one last second. And then, with a low groan of surrender, he eased her down onto the tablecloth. He unbuttoned her yellow dress, and when she was naked and waiting, taking shallow breaths to hold the tension at a safe distance, he slowly removed his own clothes.

He was even more beautiful than she had imagined. His golden skin, his powerful proportions, his hot blue eyes devouring her and his silken blond hair dangling in his face...

No wonder everyone loved him. She could love him, too, if she let herself.

He skimmed his fingers down her body, from collarbone to hip. She shivered and shifted against the tablecloth hungrily.

He knelt over her, positioning himself carefully so that their bodies met at every possible point. He brought his mouth down and took the tip of her breast between his warm lips. Arching with something that was too lovely to be pain, too piercing to be joy, she threaded her fingers through his soft hair and said his name, his beautiful name that sounded a little like a cry.

He touched her then between her legs, touched her as if he already knew her, as if her body spoke to him in a secret language only he could hear. He went slowly. He listened as her muscles quivered, as her breath trembled and moaned and snagged on its own panting pace. And then, when he was sure he understood, his fingers stroked their complicated, fiery response.

She cried out and twisted, instinctively trying to escape the terrifying thrill of such a profound intimacy.

What about tomorrow? Something frightened inside kept crying out the question. *What about tomorrow?*

But there was no tomorrow.

"Kieran," she cried, pulling at his hand. He understood—he moved quickly. He rose above her. He pressed himself into her, pushing softly at first, then harder....

"Claire?" His face was tense. He hadn't expected that he would be the first. It clearly was an agony to hold back.

Tomorrow? But the word was only a shadow now.

"It's all right," she said. She dug her fingers into his hips and pulled him in, until the barriers broke and he filled her with a groan and a flash of searing pain.

He kissed her then, and the fiery, rhythmic sparkle began all over again. She opened, and he drove into her mouth just as he was driving into her body. And in that sweet, hot wetness, she realized she had been wrong.

Kieran McClintock's lips didn't taste like home. They tasted like heaven.

And for one taste of heaven tonight, she'd gladly face hell tomorrow.

CHAPTER FOUR

THE HEYDAY HIGH SCHOOL Cheerleaders had picked the hottest June morning in Heyday history to hold their annual car wash. But at least Eddie Mackey had the consolation of knowing he wasn't the only boy dumb enough to have crawled out of bed to help them.

All the guys were here. Joe and Carter and Jeff and Mark…and even Cullen, their star quarterback, who had said last night that if his girlfriend Jana thought he was gonna be her trained lapdog, she could by God kiss his cleats. Now he was on his knees, scrubbing hubcaps, the worst job of all. In fact, as far as Eddie could tell, the boys were doing every bit of the work. The cheerleaders were just bouncing around in their wet T-shirts and waving posters to pull in the cars.

What a bunch of suckers they all were. Eddie, who had been stretched out on the leather bench seat of Doug Metzler's Cadillac, vacuuming linty bits of petrified French fries off the floor, finally got sick of the smell and rolled over with a sigh.

And found himself staring up at Binky Potter's breasts.

Binky had leaned in to wipe down the Caddy's windows, leaned right smack over him. Oh, man. She was the finest girl out here—and not just because she had the best body. She was pretty, too. All the guys were after her.

But she was his. She had been his girl for two whole months tomorrow.

He swallowed hard and decided it was all worth it—French fries, heat, sweat, stink, everything. Nothing on earth could have prevented him from being here today.

"Well, cowboy, what you looking at?"

Grinning, Binky leaned down an inch or two more, just close enough so that her necklace tickled his upper lip. He'd given her that necklace. It was a silver lariat—their little joke, because she always called him cowboy. Of course, he'd never been within spitting distance of a cow, and if anyone handed him a lariat he'd be more likely to hang himself with it than rope a steer, but so what? It sounded sexy as hell.

He caught the tip of the necklace between his teeth. "I'm looking at you, hot stuff," he said, tasting the cold sting of silver against his tongue. "Wasn't that what you had in mind?"

"Don't flatter yourself, cowboy." She pretended to try to pull away, but the lariat merely pressed lightly against his teeth, so he knew she didn't mean it. A drop of sudsy water was making its slow path down the firm mound of her left breast. If he leaned forward, he could lick it off....

His jeans suddenly seemed to become a size smaller.

He lifted his chin. His nose grazed the wet edge of her shirt. But he couldn't quite reach the drop of water.

Which, of course, was the story of his relationship with Binky. Close—so close. But then...nothing.

"Hey, Eddie, guess what? I was at Morrison's the other day, and guess what I saw?"

Morrison's was Heyday's most expensive jeweler. Binky loved jewelry. And nothing fake, either. She liked the real stuff. Eddie's jeans began to fit better as he thought of his empty wallet. He let go of the lariat.

"I don't know. What?"

"The cutest little earrings. They match my necklace exactly. Little ropes that dangle. Little ropes for big, strong cowboys to tie things up with..." She leaned down and kissed his chin, which meant that the soft flesh of her breasts momentarily pressed warm against his chest. "Anything you'd like to lasso, cowboy?"

He felt so hot and tingling all over he could hardly think straight. Hell, yes, he'd like to lasso her. Of course, she'd said the same thing when she had first seen the necklace. Some small, clear part of his brain told him that if the necklace hadn't secured her, the earrings weren't going to.

But it would be worth a try. He still had $27.50 left from last week's pay. If that wouldn't cover the earrings, well...maybe he could get another lawn job. Mrs. Tremel had said something the other day about needing help.

"Hey, get your tongue out of her cleavage, Mackey. Mr. Metzler wants his car, and besides, Coach is watching."

At the sound of Cullen's voice, Binky jerked back. Eddie twisted into a sitting position, banging his elbow hard on the steering wheel. Coach McClintock was cool, but even he wouldn't stand for Binky draping herself all over him like a human blanket.

"Hi, Coach," Binky said, twisting her lariat around her index finger and smiling so that every one of her dimples was showing. "Don't be mad at Eddie, Coach. It was my fault he took so long on the car." She tossed her blond ponytail. "I distracted him."

Coach McClintock laughed and turned back to Mr. Metzler without a real answer. Eddie growled and, putting his hands behind Binky's bare knees, tugged her toward him.

"Stop flirting with him," he said. "You've got a boyfriend, remember? Besides, he's too old for you."

Binky ruffled his hair with her pink-tipped fingers, but she was still staring at Coach. "Yeah," she sighed. "But he's just so hot, you know?"

Cullen, who had come over to work on Metzler's tires, picked up the hose and, putting his finger over the nozzle, aimed it in Binky's direction. "Down, girl," he said.

Binky squealed and dodged the spray gracefully. It fell short, and lay on the hot, dirty pavement, shining in little oily rainbows. You could almost smell the steam coming up around it. Binky stuck out her tongue at Cullen, blew a kiss to Eddie, then headed over to chat with her friends.

Eddie watched her go with mixed emotions. He could get more done if she weren't within touching distance. On the other hand, he wasn't that crazy about being alone with Cullen. The other boy had said something earlier about needing a favor. Eddie had a pretty good idea what kind of favor it was.

"So, Mackey. I was wondering." Cullen didn't look up. He stared hard at the tire he was washing and talked out of the corner of his mouth. He'd probably seen some gangsters talk that way on television. Cullen was a genius with the football, but his brains didn't work all that well off the field.

Eddie ducked his head and fiddled with the vacuum hose, trying to wind it back around its canister. He didn't say anything. If only someone would come up right now and interrupt them, God, what a break that would be. But Coach McClintock and Mr. Metzler seemed deep in conversation, and everyone else was working on cars.

"I was wondering," Cullen started again. "You know, about English. About the paper."

"What paper?"

Cullen finally looked up. He had a strong-boned face, and when he was irritated he looked mean. "What paper? You trying to be funny? Don't get the roles mixed up here, Mackey. I'm the funny guy. You're the smart guy. Remember?"

Eddie hesitated. Cullen was big, handsome and athletic, and he had the world's most extensive repertoire of sarcastic put-downs—which he loved to use on geeks who weren't cool enough to be on the football team, like Eddie.

Eddie felt like telling Cullen that Coach McClintock wanted Eddie on the team next year. That might shut him up a little. But Eddie wasn't sure yet whether he was going to say yes, so he forced himself to stay silent.

Everybody liked Cullen, though, or at least pretended to. His dad owned the local imported car dealership, and that meant he had a fancy house, a fancy car, a gorgeous girlfriend and the coolest clothes. The only thing he didn't have was a passing grade in English.

"Tennyson," Cullen said with a grin, as soon as he realized Eddie wasn't going to attempt a comeback. "Five hundred words. Not too perfect, don't want Mrs. G to smell a rat, right?" He laughed. "A C paper, that's all. Do I get a discount for a C paper, Mackey? I should. You can write a C paper in your sleep."

"I don't know, Cullen. I'm pretty slammed right now. I'm mowing about a hundred yards and—"

"I already flunked English once, Mackey. I don't intend to flunk it again." Cullen's face hardened and became all jutting bone. "What is it? You want me to pay extra? Because it's summer school? Getting kind of greedy, aren't you?"

"I don't want you to pay extra." Eddie wiped his hands on his jeans. He cleared his throat. "To tell you the truth, I really wasn't planning to do any more of that. Papers, I mean."

"Say what?" Cullen stood, and his big, beefy body blocked the sun. "You're not writing any more papers? Hey, man, that's not funny."

"I'm not trying to be funny. I'm just saying I think it's time to stop. I mean, it's cheating, and sooner or later we're going to get caught, and—"

Cullen bent over, putting his face so close to Eddie's the threat was unmistakable. "Listen, Mackey. If you want to suddenly get religious about all this, you do it after summer term is over, understand? Sure it's cheating, but you're in it up to your big red ears already, and you're not pulling out until I've passed English."

Eddie stood up, too. He didn't like being threatened. He wasn't as big as Cullen, but he worked out, and besides, he was smarter. He liked his chances against the big oaf any day. "Watch your tone, Cullen, because I don't take orders from—"

But maybe Cullen wasn't as dense as Eddie thought. His face changed suddenly, as if he'd realized there might be a better way to handle this.

He lifted his big hands and rested them on Eddie's shoulders. His fake smile was somehow more unsettling than his scowl had been.

"Hey, sorry, man," he said in a hearty tone. "I didn't mean to come on too strong. It's just that I like you. And I know Binky does, too. I mean, we'd all hate it if you weren't part of the group, you know? We'd miss you, man."

Eddie opened his mouth. But nothing came out. This wasn't an empty threat. Cullen Overton had more social power in his meaty little finger than Eddie Mackey had in his whole body. If Cullen decided Eddie was Out, then he was so Out he might as well live on Mars. And Binky Potter would be draping herself over some other guy by the end of next week.

Cullen's small green eyes were bright with triumph. He patted Eddie's shoulder a little too hard. "So it's a deal. Tell you what. I'll pay double, you know, because it's summer. And you'll write me a seriously C-type Tennyson paper. Thanks, man."

He began to walk away. But then he turned around with one last, fake smile so big his white teeth glinted in the sun. "Oh, and Jeff said he might need one, too. I'll tell him to get with you soon, so you have plenty of time, okay?"

He didn't wait for an answer.

Eddie sat back down on Mr. Metzler's front seat.

He was tired suddenly. The party hadn't wound down last night until about two in the morning, and they'd had to be out here by seven. He still had three lawns to mow this afternoon. Maybe being booted into social outer space wouldn't be so bad, really. At least then he could get some sleep.

But Binky... He heard her laughing with her friends. She had a sweet laugh, throaty and mellow, not shrill and sarcastic like the other girls. She might be a little greedy about jewelry, but he believed there was something special about her. Something worth fighting for.

Fighting for, maybe. But was she worth cheating for?

He wiped his hand over his eyes, and when he opened them again he saw that Coach McClintock was walking over to him. Oh, great. Eddie was sure he was going to get a lecture for taking so long with the Caddy, but to his surprise Coach just leaned one hip against the front fender and seemed to be admiring the sparkling windows.

"Nice job," Coach said casually.

"Thanks." Eddie hoped his voice didn't sound as pooped as he felt. He didn't want to sound indifferent. He cared what Coach thought of him. A lot.

"I hope the girls appreciate how hard you guys are working to buy them new uniforms," Coach said. "Think they'll come out and wash cars when the football team needs new helmets?"

Eddie cast another look toward Binky and her friends. One of the girls was trying to make some complicated braid thing out of Binky's long blond hair, and the others watched breathlessly, as if it were brain surgery.

"Yeah, right," he said. He looked at Coach, and the two of them smiled in perfect harmony on the subject of girls. Well, at least these girls. They were definitely not the future astronauts and Nobel Prize winners of the world. They were born to be pretty and pampered—and pointless. Like really expensive, slightly dangerous pets.

He suddenly wondered why he was killing himself trying to raise money to buy one of his own. He couldn't really imagine wanting a pet for a wife.

But damn it, he was seventeen. He didn't want any kind of wife. He wanted to get laid, just like everybody else.

"So how are things, Eddie? Everything going okay?"

Eddie looked up at Coach. His tone was weird. Did he sense something? Did he *know* something? Had he overheard what Cullen had said?

"Things seem fine." Eddie chose his words with care. "We're getting a lot of cars."

Coach gazed at him with a quiet, oddly gentle expression. "I don't mean the car wash. I mean you. You seem a little down. Everything okay?"

God, if he only knew! *Nothing* was okay.

For one insane minute, Eddie thought he was going to blurt out the whole sleazy truth. Thought he might say that he was selling his soul for a chance to get into Binky Potter's pants. That he had finally found a way to run with the big boys, and it was damn near killing him. That he was tired and trapped and sick of the whole thing.

But how could Coach help? Coach had been *born* one of the big boys. He practically owned Heyday, as his father had before him. He had no idea what it felt like to be on the outside, straining to get in.

Besides, he was so damn straitlaced. Everyone around here called him the Saint. He'd never allow the paper-selling thing to go on—and he'd never let Eddie get away unpunished.

"Eddie?"

Eddie hesitated, still unsure. Yes, telling Coach would be suicide, but at least it would be over. The temptation was almost irresistible. It would be a relief if someone like Coach could just *force* him to stop, since he didn't seem to be able to stop himself.

But in the end he didn't have the courage. He didn't have the nerve to see Coach's face when he realized Eddie was a scumball. He didn't want Coach to withdraw his offer to bring Eddie onto the team.

And he definitely didn't have the guts to give up the hope that someday Binky Potter would say yes. Maybe even tonight. They had a movie date at eight, and if he didn't get started mowing those lawns soon he'd be late. When they went to the movies, she liked to tease him, sucking slick popcorn butter from his fingers one by one till he nearly died.

No way could he give that up.

"Eddie?" Coach's voice was tighter now. Really concerned. "You can tell me. What's wrong?"

"Wrong? What could be wrong?" Eddie stood up again and tossed Coach a smile as fake as anything Cullen Overton had ever produced. "Life's sweet, man. Sweet."

KIERAN WAS DOG TIRED, and he would have given anything he owned to be able to take a long hot shower, order a sloppy pizza, open a freezing cold beer and spend the evening in front of the TV.

Instead, he had to dress up in a penguin suit and go next door to Aurora York's house, where he would spend three hours pretending he gave a damn who was elected Heyday's next parade Ringmaster and Ringmistress. Even worse, he might well be nominated himself, which would mean he'd have to pretend to be delighted.

Frankly, he wasn't sure he had "delighted" left in his bag of tricks tonight. It had been a *very* long day.

He did take the shower. That wasn't optional, not after standing in the sun all morning helping teenagers wash cars. And he got the beer, too. That wasn't optional, either, not after having spent the entire afternoon listening to the Heyday Historical Society bitch about Larry Millegrew, a newly arrived artist who had dared to paint his house orange.

Kieran didn't know how he'd stopped himself from laughing. When had this town become so darn snooty? Pretty ironic for a town that got its jump-start because of a drunken circus animal trainer to begin having apoplexy at the sight of an orange house. "Gray and white," Dolly Jenkins had kept repeating at today's meeting, sounding weak with shock. "Gray and white. Anything else is just vulgar!"

But what did they want Kieran to do about it, anyhow? He had inherited a lot of the property around here, but his dad's estate wasn't even probated yet, and besides, this wasn't feudal England. He couldn't exactly throw Mr. Millegrew in the dungeon and commandeer his absurd orange house.

Kieran tossed his towel on the bed and, still yearning for the pizza he couldn't have, he reluctantly began to assemble his tux. He hated parties. This must be one of the ways in which he took after his mother, who everyone said had been a quiet, unassuming woman. She'd died when Kieran was born, so he knew her only as a wispy, smiling face in a small watercolor painting on the living-room wall.

He certainly didn't take after his dad, who even at seventy had been all strong, primary colors, all great bold strokes in oil, like the portrait of him that hung above the fireplace mantel.

His dad could have handled Dolly Jenkins and Larry Millegrew with one hand, then tossed off tonight's party like an after-dinner cognac. Old Anderson McClintock had loved people. He'd loved parties. He'd loved power games. And, as he had every day since his father died, Kieran wished the old devil were still alive to play them.

Kieran knew he was dragging his feet and probably running late, so he wasn't surprised when the doorbell rang.

It was probably Aurora. She had asked him to come over early to help with the lights. She'd be mad as hell to discover he wasn't even dressed.

"Coming," he called as he trotted down the stairs with his dress shirt still half in, half out of his trousers. His black tie dangled between his teeth as he tried to insert his cuff links.

"Sorry, Aurora," he mumbled as he swung open the door. "But you're just in time to tie my—"

But it wasn't Aurora, who at seventy-five was still an imposing old lady. She would have stood about five-eleven, higher if you counted her heels and the feather plume she invariably wore in her hat.

This was someone younger, smaller—someone

who stood back, out of the glare of the porch lamp, clearly far less sure of her welcome than Aurora had ever been in her life.

But who…?

The woman moved awkwardly, and the creamy light washed over her.

Kieran dropped his cuff link. It was Claire Strickland.

The little ebony square clattered out onto the porch, and Claire stooped stiffly to pick it up. Watching her, Kieran pulled his tie slowly from between his teeth. He tried to gather his thoughts, which were about as disorganized as darting minnows. But it was just such a shock. What was Claire Strickland doing showing up here, unannounced, on his doorstep?

The last time he had seen her was that strange, unforgettable night in Richmond. He'd thought of her—and of the sex, of course—almost every day since. But he hadn't called. After they'd awakened in the echoing, predawn hours, she had asked him to leave. And she'd made it clear she did not want to hear from him ever again.

In the distance, he could hear the sounds of the party tuning up. Laughter, the strum of an electrified cello, the distant thud of car doors.

But here on the porch everything was silent. He felt a sudden flash of anxiety. Was she all right? He knew she wouldn't have come here without a very serious reason, not after the way she had told him goodbye….

And why was she dressed in black, her face as somber as if she had just been to a funeral? Good God, had someone else in her life died? He hadn't thought she *had* anyone else.

"Kieran, I'm… May I come in?"

"God, yes, of course. I'm sorry." He backed away from the door and let her enter. She stood there in the foyer, glancing around as if she'd never seen the inside of his house before. Which, he realized with surprise, she actually hadn't. Their relationship—or whatever embryonic version of a relationship they'd been trying to develop when Steve's death had shattered it to bits—had never progressed far enough for him to bring her here.

As she took it all in, her gaze held a strange combination of curiosity and apathy. It was as if she knew she should care what his house looked like, but she just didn't.

He tried for a second to see it through her eyes. The big, classical Georgian mansion was pristine, thanks to his housekeeper. The only item out of place was his half-empty beer bottle. He didn't have anything to feel ashamed about.

And yet, oddly, he did.

Perhaps it was just that the place was so ridiculously big. That he had so much when she had always had so little. He remembered the simple house she and Steve had shared. And that half-empty tomb she called home in Richmond.

"Claire, is everything all right? Why have you come? Do you need anything?"

She looked up at him. Her eyes were bottomless, and circled with thin, blue-shadowed skin. Her cheeks were pale, and for a moment he thought he saw her shudder. He put out his arm to steady her, but she backed away.

"Claire, what's wrong? Are you ill?"

"No," she said. "I'm pregnant."

CHAPTER FIVE

SHE HAD KNOWN, OF COURSE, that he'd be stunned—
and upset, too, especially when he realized what she
wanted to do about the pregnancy. She wasn't a fool.
She certainly hadn't been expecting him to hug her
and start passing out cigars.

But she could never have imagined the look of
pure, unadulterated horror that fell over his features.
It was as if someone had announced the end of the
world.

Strange how painful it was to see. Her face burned
as if she'd been slapped.

However, she had to pull herself together. She had
intended to be strong and businesslike, presenting her
facts and her demands unemotionally. She was furious with herself for suddenly coming across all weak
and weepy. It must be the hormone fluctuations the
doctor had warned her about.

And maybe it was also the confusion of entering
this house, which had always been the symbol of
unassailable power in Heyday. She'd felt uncomfortable even ringing the bell, like some unfortunate
chambermaid come to tell the lord of the manor he'd
done her wrong.

She'd always known Kieran was rich and important. Everyone in Heyday knew that. But knowing
an abstract fact and seeing him here, dressed in a

tuxedo, his handsome face and imposing physique so at home against the marble and the tapestries and the sheer impressive magnitude of his mansion, were two very different things.

She straightened her shoulders. Damn it, she wasn't the chambermaid. And he wasn't a lord. He wasn't even the Saint everyone had always called him. He was just a guy who'd slept around once too often and gotten himself caught.

"I'm sorry," she said, keeping her voice cool. "Maybe I shouldn't have been so blunt. I know it's a shock, but—"

"Yes," he said. "It is."

"It was for me, as well. But it's true." She let her fingers rest against the black purse that hung at her side. She realized they were trembling. "I brought documentation from the gynecologist, in case you—"

He squinted and put out his hand, as if to stop her, though he didn't actually touch her arm. "For God's sake, Claire. I don't think you're lying."

"Okay. Well, then, I assume you'll want some proof of paternity. I haven't looked into that yet. I thought it likely you'd rather work with doctors, or laboratories, of your own choosing, to ensure an un-biased—"

He shook his head tightly. "If you say it's mine, I believe you. It's just that I had thought that we— I mean I did—"

"Yes, you did. But we both know that's not ex-actly a one-hundred-percent guarantee. Again, if you have any uncertainty, I'm perfectly willing to let you establish—"

"No." He was still holding his cuff link. He was

opening and closing his fist over the thing compulsively. Other than that, he was so motionless he might have been one of the sculptures that stood at intervals along the walls of this formal foyer. "I told you, if you say this is my problem, I'll accept that."

Heat flashed through her. "You must have misunderstood me. I didn't say this was your *problem.* I said this was your *child.*"

He flushed. "I'm sorry. I didn't mean it to sound like that. It's just that—I need a little time to absorb…"

He raked his fingers through his hair, which seemed to be damp. He must have showered recently. And the tuxedo. Suddenly she realized she had interrupted preparations for something.

When she arrived, she had only half registered the men and women milling about next door, in front of Aurora York's house. Now she could put two and two together. He was on his way to a party. She was probably making him late.

Well, too bad. She hardened her heart against his obvious bewildered distress. The arrival of a baby was going to change a lot of plans, for both of them. They were just going to have to get used to it.

And if he'd been planning to meet some woman over there, some glamorous Heyday socialite who was even now impatiently awaiting his arrival… Well, it was better that he learn about the baby before he let the dancing and the drinking and the flirting go too far.

"Yes, it might be good to take a little time to think," she said. "Anyway, I can see that you're busy. I'm staying in town, at the hotel, and we can talk more tomorrow. I just thought it was important to let you know as soon as possible."

Before she lost her nerve and ran back to Richmond.

"But—are you all right?" He seemed to be waking up a bit. He looked at her with clear eyes for the first time since her announcement. He frowned, as if what he saw worried him. "You look tired. Are you well?"

"I'm fine. I have a little nausea sometimes, but that's normal."

"What about money? Do you need money?" He touched his shirt, then seemed to realize he wasn't completely dressed. "My wallet is upstairs, but if you'll—"

She lifted her chin. *Money!* Of course that was what he would think. People who owned things were always convinced the rest of the world wanted to take those things away.

"It's not about money," she said. "Don't insult me, Kieran."

He made a small sound and came toward her, holding out his hand. Then, for the first time since she'd arrived, he touched her. It wasn't much, just his palm on her shoulder, but it sent waves of weakness through her torso, and it almost loosened the emotional dam she used to hold back her tears.

"Claire—"

She backed off. What was wrong with her? Why did the slightest touch turn her steel will to mush? She had reacted the same way when the gynecologist had patted her arm and told her everything was going to be fine.

Except for the night she and Kieran had made

love, she had barely touched another human being in two years. She had thought she didn't need it, thought she was too strong to need it. Obviously she'd been wrong. Apparently she was starving for it, as weak as a baby herself.

"I don't want your money," she repeated. "You can relax. I'm not here either as a beggar or a blackmailer."

"God, of course you're not," he said roughly. "Damn it, Claire, the thought never crossed my mind. But it's just that—if you won't let me help you financially…"

She looked at him. This had seemed much easier when she rehearsed it in the car on the way here. It had seemed so simple, like a business deal where everyone paid a fair price for what they got. Crime and punishment, sin and penance, equally balanced. She had even imagined that he might suggest the obvious answer himself.

But now she saw how thoroughly she had deluded herself. St. Kieran McClintock was genuinely horrified, completely bewildered and had no idea what she wanted.

She took a deep breath.

"I want you to marry me," she said.

He recoiled. There was no other word for it. He even took a step backward, as if she'd hit him.

"Marry you?"

"Yes. You don't need to look so stunned. That's frequently what people do in situations like this."

"But—" He undid the top button of his suit, as though he suddenly weren't able to get enough air into his lungs. "Those people are usually—they have relationships. Most people who end up in this situation know each other well, have a history, have plans for a future. They're usually in—"

"In love." Her voice cracked on the word, and she tightened her throat to avoid breaking down. "I know. It's awkward. I wish being in love were a requirement for making babies, but apparently it isn't. Apparently even people who have an utterly meaningless one-night encounter can still end up pregnant."

"I—I put that wrong. I didn't mean it like that."

"It doesn't matter. What matters is that we are going to have a child. A real, living, breathing person is going to enter this world. I don't want any stigma attached to his name. I want him to *have* a name."

"Stigma?" He frowned. "That's pretty old-fashioned thinking, isn't it? I mean, in this day and age, do people really—"

"Yes. People really do." She thought of Mrs. Straine, who everyone whispered had bought her own wedding ring and sent herself flowers on an imaginary anniversary. She thought of her own mother, who had invented a marriage, then invented a divorce and cried into her pillow at night.

"I work at a very old-fashioned parochial school. I teach middle-school girls, who are becoming sexually aware themselves. I'm already on probation there for the sin of teaching them *Hamlet*. That's how repressed the environment is. Believe me, my principal would never allow an unmarried mother to be their teacher."

"Even so, there must be other schools, schools with more tolerant—"

"Perhaps. But I don't want to be chased out of my job, Kieran. I worked hard to get that position.

And I won't create an imaginary husband, either. My mother lived that lie for twenty years. I won't go through that, and neither will my child.''

He didn't pretend to be surprised. Obviously he had heard about her mother's little charade. It had been the most pitiful farce. At home, for their mother's sake, Claire and Steve had pretended that the fiction remained intact, but everyone had known.''

"But marriage." He shook his head. "Have you thought this through, Claire? Have you thought about—"

"Of course I have." She'd thought of nothing else since she'd found out. It had been an intensely lonely, agonizing mental struggle. She had no one to give her advice, no one who would help her sort through the pros and cons, help her put it all in perspective.

No one to help her step back, as Steve might have, and say, *but it's a baby! Surely that should be a happy thing.*

"This isn't some crazed plan I cooked up on the plane. I've thought through all the details. I'm not suggesting we stay married forever. I know neither of us wants that. But if we married right away, I could live in Heyday for the summer. Then, when school starts in the fall, I'd naturally have to go back to teach. If you were willing to visit a few times, meet everyone, establish the authenticity of the marriage—"

She took another deep breath. "Then we could officially separate, citing the problems of a long-distance relationship. And after the baby was born, we could get a divorce."

He didn't answer right away. He was staring, apparently right through her. She wondered what he saw. She wondered what he was thinking. Nothing happy, that much was certain. She'd never seen the charming Kieran McClintock look so devoid of all expression.

"When is that?" A muscle was moving in his jaw. "When exactly is the baby due?"

"The doctor said just after the new year. Working from…the dates I gave him, he said maybe early January."

"January." He seemed to roll the word around in his mind. He tried to smile, but she almost wished he hadn't. It didn't look right. "So we'd be married less than a year."

"Yes." She hoped he could see how little that was to ask. "Less than a year. And for most of it we wouldn't even have to be in the same city. And please, don't worry about the money. You can draw up any kind of prenuptial agreement you like. I want nothing of yours, nothing except a document that proves my child is legitimate."

His eyes seemed to narrow just a little. "Our child," he corrected without expression.

"Yes, of course. Our child would—" But she didn't have time to finish, because suddenly the large, dim foyer was filled with ringing. She jumped a little, startled. Then she realized that someone was outside, repeatedly pressing on the front doorbell.

Kieran cursed under his breath. "I'm sorry," he said. "It must be Aurora. She's probably tired of waiting for me. I'd try not answering, but she'd just break down the door."

He turned the knob, and it was like letting in a

tornado. Claire hadn't seen Aurora York in two
years, but the old lady hadn't changed a bit. Tall and
gaunt, she was dressed in a long black dress spangled
with black bugle beads. She wore high heels that
even a much-younger woman might have found
tricky, and her small sequined black hat was topped
with a big black feather that quivered wildly as Aurora, who had a touch of palsy, began to talk.

"—the most inconsiderate thing I've ever seen,
and I am glad your sainted mother isn't here to see
it. Everyone is on their second glass of champagne
already, and the nominations can't start until you get
there, of course, but where are you? Over here dil-
lydallying around with—"

She paused, turning to Claire. "Hello," she said
perfunctorily, then turned back to finish her tirade.
"Half the women at the party are whining about your
absence. It's extremely irritating, and look, you're
not even dressed yet, and—"

Suddenly she froze dramatically, like a cartoon
character who has just realized there's no ground under her feet. She turned back to Claire, her eyes wide.
"Claire? Claire Strickland?"

Claire smiled the best she could. "Yes. Hello,
Mrs. York."

Aurora smothered her in a tight hug. She was so
much taller that her bugle beads pressed painfully
into Claire's collarbone. "My heavens, I haven't
seen you since your brother's funeral, so sad that
was, so tragic. He mowed my lawn, you know. What
are you doing back in Heyday? Didn't I hear you'd
moved away?"

Claire opened her mouth to answer, but she didn't
get a word out before Aurora started up again. "And

dear heaven, why are you in black? Surely that isn't the same dress you wore to your brother's funeral? You'll have to give it up, dear. It isn't your color. It truly isn't. Is Kieran bringing you to the party? Oh, that should be interesting. Yes, that'll put a twist in a few knickers!''

Aurora rubbed her hands together as if the idea delighted her. "Kieran, get your jacket. I'll go tell everyone you're on your way."

And then she was gone, the tornado sweeping away as unpredictably as it had arrived.

Kieran looked at Claire and sighed.

"I don't think I can get out of it," he said, finally getting around to tucking in the other side of his shirt. "It's one of those things. She's been a friend of the family forever, and when my mother died she pretty much took over raising me." He began to work once more on his cuff link. "I promised her months ago that I'd act as host."

Claire nodded. "Of course. I understand. I'll just go to the hotel, and we'll talk tomorrow."

"No." He put out his hand. "She's right. You should come with me."

She frowned. He had to be kidding. "To Aurora York's party?"

"Sure. It's just the Ringmaster nomination foolishness. It'll be crazy, but we may get a few minutes to talk. Even if we don't, I can take you to the hotel afterward, and we'll have lots of time to talk on the way."

"I don't think so." She couldn't imagine herself there. It was the kind of high society snob-fest that no one would have dreamed of inviting her to two years ago. Poor young teachers from the wrong side of the tracks were not considered for admission to the Ringmistress court. "We can talk tomorrow."

"Claire, please. There's so much we haven't said, so much I haven't explained. I have a feeling I've expressed myself very badly. If you leave now, before you understand my position, you might—"

She laughed roughly. She understood his position, all right. He was dismayed that she was having his baby, horrified at her proposal that they cobble together even a short-term marriage. He couldn't have been much clearer than that. Tomorrow he might phrase it all more diplomatically, but she wondered if there was much chance that the underlying emotions would change.

Still, she couldn't give up yet. She had to believe that his conscience would be strong enough to overrule his emotions. He might eventually do the right thing—there was a reason they called him St. Kieran, after all.

He touched her arm. "I don't want you to be alone right now. I don't want to you to start feeling—to start considering—"

She knew what he was trying to say. "You don't need to worry. I intend to keep this child whether you agree to my plan or not. I won't run away, and I won't do anything stupid."

He tilted his head and smiled at her. It was his first genuine smile of the evening, and it kicked off another bout of seesawing hormones. She swallowed hard and looked away.

"I know you won't." He took her chin in his fingers and turned her face back to his. "But we have to start somewhere, don't we? If you can't spend a

single evening as my date, how can you possibly
contemplate an entire year as my wife?''

"SO IF YOU WERE TO ASK ME," Roddy Hartland said,
grinning as he joined Kieran at the patio bar, "I'd
say some sneaky old Heyday hound dog has been
keeping secrets from his best friend.''

Kieran followed Roddy's gaze to the other side of
the back yard, where Aurora was introducing Claire
Strickland to several elegantly dressed middle-age
ladies.

"I'll be careful not to ask you, then,'' he said,
plucking a beer from the white-draped table and
walking to the edge of the sparkling blue pool. He
didn't mean to be rude, but he wasn't in the mood
for Roddy's irrepressible curiosity.

Practically from the moment they arrived, Aurora
had confiscated Claire and trotted her around as if
she were the new discovery of the social season. Kieran hadn't had a minute alone with Claire to talk
about anything personal. Not that he was sure what
he'd say anyhow. His brain felt like a downed elec-
trical wire, twisting and sparking randomly, without
making any useful connections at all.

It was a little like walking through a nightmare,
although, if it were, at least he could hang on to the
distant hope that maybe he'd wake up soon.

But it all felt real enough. The people buzzing
around, talking and laughing. The musicians playing.
The anxiety in the air as every eligible young man
and woman wondered if they'd be nominated for the
Ringmaster Court.

God, did things like that still matter to anyone? To
Kieran, it all seemed like something happening on

another planet. As he stared down, a summer breeze smudged the pool's surface, blurring the reflection of tiki torches. He'd like to be under that water right now, where no sound could reach him. He'd like to swim laps until he was so tired he couldn't think.

Roddy reappeared with a beer. "Yessir," he said playfully, "the boy's been keeping secrets. And a mighty pretty little secret she is, too."

Kieran drank his beer silently. He didn't know how much alcohol he was going to need to take the edge off this irrational panic, but it was definitely more than he'd had so far.

Roddy leaned against the silver arch of the climb-out ladder. Claire was just across from them now, being entertained by two of Heyday's most courtly good old boys. She actually appeared to be laughing.

"So was she always this fine?" Roddy tilted his head. "Why didn't I notice her, you know, before? Was she always such a knockout?"

In spite of everything, Kieran had to smile. Roddy would always be Roddy, wouldn't he? On the ele-mentary-school playground, Roddy, the science teacher's six-year-old son wearing hand-me-down Levi's, had walked right up to Kieran, the million-aire's seven-year-old son, and shoved him. "You may be rich, McClintock," he'd said, "but I can set off a stink bomb that'll get us out of class for hours."

They'd been best friends ever since.

Now Roddy was rich, too. Ten years ago, some plastic conglomerate had paid him hundreds of thousands of dollars for the rights to a couple of his nutty inventions—a leftovers bag shaped like a slice of pizza, and a paper plate with its own plastic wrap attached. They'd never put his ideas into production, but Roddy had cheerfully invested their option money and turned it into millions.

But some things never changed. Roddy still noodled around trying to invent things, he still wore cheap jeans, and he still said whatever he thought. And Kieran realized that he was damn glad there was at least one corner of his world that wasn't standing on its ear.

"Yes, she was always pretty," Kieran said. "But now she's…"

What was the word? She was so much more than pretty. Her hair had grown a little since he saw her last, and it swung softly against her pale, fragile shoulders, catching amber lights from the torches. She looked sexy, mysterious and infinitely rare.

He shrugged. "She's grown up a lot."

"Hell, yes, she has." Roddy growled appreciatively. He gazed at Kieran. "So come on, tell me. Are you two seeing each other, or what? I mean, back when Stevie died, things didn't look too friendly. As I recall, when you showed up at the funeral, it took three men to keep her from clawing your eyes out."

Kieran took a swig of beer. "I shouldn't have gone. She had asked me not to."

"My point precisely. So how exactly did we get from there to here?"

"I'll be damned if I know, Roddy." Kieran put his empty beer bottle on a passing waiter's tray and grabbed another one. "I'll be damned if I know."

Roddy had another good trait. He knew when to quit. He was silent a moment, dipping the toe of his shoe in the pool. Of all the men out here, only Rod had sneakers on under his tuxedo trousers. The reflections of the fiery torches danced crazily and then died down.

"All right," Roddy said cheerfully. "Watch the diplomatic young man deftly change the subject. What do you hear from the long-lost brother Bryce— or the suddenly discovered brother Tyler? Or is the subject of brotherhood off limits, too?"

Kieran shrugged. "I don't hear much. Neither one of them seems to be terribly interested in checking out the inheritance."

Roddy nodded. "Waiting until everything's probated, no doubt. Easier that way to take the money and run."

Only Roddy could get away with being quite that blunt, but Kieran knew that the crazy McClintock soap opera had been entertaining Heyday gossips for decades. Even so, the revelations in Anderson's will had been particularly explosive.

Everyone had always known that Anderson had plenty of wives—five to be exact. Bryce was Anderson's oldest son, the child of Anderson's first wife and indisputably the black sheep of the family. Anderson had divorced Bryce's mother when the boy was only about four and had married Kieran's mother before the ink on the divorce papers was dry.

With his embittered mother, Bryce had moved away from Heyday, returning sullenly every summer merely to demonstrate his contempt for old Anderson and his new half brother Kieran, too.

Finally, the summer Bryce was eighteen, he'd ticked off old Anderson for good, and no one in Heyday had seen Bryce since—about fourteen years now. So it was a mild surprise to discover that the eldest

McClintock boy hadn't actually been disinherited at all, as Anderson had threatened.

But the most stunning revelation was the existence of a third heir. Kieran had turned thirty this year, and so had Tyler Balfour, an illegitimate McClintock son no one, including Kieran, had ever heard of. Anderson had never married Tyler Balfour's mother—even though he seemed to marry just about everyone else he slept with—and Anderson's lawyer had dryly explained why at the reading of the will.

While divorcing Bryce's mother, Anderson had found himself with two pregnant mistresses at once, Charlotte Balfour and Colleen, Kieran's mother. He couldn't marry both of them, obviously. He picked Colleen, which left Kieran the golden, beloved son, and Tyler Balfour an unacknowledged bastard.

It had taken Kieran a while to get over the sense of confused betrayal. He had loved his father. They had been close. But apparently not close enough to learn all old Anderson's secrets. Not close enough to be told about his own half brother.

He looked over at Roddy now. Roddy never really looked shocked by Kieran's family, which was soothing.

"Bryce has at least telephoned," Kieran said. "But the infamous Tyler Balfour seems to be taking his own sweet time getting down here. We're not even sure he's going to accept the inheritance."

Roddy laughed. "Yeah, right. I'd like to meet the man who could turn down—how many billion is it?—and the chance to be lord and master of his very own town." He tipped his bottle Kieran's way. "Except you, of course. You're the only saint I ever knew who actually doesn't seem to enjoy being disgustingly rich.''

Kieran smiled. "It's okay. It's not as cool as knowing how to build a stink bomb or anything."

They sat in companionable silence for a few seconds while Kieran finished another beer.

"You know," he said suddenly, "it's damn strange what it does to you, growing up in a family like mine. Your sense of what's normal really gets screwed up, you know?"

Roddy looked over, eyebrows raised. But after he looked at Kieran's face, he hid his surprise and merely nodded, as if they had this kind of conversation every day.

Kieran wasn't quite sure why he had decided to confide in Roddy. Maybe it was thinking about those early playground days, when everything had seemed so simple.

Or maybe it was the four beers in forty-five minutes.

"My father was married five times."

Roddy nodded. This was hardly news to him. "Salty old dog."

"He traded in wives like other people trade in cars. I never knew what to call them. I never knew whether to bother caring about them, for fear they wouldn't stick around."

"Yeah," Roddy said. "And the last few were so hot, too. I'll bet that was weird. Although I have to tell you, having the same old mom-monster chewing on your ass all the time isn't much fun, either."

Kieran smiled one more time. "Your mom is one of a kind." Mrs. Hartland had always been involved in one environmental campaign or another. When they were in middle-school, she'd humiliated Roddy by chaining herself to a building Kieran's father planned to tear down. It had worked. That building now housed the *Heyday Herald*.

When Roddy got rich, he had put her through law school. She was a big-time environmental lobbyist in D.C. now, and she still sent Roddy lectures through the mail.

Kieran watched Claire talking to Mallory Rackham, who owned the local bookstore. He had forgotten they'd been friends, back in the old days. He'd also forgotten how beautiful Claire's smile was.

"Anyhow, I swore I'd be different. I vowed I'd never have a string of ex-wives. Or kids I didn't raise myself. A hundred times, a *thousand*…I swore I'd never, ever be like my dad."

Kieran shut his eyes. Roddy knew all this already. Best friends heard a lot of things through the years. But it was almost as if Kieran were talking to himself.

"You know I loved him, but—one wife, one family, that was what I wanted, no matter what. I vowed my kids would never wonder who was sleeping in dad's bed this time. Or what stranger might show up at the door and say he was your brother."

Roddy must have been getting a little sloshed himself. He nodded emphatically and pointed his beer at the sky.

"Hear, hear. Defy your fate, St. Kieran. Stand up and show them you care this much—" he snapped his fingers "—for the Curse of Old Playboy McClintock. No expensive treks to divorce court. No secret girlfriends with secret babies. No illegitimate children popping out of the woodwork—"

No one ever said Roddy was stupid. Somewhere during his silly monologue, he must have realized that Kieran wasn't playing along. He paused. The silence lengthened.

Suddenly he scowled, obviously thinking so hard it hurt. He lowered his beer and turned to Kieran.

"Oh, shit."

Kieran didn't answer.

Roddy placed his beer carefully on the pool coping. "Oh, my God," he said. "You're not. I mean she's not—"

Kieran felt his heart beating too fast, as if he'd been running. "So here's the bottom line. If I absolutely had to choose… I mean, if no matter what I did, I was going to have to break one of my vows to myself. If, no matter what I decided, I was destined to become my father after all."

He stared at his empty beer bottle. "Then what the hell am I supposed to do?"

Roddy looked as if he'd been hit with a brick. He blinked. He opened his mouth, then shut it again.

"Kieran," he said with a hoarse voice. "Oh, man. I—I'm so sorry."

"Okay, ladies and gentlemen, your attention, please." Aurora's forceful voice rang out across the pool, and all heads turned in her direction. "It's time to announce the candidates for Ringmaster and Ringmistress Court."

Kieran looked, too, though he could feel Roddy's horrified stare still boring into him. He had to keep up a calm facade. He had to pretend everything was all right, at least until he could think what to do.

"We'll announce the Ringmaster candidates first. Remember, ladies and gentlemen, that being nominated for Ringmaster is the highest honor Heyday society can bestow on our young men. Our nominees must be local bachelors, at least age thirty, who set the highest possible standards in every area of their lives. Their professional ethics. Their personal behavior. Their civic responsibility.''

A low murmur hummed through the crowd, and several people looked pointedly at Kieran. St. Kieran, they called him, though rarely to his face. But he knew, and in his heart he had liked it. It had made him feel that, in spite of his father's outrageous love life, in spite of the flawed McClintock genes, Kieran could do better.

It had made him believe he could be normal.

But pride went before a fall. Everyone knew that.

Kieran could see that Claire was watching, too, obviously expecting them to call his name any minute. How ironic she must find this whole farce! She of all people knew that he wasn't Saint anything.

He was either a man who would father an illegitimate child, or he was a man who would enter into a doomed marriage, a marriage that would end, as had his father's marriages, in the petty ugliness of divorce court.

These were his only options. His only choice now was to pick the lesser of two evils.

He touched Roddy's shoulder in a wordless goodbye, and he began making his way toward Claire. She had a right to know what he had decided. Her eyes followed his progress somberly.

But before he could make his way around the pool, Aurora began to speak again.

''Our first nominee for Ringmaster is...'' The guitar player warbled out a stringy semblance of a drum roll. Aurora opened an envelope with exaggerated drama.

"Mr. Kieran McClintock!"

The applause was enthusiastic, punctuated by wolf whistles and catcalls from some of the women who had sampled a little too liberally from the well-stocked bar.

Kieran paused as people began to shake his hand and slap his shoulder. Someone grabbed him and kissed him thoroughly. He was only halfway to Claire, but he could still feel her eyes on him. He could feel her exhaustion.

Someone pushed him toward Aurora, who was holding out the microphone. He accepted it numbly, and turned, staring out at the eager, smiling faces.

Well, they had come here for excitement, and he was certainly going to provide it. For sheer entertainment value, you couldn't beat watching a saint tumble off his pedestal.

"First, I'd like to thank the committee for this very special honor," he said. He felt himself relaxing. Funny, once he got started it was so easy. It was as if he'd written this speech a million years ago and had carried it in his back pocket all his life.

"But unfortunately, I'm going to have to decline."

"What?" He could hear the whispers. He could see the startled faces turn to one another, eyes asking the question. *Why?* Why would St. Kieran, the man everyone had always known would be this year's Ringmaster, suddenly take himself out of the running?

Even Aurora looked shocked, and a little angry, as if she were a director who had just discovered her leading man hadn't learned his lines.

"You see, I'm afraid I'm not going to be eligible to become your new Ringmaster," he went on. "Because by the time our parade rolls into town, I will no longer be a bachelor."

A collective gasp. But now, strangely, there was only one face in the crowd. One pale, oval face with wide, deep brown eyes that were locked on his. She didn't seem to be breathing.

"I hope you'll all join with me in celebrating my great good fortune. Because just tonight, less than an hour ago, Miss Claire Strickland did me the honor of agreeing to become my wife."

CHAPTER SIX

THE PARTY WAS FINALLY OVER, thank goodness.

Claire's mouth felt stretched to the aching point by all the forced smiling and polite laughter. After his announcement, Kieran had been attentive and thoughtful, but they never had any time to talk alone. Everyone had seemed thrilled—you'd think the whole town had just been waiting for the chance to celebrate Kieran's engagement.

And they had such excellent manners—not one person had even subtly hinted that Kieran's choice of fiancée was a shock.

Still, Claire longed to go somewhere quiet and lie down. She needed to sort through all the changes this strange evening was going to bring to her life.

Unfortunately, at the very last minute one of the power couples in attendance, two taut, fast-talking lawyers named Gordon, realized they had misplaced their eight-year-old daughter.

Kieran checked the pool first, but its glowing sapphire rectangle was undisturbed. That calmed the mother significantly, and she began to get cross, alternately calling ''Erica!'' loudly and informing the others that the little girl did this kind of thing all the time.

''Ought to keep her on a leash, then,'' Aurora retorted, her feather bobbing, ''if you can't teach her common sense. In my day, kids did what they were told, they didn't go wandering around getting lost in other people's—''

"She probably just fell asleep somewhere," Kieran suggested. "Why don't we divvy up the house and launch a hunt?" He turned to Claire. "I know you must be tired. Would you like to wait for us in the library? The chairs are comfortable there."

Claire nodded gratefully. She wasn't sure how helpful she could be anyhow. She didn't know the layout of the mansion, and she didn't have any idea where the good hiding places might be.

But the others had been gone only about five minutes when she heard a noise just outside the library door, where the caterers had set up a cloth-covered table. Claire listened, and she heard it again. A scraping sound...something against wood, then metal against glass. Deciding that neither rats nor poltergeists would be audacious enough to invade Aurora York's territory, Claire went to investigate.

She reached the table quietly, and then she bent down and lifted the soft white cloth. Nothing. But then she noticed that the table stood a little crooked in the hall, and that it backed up to a built-in closet, and the door was askew.

She peeked in the door. Sure enough, a little girl sat cross-legged on the floor, sniffling as she ran a spoon along the sides of a custard dish, trying to get the last bits of a crème brûlée.

"Hi," Claire said. "Are you Erica?"

The little girl looked up, and to Claire's surprise her eyes were red, her cheeks wet with tears. She scowled. "No, I'm the *other* eight-year-old kid who ran away."

"Oh." Claire bit back a smile. It had been a dumb question. "Okay." They looked at each other a moment. Claire had just started to move away when the little girl spoke again.

"Are you going to tell them where I am?" Her voice was no less fierce than before.

Claire hesitated. "Don't you think I should? Your mom and dad seem pretty worried."

Erica shrugged. "I don't care. If you tell them, I'll just run away again before they get here."

Well, that wouldn't do. Claire wondered why the little girl had been crying, but she could tell it wouldn't be a welcome question. In fact, she probably could safely assume that eight-year-old girls were a lot like the middle-school girls she taught— full of defensive pride and embarrassed by everything.

Still, she couldn't afford to lose her. And something about her candid spunk appealed to Claire. If the truth were told, there had been plenty of times tonight that she, too, would have liked to hide in a closet.

So if Claire couldn't coax Erica out, she might as well keep an eye on her from the inside. She scanned the area, which was huge. Nothing in this house had stingy proportions, even the closets.

"Got any more of those custards?"

Erica squinted suspiciously. "I'm not supposed to eat too many," she said without really answering the question. "Or I'll get sick."

But Claire had already figured out that the little girl's skirt was strangely lumpy. She'd be willing to bet she was hiding at least a couple more desserts. Claire, who had been nauseated through most of the party and unable to eat, suddenly realized she was ravenous.

"Then maybe it would be a good idea to share." Claire tilted the table a little farther out into the room—when the others came by, that would be enough to alert them. She joined Erica in the big, empty closet, leaving the door open enough to let in lots of light, and sat on the floor beside her.

As she'd predicted, there was plenty of room. In fact, Kieran and Aurora could have joined them without being cramped. Claire smiled at the thought.

Erica looked surprised, but after a minute she edged her skirt sideways, exposing three more crème brûlées, all uneaten, and a small crystal wineglass that had been snapped at the stem.

Ah. That probably accounted for the crying.

"My mom's gonna kill me about that," Erica said glumly, staring at the broken glass. "I never, ever watch where I'm going."

Claire picked it up. "Looks like a clean break. I bet it could be fixed."

"Really?" Apparently comforted by Claire's nod, Erica picked up one of the crème brûlées and handed it to her. "We'll have to share the spoon."

After munching a few seconds in silence, Erica gave Claire an appraising look. "Hey, I know who you are. You're that lady who is going to marry Kieran."

Claire smiled. "Yes. Do you know Kieran?"

"Sure. My dad is his lawyer. He comes over all the time. I like him, even if he does own us. My dad says he's a benevolent despot."

"Oh." Claire took another bite, wondering if Erica had any idea what a despot was, benevolent or otherwise. She clearly loved to talk, but she was like a little myna bird, repeating sounds without meaning.

"So, tell me," Erica went on eagerly. "It is really true you have a shotgun?"

Claire swallowed her last bite without chewing. "Of course not. Where did you get such an idea?"

"I heard somebody say you did. I hear all kinds of stuff under here. They said that's how you got Kieran to marry you, with your shotgun. Then somebody else said, yeah, a shotgun named Steve."

A shotgun named Steve...

Claire was so stunned she couldn't even pretend it didn't matter. She just stared at Erica, feeling herself flushing all over. So that's what they had been saying, in whispers, in corners, when they knew she couldn't hear. When they were finished smiling to her face.

Erica, who was too smart to miss the implications of Claire's shock, rolled her eyes and groaned. "I guess I shouldn't have told you, huh? Was it rude? People say rude things about me, too. Like when Mrs. York said I should have to wear a leash like a dog."

Claire couldn't think how to respond. She ought to come up with something, just to make Erica less uncomfortable, but apparently Claire didn't have a brain at all, just a head full of anger and shame.

"It's okay," Claire finally said. "It just surprised me, that's all."

Suddenly there were footsteps in the hall behind them. And voices.

Kieran was talking. "Aurora, I know you mean well, but Claire and I were thinking just a quiet ceremony, just the two of us at the justice of the peace."

"Nonsense. Your mother would turn over in her grave if I let that happen, Kieran McClintock, and you know it. If you're really going to marry that girl, and I'm not saying you shouldn't, her brother was a good kid, and I've always thought she had real spunk, ever since she went for your throat at his funeral."

"Aurora—"

"You owe this to me, Kieran. You owe it to your mother's memory. If you're going to marry that girl, you're not going to do it in the dead of night, like something you're ashamed of. I'm going to give the two of you a proper wedding."

Aurora paused. "You're *not* ashamed of it, are you, Kieran?"

Oh, God. Claire moved to her knees, rushing to climb out and announce their presence. She didn't want to hear Kieran's answer. She might hear something that would make it even more difficult to do the one thing she knew she absolutely must do: provide a name for her unborn child.

Don't say anything, Kieran, she prayed silently. *I don't want to know.*

It was enough to know that he had hesitated, that he had not been willing—or able—to rush in with a denial.

She began to press on the door.

Erica lay her hand on Claire's arm. "Hey, if we wait," she whispered, excited, "we might hear some more cool stuff."

"That," Claire whispered back, somehow managing to soften it with a smile, "is exactly what I'm afraid of."

ON SUNDAY AFTERNOON, Eddie went to Morrison's Fine Jewelers and checked out the price tag on Binky's lariat earrings.

Two hundred dollars.

He was too surprised even to blink. While he stood there like a stooge, with his mouth hanging open, Mr. Morrison put the earrings back in the case, returned to his desk and screwed his spooky jeweler's monocle back into his eye.

The dang monocle probably gave him some kind of X-ray vision. Mr. Morrison had probably known from the minute Eddie walked in the shop that he had exactly $27.50 in his pocket.

But damn it. Who paid two hundred dollars for earrings?

Eddie thought of all the things he could buy with two hundred dollars. A used guitar. An Xbox. A stereo for his car. Tickets to the next great concert in Richmond.

Hamburgers at The Big Top for the rest of the *year.*

But then he thought of Binky.

He hadn't seen a single frame of the movie last night. While the U.S. Air Force blasted the incoming aliens with great big exploding guns, Binky had fed Eddie popcorn, piece by piece, from her fingertips to his lips.

Then, when he was pretty much ready to explode himself, she had begun to put the pieces on the tip of her tongue, and let him come and get them.

By the time the last alien went up in smoke, Eddie was a wreck. He'd probably never be able to smell butter again without getting turned on and stuttering like a moron.

"Anything else I can show you, son?"

Eddie flushed at Mr. Morrison's tone. The question wasn't serious. Mr. Morrison hadn't moved a muscle. He didn't intend to show dead-broke Eddie Mackey anything at all, except where the door was.

But at that moment the bell over the glass entrance jangled, and in walked Mrs. Tremel, dressed in a tight blue summer dress that just barely covered the important spots.

Eddie wondered if the fates had sent her to him. She had said something the other day about needing a guy to mow her lawn. At the time, he had told her he was completely booked up. He didn't see how he could fit another customer into his weekends.

How stupid had that been? Shoot, he didn't need to sleep late on Saturdays. He could always get up a couple of hours earlier.

If only she hadn't already hired someone else…

"Hi, Mrs. Tremel," Eddie said, smiling politely. "I'm really glad you came in. I was just about to call you."

"You were? That's nice." She smiled at him, her slick red lipstick revealing very large, very straight white teeth. She had a dimple, too, just like Binky, but Mrs. Tremel's hair was big around her face, kind of messed up in a super-expensive way.

She was an awesome-looking woman, considering she had to be at least, what, almost thirty? And she'd already been married and divorced.

Man, what kind of guy divorced a hot woman like that? Her breasts stuck out as round and firm as beach balls, and her ass was exactly the right shape to get the palms of your hand around.

Damn it, Mackey. Chill! He mentally shook the

image out of his mind and forced his gaze to focus just over her left shoulder. She'd never hire him if she thought he was a little creep.

"Yes, ma'am, I was wondering if you still need someone to do your lawn. I was thinking, if you did, that maybe I could squeeze you in."

She smiled slowly. He flushed, wondering if she thought he had meant something dirty. But then he remembered that grown-ups didn't do that, didn't read sexual innuendos into every single word.

Must be nice to be a grown-up. Frankly, it would be a lot less stressful to think about something other than sex.

"That's great, Eddie," she said, grinning. "I would be very happy to be squeezed!" She laughed slightly, as if they had shared a cute joke.

He laughed, too. *Ha ha. Nice one, Mrs. Tremel.*

"Let's see," she said. "I guess now we just need to agree on a price. Exactly what do you offer?" She held out her hands, palms up. "I think I'm going to need everything you've got. I haven't had a service in a very long time."

Eddie took a deep breath and focused on being a grown-up. *She's not coming on to you, moron.* It was just that last night with Binky had left him all revved up and nowhere to race. His mind was one big cloud of sex fumes.

But he noticed that even Mr. Morrison was listening curiously, forgetting to study his tiny little watch workings. And Mrs. Tremel was still smiling.

Well, okay, maybe she *was* flirting with him a little. She was that type. She was gorgeous, and she liked men. He realized that the idea made him feel kind of cool. He wished Binky were here to see it.

"I can do whatever you want, Mrs. Tremel," he said. He put on his most professional voice, eager to show her he was practically an adult who took his job seriously. It was true. He'd be eighteen in a couple of weeks. That was an adult, in every way that mattered.

"I have a riding mower and an electric edger and a grass whip. For your yard, I'd probably charge a hundred a month. I'd come every week from now to October, then twice a month in the winter."

She tilted her head. "That sounds great. Although I should warn you, sometimes I need a little extra attention. If I'm going to have a party or something I might need you to come an additional time or two."

"Of course," he said. "That's how it is with all my customers."

Still smiling, Mrs. Tremel dug in her purse and pulled out a wad of twenties. She held out her hand. "Then it's a deal, Mr. Mackey. And here's the first month in advance, just to make things official."

He started to say no, no that wasn't necessary. No one paid in advance. But then he thought about the earrings. A hundred dollars would put them on hold. Next week the Gordons would pay him for June, and then the little silver lariats would be his.

And Binky Potter, too.

Although suddenly he wasn't sure prissy Binky Potter was quite woman enough for a man like him.

AURORA YORK'S ELEGANT four-poster with satin sheets and down comforters just might be the most comfortable bed Claire had ever slept in.

Or maybe it was simply that, for once, Claire didn't have to toss and turn all night, wrestling with unanswerable questions. Her path, right or wrong, had been chosen. She was going to marry Kieran McClintock, and she was going to do it in a small ceremony two weeks from today, orchestrated by Aurora York.

Whatever the reason, it was the best night's sleep Claire had had in a long time, and she was very glad she'd let Aurora talk her into staying here instead of at the hotel.

Though she woke once, around seven, she had felt no morning sickness at all. She hadn't heard anyone stirring in the house, so she lay back down. To her amazement, she didn't wake up again until almost one in the afternoon.

Sunlight was pouring through her third-story window, dappled gold and green by the nearby sourwood tree. More than sixty feet tall, it towered over the house, and yet it was near enough that Claire could have reached out and picked one of its delicate white clusters of flowers, which looked so much like lily of the valley.

Through its branches, she could almost see into the third-floor windows of Kieran's house next door. She could have stayed there, of course—it was plenty big enough. But Aurora wouldn't hear of it. It might be the twenty-first century, with a whole new social-moral code, but in Aurora York's world it was still completely unacceptable for a young woman to spend an unchaperoned night under her fiancé's roof.

The houses were so close, however, that it was almost a technicality. Here, just blocks from the center of town, even the mansions rubbed elbows with one another. It wasn't until you got several miles outside Heyday that you found the old farms and plantations, many of them run-down and abandoned.

Kieran's house, on the other hand, had been maintained like the architectural jewel it was. It was a classic Federal-period mansion, painted a creamy coffee color with white accents on column and cornice. Deep-brown shutters flanked each window, matching the front door and roof.

On the street side, the house was serenely simple. Its front porch was narrow but elegant, with Ionic columns rising to a formal, filigreed cornice. Looking down at it now, Claire could hardly believe she had found the courage to mount that porch last night and ring that intimidating bell.

From this vantage point, she had her first glimpse of the beauty behind the house, away from the prying eyes of solicitors, tourists and envious nobodies.

In the long, narrow backyard a geometric sculpted garden drew intricate patterns of greenery around an oval swimming pool. A tiny octagonal summerhouse, flowers winding through its latticed walls, anchored the far end of the formal garden. Just far enough from the main house to be perfect for assignations.

But that wasn't all. Behind the summerhouse, an overgrown flagstone path led to one last shady alcove, where she could just glimpse a wrought-iron bench and a trickling fountain between the drooping branches of a weeping willow.

Secrets behind secrets. This was where the real lives were played out, hidden behind the placid facades these eighteenth-century mansions presented to the street. Claire wondered what it would be like to go beneath the surface. To enter those secret gardens, to learn the private truths behind the public faces.

"Ah, you are up!" Aurora knocked once at the bedroom door, then entered without waiting for an answer.

Claire turned from the window and smiled.

"Yes," she said. "Finally. I'm sorry to have slept so late. I can't imagine what got into me."

"Too much excitement." Aurora had brought a tray with her, and she put it on one of the tables in the room. It seemed to be loaded down with fruit and cheese and sandwiches. "People forget that even thrilling changes are stressful. I told Kieran that when he showed up this morning. Let her be, I said. She's sleeping, and she's going to stay sleeping. Go bother someone else."

Claire smiled. Imagine anyone talking like that to a McClintock. Kieran said Aurora had been like a grandmother to him. Apparently he hadn't been kidding. "How did he take it? What did he say?"

"He said I was an infuriating old tyrant, which is true, of course, and he said to tell you that he had to go out of town to talk to somebody about something, I forget exactly what, something about Anderson's will, I think. Stupid will, bringing in that bastard son after all this time. Anderson never breathed a word to me about it, I'll tell you. If he had, I would have given him a piece of my mind."

Aurora waved her hand at the tray. "So, what are you waiting for? Eat up. You're too skinny."

"Yes, ma'am." Claire sat down next to the table and wondered what was most likely to stay down. She settled for a wedge of cantaloupe. "This looks wonderful. But you didn't have to. I don't want to be a nuisance. I really could stay at the—''

"It's no bother. Cook did it. I just carried it. And I told you already, Kieran's fiancée will not be staying at any hotel, not while I'm around. We went through all that quite thoroughly last night.''

That wasn't technically true. Claire and Kieran had *tried* to go through it last night, but Aurora had refused to listen. Finally, after arguing endlessly and getting nowhere, they had given up and allowed her to win. At the time, it had seemed like their only hope of getting any sleep at all.

Claire had expected to discuss it further with Kieran the next time they were alone. Was he really willing to let Aurora host a wedding ceremony? Didn't that take the charade to a new, uncomfortable level? Aurora had promised to keep it simple, something she could arrange in two weeks, not a day longer. And just a few people. Just their very best friends.

Not that Claire had any friends in Heyday, really. She didn't have many in Richmond, either. What would Aurora make of that?

Clearly, Claire needed to talk to Kieran, but still she had been dreading it. How should they act? The situation was without precedent, at least in her life.

They would have to appear affectionate in public—they had already begun that part of the charade last night when they had stood together, his arm around her shoulders as they accepted congratulations. But when they were alone...then what? Would he decide to keep it cool and practical, like business partners or roommates? Or would he decide to be warm and friendly? Which would ultimately be easier for them both?

It was like embarking on a very long, very complicated theatrical event…a performance on which her child's future depended.

"Did he say when he'd be back?"

Aurora was bustling about opening drapes and running her fingers across the glossy wooden furniture, as if double-checking her housekeeper's dusting. Claire had never seen a seventy-five-year-old woman with so much vitality.

"Who? Kieran? Not really. Late tonight? Tomorrow? Soon, anyhow. But you and I are going wedding-dress shopping, so he can just be patient."

Claire set down her cantaloupe. "Wedding-dress shopping? Today?"

"Heavens, no. The stores we want aren't open on Sundays. Did you think we were going to buy your wedding dress at K-Mart?" Aurora laughed, enjoying her little joke. "We'll shop tomorrow. Actually, today I have a Garden Club meeting. Would you like to come with me? Don't worry—we don't waste time talking about flowers and such. We go straight to the juiciest gossip."

And today Claire herself would undoubtedly be the main course. She tried not to shudder, imagining it. "Thanks," she said, "but I have a few things I need to do around town, if you don't mind."

"Of course not," Aurora said. "You probably have friends to visit, too, young people. We're all a hundred years old at the garden club. But mind you don't overtire yourself. We're going to be very busy. I told Kieran that this morning. I said, we've got a lot to do, so don't you get in the way. I said you're going to have the rest of your life with that girl, so you might as well let someone else have the next couple of weeks.''

She sat down in the chair next to Claire and plucked a sandwich from the tray.

''Besides,'' she added, peeling apart the bread, apparently determined to investigate whether the cook had assembled the proper ingredients. ''You and I definitely need some time to get to know each other better.''

Claire smiled weakly, glad that her mouth was full, and she couldn't politely respond.

Time to get to know each other better.

If only Aurora knew the truth. That was exactly what Claire and Kieran needed, too.

CHAPTER SEVEN

BY MIDAFTERNOON, the wind had picked up, and the sun had hidden behind a bank of pewter clouds. The storm had seemed almost charming in Kieran's hilly Riverside Park neighborhood, where the raindrops fell in diamond chains through the leaves of the stately elms and then nestled, scattered and twinkling, on the velvety green lawns.

But in the dingy lowlands of East Yarrow Street, things were very different.

The sky seemed lower here, as if the lack of trees had let the gray clouds sink oppressively toward the earth. Lawns were spotty, and the rain splashed up from muddy puddles to stain the rusty wheels of overturned tricycles and the fat legs of plastic gnomes.

The neighborhood looked exactly the same as the day Claire had left. And not very different from the day, fifteen years ago, that she, her mother and Steve had moved into it.

She remembered how proud and happy her mother had been that day. The square brick house might be uninspired and, compared to the historic mansions of Kieran's street, a little tawdry, but it had been their own.

Their first real house. No more apartments. No more landlords, no more footsteps stomping overhead, no more loud music pumping through thin walls in the middle of the night.

Only in the past couple of years had Claire fully appreciated what a major accomplishment buying a home was for her mother, an underpaid legal secretary, a single parent with two young children to care for.

Claire parked just down the street from her old house, not wanting to draw attention to herself, even though the house looked empty. She debated whether to get out. She hadn't brought an umbrella, and what was there to see, anyhow? A For Sale sign had been planted in the front yard, with an attached plastic tube full of flyers that looked untouched.

But after a few minutes the rain began to let up a little, and she realized she couldn't resist getting a closer look. She opened her car door and, carefully stepping around a pothole, she made her way up the cracked sidewalk to get one of the flyers. That seemed legitimate enough, in case anyone saw her.

Seen up close, the house appeared fairly well cared for. Someone had painted it. She wasn't surprised that it was for sale, though the current owners had bought it from her just over a year ago. They had paid a ridiculously low price, even for Yarrow Estates, and they'd probably always planned to resell for a quick profit. Had they ever lived here at all?

She had just extracted one of the soft, damp pieces of paper from the tube when, to her shock, she heard a shrill voice coming through one of the open windows.

"I don't give a good goddamn if there's a *hurricane* outside. You promised you were going to fix that back step today, and if you don't drag your ass here in the next ten minutes, don't bother bringing it home at all.''

The sound of a phone slamming into its base cracked like thunder. And then a baby began to squall.

"Shut up!" The woman sounded beside herself with fury. "Just shut up!"

Claire looked at the front door, horrified, wondering if she should intervene. She was surprised at how indignant she felt. How could these vicious vibes be coming from *her* house?

The little Strickland family had known plenty of tough times here. Claire and Steve had bickered, like any children, and their mother had scolded and fussed, especially when she was overburdened. Claire remembered one winter when the power had been cut off briefly until the next paycheck came through, and their mother had let them roast marshmallows and sleep by the fireplace, turning it into an adventure. But later that night Claire had heard her crying softly, when she thought no one would hear.

It had never been easy. And, of course, the house had been witness to two unnecessary deaths, and the unspeakable pain that followed.

But it had never known this kind of bitterness. It had never been so utterly devoid of warmth and love.

The volume went up on the baby's cries. Claire heard the sound of something breaking. She began to back away, staring at the door, the door she no longer had a right to enter. It was raining again, harder than ever.

She shouldn't have come. Steve was gone, and so was his memory. These pitiful, shrewish people had driven it away.

After only about four steps, though, she collided with another body. She turned, gasping.

It was Kieran. He put his hands on her wet shoulders. "Steady," he said. "I didn't mean to startle you."

"You didn't," she said. "You didn't. I was just— I was just leaving."

But suddenly the front door opened. Claire glanced around long enough to see a thin, nicely dressed woman standing there peering at them through the rain.

"You two want to see the house?"

Kieran looked at Claire, a question in his eyes. She kept her back to the house. The baby was still screaming. Almost imperceptibly Claire shook her head, hoping Kieran would understand. He must have, because he eased the flyer out of her hand and held it up cheerfully.

"No, thanks, not right now," he said. "We just came by to pick up an information sheet."

"You don't need an appointment. I can show you around."

"Thanks, but we really haven't got much time right now. We'll call later, if that's okay."

"Sure." The woman seemed to hesitate. "You call later, then."

Kieran nodded. He turned around, put his arm across Claire's shoulders and began walking her back to his car, which was closer than hers. He opened the passenger door and helped her in. Then he went around to the driver's side, climbed in and shut the door.

"Just till it lets up," he said. "Then I'll drive you to your own car."

She nodded. "Thanks."

For a minute after that they didn't speak at all. He reached across her, opened the glove compartment and pulled out a small pack of tissues. He peeled off a few for himself, then handed the rest to her.

"Thanks." Carefully opening the tissues, she began to wipe her cheeks and throat dry. By the time she got to her forearms, the tissues were falling apart.

She looked over at him. He seemed relaxed, interested only in drying himself off a little.

"I didn't mean to be jumpy like that," she said. "I was just surprised to see you. I thought you had gone out of town."

As she said the words, she realized suddenly that his absence was the main reason she'd chosen this afternoon to make her pilgrimage. She had assumed he'd never know. And if the memories upset her, she'd have time to recover before she needed to face him again.

"Yes, but I only went to Grupton," he said. Grupton was the next little township over, not more than twenty minutes outside the Heyday city limits. The McClintocks owned almost as much of Grupton as they did of Heyday. "I was only gone a couple of hours."

"Oh. I see." She wadded the soggy tissue up in the palm of her hand. She looked out the rain-drenched window. The drops were running so thick she almost couldn't see the house anymore. "How did you know I'd be here? I didn't mention it to Aurora."

"I didn't know for sure," he answered, speaking a little slowly. "I tried the cemetery first. I thought maybe you'd want to—"

"No," she said. She swallowed. "Not yet."

He paused. "Well, anyhow, then I went to…I checked a couple of other places…."

She knew what he meant—she could tell by the discomfort in his voice. He thought she might have driven by Poplar Hill.

Why would she have gone there? To see the slashing scar in the tree that had ended Steve's life? Kieran really didn't understand her, did he? She had no interest in haunting the places she associated with Steve's death. If she decided to revisit the past, she'd want to go back to where he'd been alive and happy.

"Anyhow, then I remembered about your old house, so I came here."

"Why were you out looking for me at all? Did you need something?"

He lifted one shoulder. "I thought maybe you'd like to talk. It's going to be kind of difficult to get time alone now that Aurora has commandeered the situation."

Claire tried to smile. "Yes, she's a bit of a dragon, isn't she? But she seems devoted to you."

"She's extraordinary." He took a deep breath. "She pretty much took over the role of mother in my life from the time my real mother died. My father's wives were, for the most part, not very well suited to that job."

Like everyone else in Heyday, Claire knew all about Anderson McClintock's serial marriages. Each wife younger and flightier than the last.

"And that's why you feel you have to let Aurora put on a wedding?"

He looked at her calmly. "That's why I'd *like* to let her." He smiled. "I think she's been dreaming of this for years. But if the idea makes you uncomfortable, I probably can talk her out of it."

Of course the idea made her uncomfortable, especially now that she knew the entire town of Heyday had instantly deduced this was a "shotgun" wedding. She'd be standing up there in satin and baby's breath, and the people behind her would be snickering about her choice of bridal white and speculating about the exact measurements of her waistband.

But how could she tell him to hurt his dear friend just because it made her uncomfortable? She had understood when she came here that her proposed solution wouldn't be the "easy" path. Just the right one.

"No," she said. "If you can live with it, I can, too. I just—I just would like to generate as little gossip as possible."

His answering smile was wry. "You might as well try to stop a dog from chewing on a bone. I'm afraid our situation presents too much fresh meat. Especially with—our past."

Of course. Their past.

But what was that, exactly? One date, one death, and then one stupid, stupid night in each other's arms. How could that simple, terrible recipe have created such disaster?

Unable to answer him, she delayed by dabbing at the wet piece of paper he'd put on the seat between them. It was blurred, but the words were still legible. "Sturdy fixer-upper, family house, 3/2, 1,300 sq ft. Good schools."

A fuzzy photo—and then the price. Her eyes widened. The new owners were asking twice what they'd paid her for this house only a year ago.

Now that she had this new responsibility, this child who would arrive so soon and need so much, she realized she'd been shortsighted to sell her one big asset cheaply. But back then she had simply wanted to get rid of it. She'd been desperate to sever any ties that connected her to this street, to this town, to the haunted football field and the scarred tree and the little marble cross in the shady corner of Forestlawn Cemetery.

She had just wanted to run. And she'd almost made it.

Ironic, wasn't it? Now, because she had been weak and stupid, because she had fallen into Kieran's arms that one fateful night in Richmond, she would never be free of Heyday. Now her child, her own flesh and blood, would be a McClintock.

And the McClintocks didn't just own Heyday. They *were* Heyday.

"APPARENTLY THE RUMORS ARE TRUE," John Gordon said as he and Kieran came out of the city manager's office into the Monday morning summer sunshine. "You really are a saint."

"Shut up, John." Kieran rolled his eyes. "You're my lawyer. You know better than that. What's saintly about giving things away when you already have more than you could possibly use?"

"You've got a point. Still, can you imagine your brother Bryce giving away his inheritance? When everything finally makes it through probate, he'll probably just sell every square inch of it. And get top dollar, too. The devil has damn little love for Heyday. He hasn't set foot in it in, what, twenty years?''

"Fourteen. But who's counting?'' Kieran shrugged. "Bryce has his reasons, though, John. The last time he was here, things got pretty ugly.''

John nodded, and for a minute, Kieran thought the lawyer might ask him for details. The gossips had about six different and increasingly salacious versions of Bryce McClintock's final summer in Heyday, but people knew better than to talk about it in front of Kieran.

Bryce had always carried around a chip the size of a boulder on his shoulder, and he had never shown the slightest affection for any of the other McClintocks. But still, like it or not, they were brothers, and Kieran wasn't going to trade juicy Bryce stories with anyone.

"You may be right, though,'' Kieran said. "Bryce doesn't have a sentimental bone in his body. Owning a little town like this would probably strike him as just too ridiculous.''

It struck him that way, too, sometimes. Kieran looked around the little municipal complex they'd just exited, trying to comprehend the notion that everything in sight actually belonged to him—well, to him and Bryce and that unknown quantity, Tyler Balfour.

Four-fifths of all the land in the Heyday city limits. Half the buildings. The library, the bank, the bookstore and the beauty salon.

The police department, the fire department, city hall and the plots those buildings stood on… Some people even said that the politicians working inside city hall had been listed assets in his dad's will, too, although that part was pure spite.

Kieran gazed at the neat little fire department, a brick building that pretty much consisted of a huge garage and a brightly lit common room above it.

"Hey, John," he said. "Did you know I used to want to be a fireman?"

John grinned. "No kidding."

"No kidding. When I was about ten, I thought sliding down that pole and holding that huge hose would just about be heaven."

"Very Freudian." John winked. "So how come you didn't? You decided there was more money in the saint business, or what?"

"My dad didn't like the idea. He said McClintocks weren't civil servants."

John laughed. Old Anderson's snobbery had been well-known. For instance, he had at first refused to hire John and Evelyn Gordon's excellent law firm just because the Gordons hadn't been born in Heyday.

But John didn't care. Anderson had hired him in the end, because Anderson valued talent even more than pedigree. John also knew that Anderson and Kieran had been as close as father and son could be, in spite of all the old man's idiosyncrasies.

"He really said that?" John's expression was mischievous, making him look much younger than his nearly fifty years. Kieran could see why John had snagged a beautiful wife twenty years his junior. "And you let the old man just stomp out your dream?"

"Hey, I was only ten. I didn't have the courage

of my convictions. He threatened to take the TV out of my room.''

''I guess he wasn't that thrilled when you became a high-school football coach, then. Not much more socially upper crust than fireman, actually.''

''Nope. He was mad as hell. But I was twenty by then. I'd grown a little backbone. Plus, I'd discovered there was a TV down at Sam's Pierside that anybody could watch.''

And anyhow, Kieran had always known that Anderson's tirades were more noise than substance. Especially about the coaching job. Before long he had become Kieran's biggest fan. Until his heart got too bad to let him climb the bleachers, he had attended every Heyday High game Kieran coached.

Crusty old crow. Kieran would give a hell of a lot to look up and see that craggy, arrogant face in the crowd again this September.

But he refused to turn maudlin. That wasn't what Anderson had wanted. ''Just get busy and get on with your life,'' he'd told Kieran when he had finally accepted that he was dying. ''Your life. Your way. Forget everything I told you. I never knew what the hell I was talking about anyhow.''

So, in honor of his father, Kieran had done exactly that. Starting this morning.

''Seriously, though,'' John went on, ''I'm mighty glad Anderson wasn't here today to see you giving all that land away.''

Kieran grinned. ''Me, too.'' He remembered the first time he'd mentioned this idea to his father. Ten acres of prime downtown property, prime money-making land, which Kieran had inherited from his mother—and Kieran thought it should be donated to the city for a park.

His father, who hadn't left his bed for more than a month, had nearly jumped up and strangled him.

No, Anderson hadn't much believed in giving anything away. But Kieran knew the town needed it. And when the Little League program chairmen approached him last week, explaining how desperately they needed a new ball field, Kieran simply decided it was time to make it official.

He'd never miss the land. And if he did, well, he was a Heyday taxpayer. He could sit on the benches whenever he wanted to.

"Thanks for helping me out with the paperwork on this," Kieran said, holding out his hand as the two men drew near their cars and prepared to part. "I was particularly impressed with the way you set up the tax situation."

John shook his hand. "I'll pass that thank-you on to Evelyn. She drew up the documents. She's the money expert in the firm. I'm actually just supposed to be the mop-up man for your personal life." He sighed, an exaggerated heaving. "However, when you work for a saint, there's not much mopping up to do."

Kieran touched his shoulder. "If it'll make you happy," he said, "I'll try to be a little more decadent."

"Too late for that," John said wryly. "Isn't that your lovely fiancée heading this way?"

Kieran turned. It took a minute to answer, because, as incredible as it sounded, he almost didn't recognize Claire as she strolled toward them, only a block away.

But he had forgotten exactly how petite she was, compared to other women. If he'd ever noticed that she carried her shoulders tightly back when she walked, he'd forgotten it. He was pretty sure he'd never realized that her hair picked up so many golden highlights from the sun.

Besides, she looked so different from the drained, angry woman who had rung his bell Saturday night. Different, too, from the polite mannequin accepting congratulations from his friends with formulaic phrases and robot smiles. And definitely different from the rain-drenched mourner he'd found standing half-dazed outside the house in Yarrow Estates.

The sad truth was that, though they were to be married in twelve days, he simply didn't know her well enough to recognize her in all her moods.

Today she was like walking sunshine. She was utterly lovely and disarmingly young in a sleeveless dress as yellow as the honeysuckle that grew up the back wall of his house.

"Yes," he said belatedly, but with an illogical sense of pride. "That's Claire."

John gave him a serious look. "Well, at least you'll have one job for me. I'll be busy drawing up an ironclad prenup. Right?"

Kieran cocked his head. "What?"

"Prenup. A little piece of paper that protects your ass, I mean your assets, just in case the marriage doesn't quite last until death do you part. Every wedding ring should come wrapped in one."

"Oh. That. Yeah, maybe."

"*Maybe?*" John's whisper was filled with incredulity. "Not maybe, McClintock. Definitely. You're a very rich—"

"Hi, Claire," Kieran said with a welcoming smile, hoping his greeting would drown out John's words. "I was just headed back up to Aurora's house to see you. I don't know if you've met John Gordon."

Claire held out her hand. "Of course. We met at the party. How's Erica doing, John? Has she recovered from the crème brûlées?"

John's face was returning to its normal color. He took Claire's hand and gave her a smile that said he remembered well how cleverly she had corralled his obstreperous daughter.

"She had a pretty vicious stomachache yesterday," he said. "But she's back to normal now, God help us." He grinned. "Good thing my wife is still a young woman. I wouldn't ever have had a child so late in life if I'd known she'd be like Erica."

Claire laughed. "I thought she was adorable. Just be careful what you say around her. She repeats everything she hears. She's actually frighteningly smart."

"She thought you were terrific, too. She keeps asking when she'll get to see you again. I told her we'd have you and Kieran over for dinner soon." He glanced at Kieran. "That sound good?"

Kieran exchanged a wry smile with Claire. "We'll have to check with Aurora. Claire is pretty much her prisoner between now and the wedding." He glanced toward the street, where Aurora's long white Cadillac was purring to a stop beside them. "See what I mean?"

He moved to the curb just as Aurora rolled down the back window and peered out.

"Hi, there," he said, leaning in to kiss the old lady. "I was just telling John what a strict chaperone you are. I told him if I want to see Claire alone, I'm going to have to sneak up the trellis like a teenager.''

"Do it, McClintock, and I'll sic the hounds on you,'' Aurora said with a grin so devilish it wrinkled her whole face. "This girl is under *my* protection now. Besides, I'm not exactly the wicked witch. I let her walk down here just now, didn't I? So that she could say hello to you before we got started for the day.''

"Hello? I get one hello a day from my fiancée?''

"That should be plenty.'' The driver had climbed out of the car and was now standing at Aurora's door, holding it open. Aurora waved one be-ringed finger in Claire's direction. "Come, my dear. We are going to have lunch at Bennini's before we shop. We will not rest until we've found the perfect gown, so we must fortify ourselves for a long afternoon.''

Claire cast one last, helpless look at Kieran, and then obediently bent down and folded herself into the car.

"Hey, what about me?'' Kieran frowned playfully. "I'm hungry, too, you know.''

Aurora signaled her driver to close the door. "Nonsense,'' she said as she slowly rolled her window up. "Saintly young men who have just become engaged are expected to live on love.''

CHAPTER EIGHT

LUNCH WAS EFFICIENT and uneventful, but at the very first bridal boutique Claire and Aurora encountered a hitch.

The hitch was one of the other customers, a highly polished blonde whom Claire recognized as Linda Reavis. Two years ago Claire and Linda had both been novice teachers at Heyday Middle School.

Unfortunately, Aurora seemed to recognize the blonde, too, and obviously considered the encounter highly undesirable.

"Linda Tremel, of all people! Oh, will you just look at that alley cat! What's she doing here? Not buying a wedding dress, I assure you. Waiting like a spider for us to stumble into her web, that's what. Pretend you don't see her, dear. She's just trying to ferret out the newest gossip."

A spider and a ferret *and* a cat? Apparently Aurora couldn't adequately express her irritation without using every metaphor and simile in her repertoire. But Claire had no intention of snubbing Linda just because Aurora York told her to. Two years ago, Aurora probably would have pretended not to see Claire, either. Or maybe she really *wouldn't* have seen her, the way the very rich don't see waiters or servants or salesclerks.

Linda Reavis, on the other hand, had always been

friendly to Claire. When they had started teaching across the hall from one another, Linda had just fallen desperately in love with a young lawyer named Austin Tremel. Claire remembered being worried for her. Linda's infatuation had seemed so intense, and Austin Tremel was one of Heyday's elite, traveling in an entirely different social orbit.

But if she was Linda Tremel now, she must have somehow leapt that gap. Apparently congratulations were in order.

"I'm sorry, Aurora," Claire murmured. "I can't do that. Linda's an old friend."

She went up to the other woman and touched her on the hand, noting the gigantic diamond ring, the unnaturally bronze tan, and the elegantly manicured fingertips. Oh, yes, Linda had definitely been pulled into Austin Tremel's gravitational field.

"Linda? It's Claire Strickland. How are you? It's been a long time."

Linda turned, and instantly Claire saw that all the changes were stamped on her face, too. She looked gorgeous but strangely artificial, almost doll-like. She was so thin her cheekbones threatened to break through her stretched skin. And, this close, Claire smelled something that was either the strangest perfume in the world, or plain old vodka.

Maybe, Claire thought, she should hold off on those congratulations.

"Well, hey there, honey," Linda said, giving Claire a hug, nothing so physical it risked mussing her lipstick or hair. "I heard you were back. Ready to ride the old matrimonial merry-go-round, I understand. I took a spin on that myself." She wiggled her ring finger. "Of course I couldn't hold on. But, luckily, when I fell off, some of the dear boy's stock portfolio fell off with me.''

Claire couldn't hide her surprise. ''You and Austin Tremel are divorced?''

Already?

''Yeah, apparently he married me primarily to tick off Tremel Senior, and when the old guy died I guess that rendered me obsolete.''

''Oh, Linda, surely—''

''No biggie,'' Linda said, smiling. ''I ended up with the mansion, right there on Big Shot Street, which means that once you tie the knot I'll be your next-door neighbor, twice removed. Hers, too.''

She waved merrily at Aurora, who sat in a throne-like chair by the wedding dresses, being fawned over by the young saleswoman, who obviously had no trouble identifying the biggest bank account in the room.

''Hi, neighbor,'' Linda called. She tilted her head toward Claire again and whispered, ''She tolerated me until Austin split. Apparently he provided my get-in-free card, and now that he's gone I'm just another tacky interloper. You might want to remember that. She's leading you around like her new pet poodle now, but when you and St. Kieran call it quits—''

'''*When?*''' Claire tried to smile, but this level of cynicism was a surprise. ''Not even '*if?*'''

''Hey, don't kid a kidder, honey. I've—''

''Claire!'' Aurora's summons was imperious. The blue feather on her pillbox hat shook, as if it echoed her indignation. ''Come and look at these gowns. We have several establishments to visit this afternoon. We mustn't let ourselves get bogged down in the very first one.''

"We'll be right there, Aurora," Linda said, clearly pretending she thought the invitation included them both. She gave Claire a grin, and for a minute she looked like her old self.

Claire had to smile back. Ordinarily, she didn't much care for women as lacquered and insinuating as Linda Tremel had become. But Aurora was being a snob. Claire appreciated being taken under the older woman's wing, but Aurora might as well understand now that Claire didn't plan to adopt her elitist views.

Together, Claire and Linda walked over to the wedding gowns, which were lovely, and entirely out of Claire's price range. The saleswoman looked at Claire, then touched Aurora's arm, as if overcome with delight.

"Oh, you're right, she'll make a beautiful bride. I know we have something that you'll like, Ms. York." She beamed. "You may find that you don't need to visit those other establishments after all."

Claire looked at one of the price tags. "Aurora, I can't possibly afford—"

Aurora's feather wobbled emphatically. "Nonsense. *I'm* putting on this wedding, on behalf of Kieran's dear mother. You're not allowed to worry about a single thing, my dear."

As if that settled it, Aurora turned toward the saleswoman. "I think her coloring calls for ivory, don't you? Long, of course. And demure. But watch the lace. Her face is feminine enough. She doesn't need to fuss."

The saleswoman nodded as if Aurora had spoken pearls of great wisdom. "I know exactly," she said. "I'll be right back."

Linda Tremel had been sifting through the dresses while Aurora gave orders. She watched the departing saleswoman and grimaced. "She's going to bring back every hackneyed old Edwardian princess gown she's got. Look how tiny Claire is. If she wears some monster gown, she's going to look as if the damn dress is eating her alive."

Aurora tilted her head so far back her feather bumped into the wall. "And what exactly are you doing in this establishment, Linda?"

"Checking on my own dress. They're selling it for me—God knows I don't want it. Don't worry, all the used stuff is over there, in the consignment area. No risk of letting Claire here buy damaged goods." She winked at Claire.

"I see." Aurora still stared piercingly down her nose. "And...I don't remember. Did I request assistance with this decision, Linda?"

"No, but you need it. You didn't mention *sexy* on your list of requirements. You don't want Kieran to think he's married a frump, do you? Now this—" She pulled out a gown and, folding the hanger out of the way, held it against Claire's torso. "This would look just awesome."

The gown was very dramatic. It looked, in fact, as if it had been designed for the Marquis de Sade's wedding. It had a fitted boned bodice like a corset and a ruched skirt so tight Claire wouldn't have been able to walk.

"Yes," Aurora said thinly. "All it needs is a little white whip."

Linda studied the dress for a moment, and then she laughed out loud. "Okay," she said, still chuckling. "Point taken. We'll tone it down, then. How about…this?"

It was better, but still loaded with overt sexuality. Claire privately thought of it as an "off" dress. Off white, off the shoulder, off the back, darn near entirely off the body.

But, to Claire's surprise, Aurora studied it a moment before reacting.

"It doesn't leave much to the imagination, though, does it?" Aurora glanced at Claire. "And I think we really must give Kieran credit for possessing a bit of that."

Linda laughed. "Must we?"

Aurora fingered the satin. "Yes," she said finally. "Yes, I think we must."

Claire looked at the two of them, incredulous. Was it possible that the stiff old aristocrat and the brash young divorcée were actually understanding one another rather well? The bride-to-be seemed, for the moment, completely irrelevant.

Which was just as well. Her hormones must be going through another swing. Claire suddenly felt a little sick, as if the soup she'd had for lunch might be going to stage a revolt.

Not here, she prayed silently, pretending an interest in the row of gowns. The irony would be intolerable.

The saleswoman finally reappeared, her arms laden with dresses. She hung them on rods around the area, all facing out, so that the women suddenly seemed to be drowning in a perfumed white sea of organza, crepe de Chine, satin and lace. Claire thought she'd never in her life seen so many crystal beads and seed pearls in one place.

Linda and Aurora looked them over silently.

"Told ya," Linda said. She yawned.

Aurora tapped her index finger against her purse. Her eyes were narrowed, her lips set. Finally, with a sigh, she turned to Linda.

"If I allow you to accompany us on this expedition, do I have your assurance that you will not endeavor to send Kieran's bride to the altar looking like a trollop?"

Linda smiled. "If I have your assurance that you won't try to send her up there looking like somebody's great-great-grandmother."

"Very well." Aurora inclined her head. "I believe there is a possibility we might be able to find some middle ground."

Claire made a small sound. "I don't suppose anyone cares what I think?"

The other women both spoke at once.

"Of course we do, dear," Aurora soothed.

"Not really," Linda said, more honestly.

"That's what I thought." Claire squared her shoulders, ignoring the fact that her upper lip felt a little clammy, and her head had begun to feel light. She felt claustrophobic, penned in by heavily scented satin.

"But there is one thing you both need to know. I have a limited amount of money to spend on this, so whatever you two decide, you'd better put the whole costume together for less than six hundred dollars."

"Six hundred dollars?" Aurora laughed softly. "Oh, my dear, just don't you worry about a—"

Oh, no. The room began to tilt.

"I'm sorry, Aurora." Claire turned to the saleswoman. "Do you have a rest room?"

"Sure," she said, pointing. "Through there."

The sickness was brief and miserable, even though Claire had hardly eaten anything all day. The small rest room's wallpaper of pink and red roses swam as her eyes watered, and the little bowl of rose potpourri just made things worse.

When she finally stood up, her legs were shaking. She rinsed her mouth in the old-fashioned white basin and checked her face in the fancy antique-gold-framed mirror.

She thought maybe she could pull it off. Her eyes were shining a little, and her cheeks were very pale. But maybe, if she redid her lipstick, no one would notice.

When she returned to the sales floor, Aurora was already out at the Cadillac. Through the picture window, Claire could see the driver helping her into the back seat.

Linda had hung back, waiting, and she scrutinized Claire's face as she approached. "You okay?"

"Yes, I'm fine." Now that she felt steadier, Claire assumed that the less said the better. Overexplaining would just look suspicious.

But maybe she should have made something up—bad food from lunch, a need to take a pill, anything—because Linda kept studying her, and finally her gaze flicked down to Claire's waist. Though Claire knew her stomach was entirely flat—it was much too early for anything to show—she flushed.

Linda clearly saw that, too. "Oh," she said. "Oh, dear."

Claire raised her chin and took a step backward. But Linda didn't accept the silent rebuff. She chuckled softly and slipped her arm through Claire's, grinning like the Cheshire cat.

"Well, well, it's a good thing you ran into me," she said. "I tell you what. As soon as I'm through saving your butt on this dress issue, I'll give you a few tips on negotiating the ironclad prenup."

"Linda, I don't—"

"Oh, yes, you do." Linda glanced at Claire's midsection one more time. "Because, sweetheart, I was right, wasn't I? The only question about the end of this particular marriage is *when*. Not *if*."

SIX HOURS LATER, when the sun was sinking behind the sturdy silhouettes of the Riverside Park mansions, Claire knocked on Kieran's front door one more time.

He'd left a message on Aurora's answering machine, saying he needed to see Claire as soon as they returned. Aurora had announced that she'd go along as chaperone, but just then her telephone had rung. While Aurora was absorbed in the call, Claire had made her escape.

Still, she hoped Kieran would hurry. You never knew what the old lady might do. She could easily come storming over here and try to snatch Claire back into protective custody.

Kieran opened the door within seconds, as if he'd been waiting for her. He was casually dressed in jeans and a broadcloth shirt. He'd rolled the sleeves back, and she recognized the look. It was the way he always dressed for coaching football practice.

"Hi," he said with a smile. He stuck his head out and checked both directions. "Where's the warden?"

"On the telephone," she said. "Apparently it's time to start choosing the food for the reception. We just five minutes ago returned from the great wedding dress safari."

He laughed. "Did you bag one?"

She shook her head, but not for long. She had a vicious headache, and any movement was excruciating. "No. You see, Linda Tremel went with us."

He opened his eyes wide. "Oh, my God."

"Yes. It seemed okay at first, but by the fourth store they were like two tigers trapped in one cage. They couldn't agree on anything. It was pure insanity. Honestly, Kieran. Do you care whether I wear satin-edged lace or lace-edged satin?"

He gave her a twisted smile. "Hell, no."

"Well, they do. Passionately."

Chuckling, he put his hand out and captured hers.

"Come on in," he said. "There's something I want to show you, and I'd like to be alone for once. I'll lock the door. Aurora helped a lot when my dad was sick, so she has a key. But there's a dead bolt I use for emergencies."

Claire followed him into the house. Strange, she couldn't remember ever having been so passive in her life. But then she couldn't ever remember feeling so physically wiped out.

He positioned her under the crystal foyer chandelier and studied her face.

"Damn Aurora," he said. "She ought to know better than to drag you around all day. You looked fine this morning, and now you're clearly exhausted again."

"I'm okay," she said. "I have a headache, that's all. Besides, Aurora doesn't have any reason to believe I can't keep up with a seventy-five-year-old woman." She smiled. "Remember, she doesn't know I'm pregnant."

He took a deep breath. "I guess you're right. But I'll have to think of something to tell her. She can't be allowed to wear you out like this."

It was nice, she thought, shutting her eyes against the painful stabbing light of the huge chandelier. Nice to have someone who wanted to protect you. Especially when your whole body seemed to be working against you. Nausea one minute, irrational tears the next. And always this sapping, head-to-toe lethargy.

"Come in here," he said, taking her hand again and tugging her toward one of the adjacent rooms. "You look as if you're going to fall over any minute."

He led her into the library, the kind of huge, cherry-wood-and-leather library seen in movies and books. Three walls had ceiling-to-floor, built-in shelves. The western wall held a long, red-cushioned window seat that looked out through a mullioned bay window onto a little bricked-in garden. The sunset was turning the garden crimson and gold.

"It's very beautiful," she said.

"Thanks." He glanced around the room as if he were trying to see it through her eyes. "It was my father's favorite room. He loved to read."

Her mother had loved books, too. Buying books had been her one indulgence. When she died, Claire and Steve had counted them. She had owned one hundred. Not even enough to fill one shelf on one wall in this room.

"I meant to tell you," Claire said. "I'm very sorry

about your father. I didn't realize he'd died so recently until someone mentioned it today.''

"Yes. It was less than four months ago. He was a difficult old tyrant, but I miss him a lot.''

Only four months? Then old Anderson McClintock had been gone just over a month when Kieran came to Richmond. For the first time Claire wondered if Kieran, too, might have been battling loneliness and loss that night.

"Sit down,'' Kieran said gently. "I have something I want to give you.''

He pointed to a leather armchair that looked as if it still held his own body's imprint. She saw a book open, facedown, on the end table beside the chair.

Fair, Not Foolish: The Essential Prenuptial Planner.

Was that what he wanted to give her tonight—the prenuptial agreement? She didn't mind that. She had expected him to draw one up. She'd seen the speculation in John Gordon's eyes this morning, and she'd realized that any good lawyer would insist on it being done immediately. Kieran couldn't just take her word that she didn't want to rip him off. He had no idea whether her word was worth anything at all.

But this was almost too fast. Shouldn't they have talked over the custody situation first, and included all the details in one agreement?

She sat in the still-warm chair and waited while Kieran went over to the big cherry-wood desk and opened one of the top drawers. She shut her eyes, wishing her headache would go away long enough for her to think.

The details were important. She didn't want Kieran's real estate or his stocks, or his leather-bound library, but she wanted her child. She wouldn't allow any cagey lawyer to slip in phrases that might compromise her custody situation.

She heard the drawer close.

"Here," Kieran said. "I wanted to give you this. I picked it up in Grupton yesterday. It was among the things I keep in a bank over there."

She opened her eyes. He was holding out a small velvet box. She felt stupid, but for a couple of seconds she couldn't take it in. She had been so sure it would be an envelope or a document.

"What is it?"

"Well, it's not a rattlesnake," he said with a hint of laughter in his voice. "It's all right for you to touch it."

She put out her hand and took it. She ran her fingertips over the soft scratchiness of the rounded velvet top. Finally, taking a bracing breath she hoped he wouldn't notice, she opened the box.

"Oh!" She almost dropped it. She'd never seen diamonds this beautiful in her life. She looked up at him. "Oh, Kieran. No."

He raised one eyebrow and smiled slightly. "Why not?"

"It's too—too much. It's too expensive. For a marriage like ours, just a temporary arrangement, you don't need to—"

"You want this marriage to look real to the rest of the world, don't you?"

"Yes, but…"

"This is what I always planned to give the woman I married. Lots of people know that. Aurora, John Gordon, Roddy…just for starters. Even Linda Tremel knows, which means the whole town knows."

"Well, couldn't we say that I didn't want it, that I wanted something—"

"No one would believe it. You see, this was my mother's wedding set. It's been sitting in a vault in Grupton for thirty years, waiting for this day."

Oh, God, the tears were launching another surprise attack. She blinked hard and swallowed a large, jagged lump of them.

"I can't," she said.

"Of course you can." He reached over and took out the engagement ring. It was an exquisite, rainbowed diamond set in a small platinum band with delicate old-fashioned carvings on either side.

He picked up her left hand. "I think it will fit," he said. "Let's see."

The ring slipped on easily, but amazingly it didn't swim on her small finger. His mother must have been petite, too.

"It's perfect," he said, holding her hand up and rotating the band back and forth to be sure it wasn't too tight. The diamond caught lights and tossed them everywhere. "Of course, I know the setting is dated. If you'd like something more modern, we can always reset it and—"

"No," she said. "It's—it's perfect. But—"

"But what?"

What could she say? That she'd never once considered that he'd have to give her a ring? How dumb would that sound?

She had been so sure she'd thought the whole idea through completely. But she realized now that it was only the implications on *her* life that she'd anticipated down to the last detail. *His* life had been a shadowy, out-of-focus piece of the puzzle that she hadn't really understood at all.

She suddenly felt a little bit ashamed.

"I'm sorry," she said awkwardly. "I know this wasn't how you'd imagined using this ring. And I want you to know that I'll return it to you safely. When it's over, you don't need to worry, I'll make sure you get it back."

He gave her a strange look. "Why? So that I can use it again next time? I don't think that's how it works, Claire."

She stared at him, dismayed. Oh, what could she do? She couldn't wish the baby away. She'd tried that, in the first few days after she'd discovered she was pregnant. And she couldn't condemn her child to a confused life of fatherless illegitimacy just because she didn't have the courage to see this through.

But it was so much more complicated than she had ever imagined. Was there no way to remedy this that wouldn't create even more tragedy and heartbreak? She closed her eyes, feeling slightly sick all over again.

Kieran brushed her hair from her damp forehead. She looked at him helplessly. "I don't know what to do," she said.

He took her hand and folded her fingers down over the little box. Then he touched the ring, which sparkled orange and violet in the fiery sunset that poured in through the bay window.

"I want you to keep it," he said. "I know you won't want to wear it—after. But our child will grow up eventually, and then, when he is ready to get married, you can give it to him."

She made a small sound, but Kieran tightened his hand.

"Or her," he amended. His eyes were dark in the dying light, but Claire thought he was trying to smile. "It may take a few generations, but surely someday a McClintock will come along and get this love thing right."

DOING MRS. TREMEL'S LAWN was the sweetest job Eddie had ever had.

She had told him not to worry about trimming the bushes and weeding the fancier gardens in the back. She still had a landscaping service that did all that, though they didn't do the mowing. That was kind of weird, but he wasn't complaining. All he had to do was mow and edge around the sidewalk, which was a snap.

What a swanky place! Eddie's father was just a regular dentist, not poor but hardly super-rich. Since most of Eddie's jobs were in his own neighborhood, a new, middle-class subdivision, he was used to scrawny trees and lumpy lawns that hadn't been leveled out that well when they went in.

Eddie hadn't really minded before. In fact, he hadn't even noticed. This was the first big break— his first house in the old-money Riverside Park.

He couldn't believe the difference.

The lawns here were so thick and smooth you could sleep on them. When you were mowing, you never ran over a dead spot that threw dirt up in your face. And these elm trees were bigger than the houses. Their leafy branches turned a hot, nasty job into a shady walk in the park.

He looked up and down the quiet street, at the long

lines of houses just like Mrs. Tremel's. Sure would be sweet if some of her neighbors would hire him, too.

He looked up and saw that Mrs. Tremel was standing on the front portico. He killed the gas on his edger and smiled at her politely.

"Hi, there," she said. She was wearing nothing but a little blue bikini. She had been lying out by the pool when Eddie got there about an hour ago, and apparently she was just going to wear that all day.

"Hi," he said. He wiped his face so he wouldn't look gross. He raked his fingers through his hair, which had an annoying way of sticking up in spikes whenever he sweated.

"I wondered if you'd like to take a break," she said. "Maybe come in and have a cola."

That was different, too. Some of his other customers put out a pitcher of water for him—they were nice people. But no one had ever invited him into the house. This was the second time in an hour that Mrs. Tremel had done it.

"I'd better keep going," he said, smiling to show he still appreciated the offer. "I've got four more lawns to do, so…"

"You're absolutely amazing," she said. "I honestly don't know how you keep it up. It's so darn hot today."

She held a glass of clear liquid in one hand, and she rubbed it slowly against her neck. It dribbled a trail of condensation down into her cleavage. She was so fine. He couldn't believe a twenty-six-year-old divorcée—she'd told him how old she was—could be so damn hot.

"I guess it's because you're so young," she said,

letting her gaze slide up and down his shirtless body. "And you're in such great shape."

Eddie looked away, embarrassed that she was acting like this but getting kind of a thrill out of it, too.

It did occur to him, though, that the neighbors around here weren't very likely to take her advice about lawn boys. Or anything else. He wasn't so dumb he didn't know most of the Riverside Park people probably thought Mrs. Tremel was trashy. The people in his neighborhood thought so, too. Even Eddie's dad, who thought Eddie should mow lawns 24/7, hadn't been very happy when he heard about this new job.

"Yeah, well..." He shifted the edger nervously. "It's not that hard."

She smiled with sleepy eyes, kind of like a cat. "Really? It sure *looks* hard."

Oh, man... He fought the urge to glance down at his shorts. But he felt kind of hot-faced and flustered. A little bit angry, even. Why was she playing with him like this? He was seventeen, for God's sake. He got turned on when Binky Potter leaned over to pick up a pencil in math. If Mrs. Tremel was going to come out here half-naked and start rubbing that glass all over herself, what did she expect?

Or was he imagining the whole thing? She'd probably laugh if she realized he thought she was coming on to a teenager.

Still. It felt weird. He had no idea what to say now.

He never thought he'd be happy to see Cullen Overton, but this time the sight of Cullen's fire-engine-red BMW coming down the street was as welcome as a reprieve from the governor.

Cullen pulled to a stop in front of the house. "Hey,

Mackey," he called. "You got something for me or what?"

Eddie glanced toward the house, but Mrs. Tremel had disappeared into its cool depths. She'd left a Coke on the banister.

"Yeah, I've got it," Eddie said. "Can't you wait till later? It's in my car."

"Your car?" Cullen climbed out of the BMW and pretended to search the vicinity with a confused gaze. Finally he stopped at Eddie's Ford. "Oh, that. I thought that was your mom's car."

Cullen loved that joke. He'd probably used it a hundred times. It *had* been Eddie's mother's car, of course. She'd let him have it for the price of the last ten monthly payments. It was a dumb car, a white minivan. But it was all Eddie could afford.

"Don't be such a fathead, Cullen. Get some new material." Eddie toyed with the switch on the edger. "I'm working right now. I'll come by your house later and drop it off."

"No, man, I need it now. I have to retype it on my own computer. Mrs. G knows my work. You are such a hopeless A student you probably couldn't mess up a semicolon if you tried."

"Hey, don't worry. Just because I'm not a cretin doesn't mean I can't write like one. You said a C paper. You'll be lucky if this sucker gets that much."

Cullen shrugged and looked at his watch. "I need it now, man."

Eddie knew from long experience how stubborn Cullen could be. He shot a quick glance at the door to be sure Mrs. Tremel had really gone away. Cullen was such a screw-up no one would bat an eye if it was revealed he'd been cheating, but expectations were higher for Eddie. His dad would kill him—but even worse, a lot of his teachers, and Coach McClintock, too, would be really shocked and disappointed.

"He-llooo?" Cullen sighed. "Now means now, man. Not after you get through picking your nose."

Eddie put the edger down carefully and walked over to his car. He unlocked it, unzipped his backpack, and pulled out Cullen's paper. It was a C paper, all right. He'd even misspelled Tennyson, though Cullen would probably never notice that.

"There you go," he said. "Now I think you owe *me* something."

Cullen flipped through the four pages casually. "Bibliography?"

"Of course."

Cullen tossed the paper through the open window of his car. He dug around in his pocket and pulled out three twenties. He looked annoyed now that he had to pay up.

"You know, I could get it on the Internet for ten bucks," he complained.

Eddie wasn't impressed. "Yeah, and so could Mrs. G."

They'd been through this before. Cullen shrugged, handed Eddie the money with a smile, then got back in his car and peeled away.

As he picked up his edger, Eddie felt an intense sense of relief mixed in with his usual guilt. That was the last job he'd committed to. Now that he had an extra lawn to mow, maybe, just maybe, he could finally get free of this quicksand.

But then he looked at Mrs. Tremel's house, and

his heart did a big, looping dive right down into his cross-trainers.

She was standing at the window, her blue bikini conspicuous in a ray of sunlight that found its way through the trees. She still had her drink in one hand, but she had her other hand on the curtain, pulling it aside for a better view.

She had, quite clearly, watched the whole damn thing.

CHAPTER NINE

CLAIRE SHOULDN'T HAVE BEEN surprised to see Principal Straine purring like a kitten and smiling at Kieran with the special warmth usually reserved for people who'd just written a very large check made out to Haversham Girls' Academy.

Kieran had that effect on most people even when he wasn't trying.

And today he was trying.

It had been his idea to make the drive to Richmond so that he could meet Mrs. Straine. "A preemptive strike," he'd called it. "Let's invite her to the wedding. If she's there, she can't exactly doubt that it ever happened. And she'll be eager to tell everyone that she alone was important enough to make the A list."

It made sense. So, though Claire dreaded the thought of Gillian Straine witnessing this charade of a marriage, she had agreed.

For once, the fates were on her side. Unfortunately, Mrs. Straine would be out of the country and unable to attend.

"I wish so much that I could alter my plans," the woman said. "I'd love to be there to wish our Claire joy. But I'm afraid my commitments are of long standing, and I must honor them."

"Of course you must. We wouldn't dream of ask-

ing you to disappoint someone else on our behalf.''
Kieran smiled, as if he admired her code of ethics
tremendously.

"So…'' Mrs. Straine relaxed a little, the first time
Claire had ever seen her back actually touch the
chair. Kieran really had melted her, hadn't he? "You
and Claire have known each other a long time?''

Kieran took Claire's hand. "Oh, yes, for years. In
a town as small as Heyday, everyone knows everyone. And, of course, I was her—''

Claire squeezed his fingers carefully. No one at the
Academy even knew she'd had a brother. She had
never mentioned Steve to anyone.

"—her biggest admirer long before we began to
date. I have to admit, it was hard for me when she
moved here to Richmond. Eventually it was simply
too hard. I found that I couldn't live without her.
After that, it all happened pretty quickly.''

He smiled at Claire. She smiled back, grateful that
he had picked up on the problem so effortlessly. She
squeezed his hand again, thanking him.

As she watched them, Mrs. Straine looked a little
misty-eyed. Amazed, Claire wondered if there might
be a thwarted romantic hiding under that buttoned-
up exterior.

"How will you manage the distance? I know you
said Claire intends to continue working here at HGA,
but it's quite a long commute, isn't it?''

"We're not sure yet." Kieran leaned back in his
chair. "I may stay in Richmond during the week,
then bring her home on the weekends. Although…I
have a lot of property and investments in Heyday that
I really need to monitor. They're actually extensive
enough to be quite a headache.''

He looked pointedly around the elegant room and then shot Mrs. Straine a knowing smile. "I'm sure you're familiar with all that."

Claire gave him another mental round of applause. He didn't ordinarily brag about his assets—he rarely even mentioned them. He must have intuited that Mrs. Straine would treat the soon-to-be-advantageously-wed Clair better than the unprotected, single Claire. And that she was snob enough to love being treated as an equal, a woman who understood all about the trials of wealth and responsibility.

Best of all, the ties to Heyday would explain his extended absences when that became necessary.

"Yes," Mrs. Straine said with a world-weary shrug of her shoulders. "Heavy obligations are a mixed blessing."

She turned to Claire. "Are you sure you want to continue teaching? It sounds as if your husband would be happy to keep you at home with him."

Rich enough to keep me at home, you mean. But Claire just smiled. "I'm sure, Mrs. Straine."

"She's determined to remain her own woman." Kieran gazed at Claire. "It's part of what makes her special, so I know I mustn't try to change her. Actually, I've thought of buying a home somewhere in between."

The meeting dragged on. Mrs. Straine ate the attention up like a cat with a saucer of milk. Apparently reluctant to let them go, she even gave Kieran about twenty minutes of advice about home buying that he pretended to appreciate.

Finally, though, they were free. Claire practically

ran to the car. Kieran followed more calmly, but his eyes were full of laughter.

He opened the door for her. "Thanks," she said. She hesitated, then touched his hand. "You were great in there. You handled her perfectly."

"Ah, yes." He sighed and put his other hand over his heart. "Heavy obligations are a mixed blessing. But one does what one can."

Chuckling, he climbed in, too, and put the key in the ignition. "So you think she's convinced?"

"Absolutely," she said. "Frankly, Mr. Mc-Clintock, it was something of a shock to see what a good liar you are."

He turned to her, still smiling. "Who said I was lying?"

For a minute, behind the smile, she thought she saw something darkly serious.

"What do you mean?"

"I mean…I actually am thinking of buying a house somewhere in between. I thought it might make—" He hesitated. "Custody issues a little easier."

She didn't answer right away. She was briefly tangled up in a snarl of images. What exactly would their lives be like, once the baby was born, once the divorce was final?

They had agreed without any debate that joint custody would be the only answer. Her soul ached at the thought of juggling a child's heart between two homes, trying desperately not to break it. But it had to be done. She couldn't imagine denying Kieran the right to know his own child.

John Gordon, Kieran's lawyer, had made it clear he thought the lack of a prenuptial agreement was a big mistake. She could only imagine his horror if he knew Kieran had also decided not to rush the decision about custody.

"Are you sure you don't want to have something drawn up before the ceremony?" She smiled a little. "You know I don't mind. There's still time. I don't mind if John Gordon knows about the baby. He could have documents ready in a nanosecond."

Kieran shook his head. "We've been through this. If you're comfortable with the arrangements as they stand, so am I."

"But John says—"

"I know you better than John Gordon does. If you had wanted to exclude me from the baby's life, you never had to tell me you were pregnant."

That was true. She could have disappeared forever.

On her side, Linda Tremel had warned Claire that she was the one who was being naive. She'd warned that Claire should get something in writing, something that promised Kieran wouldn't try to shut her out someday.

But Claire simply didn't believe that Kieran would ever do that. In her heart, Linda Tremel probably didn't believe it, either.

Claire touched the exquisite ring Kieran had put on her finger less than a week ago. His mother's ring.

"I guess we've both made it clear we want this child to have the happiest life we can manage." She steadied her voice. "Under the circumstances."

He started the car. "Okay. That's settled, then," he said. "Now, do you want to go by your apartment?"

When they'd decided to go to Richmond, she had asked him if he'd mind making the extra stop. She'd been so emotionally knotted up when she left—she hadn't been thinking about what she might need for a wedding. The only thing she'd been thinking about was the doctor's note in her purse that confirmed her pregnancy.

Funny to remember that she'd thought she'd need it as proof. Funny to remember that, only a week ago, she had thought he might throw her out and call her a liar.

When they parked in front of her complex, she got out, bent down and looked at Kieran, who to her surprise was not moving from behind the wheel.

"I thought I'd wait here," he said casually. "Unless you need me to carry something down for you."

"No, no, there's nothing big," she said, embarrassed. She knew what he was thinking. If he went in, they'd be together, alone, in the place where they had made their terrible mistake. He obviously didn't want to face that memory right now.

"Thanks. I'm sure I can manage. I won't be long."

But the minute Claire opened the door, and the stale air rushed out at her, she wished she had asked him to come with her anyhow.

It was so dark, so stuffy...so lifeless. She felt the strangest reluctance even to enter the foyer, as if there were something to fear here.

After just a week in Aurora's lovely house, which was filled with charming clutter, priceless heirlooms and sentimental geegaws, Claire found this blank emptiness to be almost suffocating.

Had anyone ever really lived here?

The answer, of course, was no. What she had done in this apartment couldn't be called living. It had been a form of mindless survival, and she had moved through these rooms like a cold, blind thing, leaving no warmth behind, hardly even disturbing the air.

But as she stood in the shadowed foyer now, she realized that in some intangible but profound way, everything was different.

She was different.

It was as if the tiny life that slept unseen inside her body had brought her back to life as well.

She touched her stomach. Her child. And suddenly, without any warning, warm tears began to slide down her cheeks, like sap from the sweet, deep core of a frozen winter tree.

Her fingers couldn't actually feel any sign of the baby—it was too soon. But she knew that somewhere under her hand a little heart was beating, fast and trusting and sure.

And, because it did, her own half-broken heart had begun to beat again as well.

THE RINGMASTER CARNIVAL and parade didn't officially arrive in Heyday for another week. But on that sunny Monday morning, just three days after Kieran had taken Claire to Richmond, just five days before their wedding, he took her downtown to see the Ringmaster announcement.

The scene bustled with all the excitement and chaos of a full-fledged circus. At noon the mayor would officially reveal Heyday's next Ringmaster and Ringmistress. Though Kieran knew Claire thought the whole thing was silly, he was glad she had agreed to come. He thought it was pretty silly himself, but, after having turned down the honor, it would have seemed grudging for the two of them to miss the announcement.

Besides, he was pretty sure that Roddy, who used to poke more fun at the tradition than anyone, was going to be named Ringmaster, and Kieran couldn't wait to razz him about it.

The names of the five nominees chosen at Aurora's party had been sent to the Zebra Committee, which consisted exclusively of former Ringmasters. Former Ringmistresses weren't allowed to vote, which annoyed some of the more vocal women, like Aurora, who had been one. Now only the Head High Zebra himself knew the results.

The announcement was always a colorful event, complete with banners and music and balloons and strolling clowns to keep the audience's anticipation high. But the scene this year was even crazier than usual. In addition to the eager nominees, their families and friends, and all the chamber of commerce types who made so much money from this parade, the crowd now included a small but vocal contingent of protestors.

About a dozen young women stalked back and forth beside the gathering, carrying posters that shouted insults in stenciled red letters.

KEEP YOUR RING—I'M NOBODY'S MISTRESS!

HEYDAY—WHERE TIME STANDS STILL AND WOMEN STILL CAN'T VOTE.

Claire laughed a little as she read the signs.

"Wow," she said. "I *have* been gone a long time. Has Heyday actually entered the twenty-first century?"

Kieran grinned. "Well, a dozen of us have, anyhow. But that's better than last year. Last year there were only two brave souls out here chanting their hearts out.''

One of the protesters was a young mother, who carried a sleeping infant in a sling on her back like a papoose. She had taped a sign to the carrier that read, I'm a Girl, and in 18 Years, I'll Be Voting, Too.

Kieran laughed softly, and Claire smiled, too. He could tell that both of them were mesmerized by the sight of the tiny baby, her soft face pink and placid as she bobbed along to the rhythm of her mother's marching.

''I wonder whether it'll be a girl or boy,'' Claire said quietly, touching her stomach almost unconsciously. She looked up at him. ''It's too early to tell, but have you ever thought about that?''

He was almost ashamed to admit he hadn't. He didn't even entirely believe, just yet, that this wasn't all a dream. He supposed that, to the mother, the existence of the child was very real from the first instant. The mother's body altered almost immediately. Her normal cycles ceased, she developed tender places and morning sickness and God only knew what else. For the father, it was just an announcement, a word, a concept.

''It doesn't really matter to me,'' he said. That much was true. If only this child could be blessed with health and happiness, he would be satisfied. And he made a vow on the spot to do whatever he could to ensure them both.

But suddenly, looking down at Claire's somber face, he realized that she had read his answer differently. She assumed he was indifferent because he planned to have very little contact with the child anyhow.

Oh, great. He just couldn't get the hang of this. He would have explained himself a little better, but he knew too many people here. Everyone who passed seemed to want to shake hands and say hello.

Finally they were able to move again, but he noticed that she watched the protesters until they rounded the corner. He wondered if, as something of an outsider herself, she felt a certain sympathy with their cause. The whole Ringmaster Parade thing really was a throwback to the good-old-boy days.

"Everyone says you would have been the Ringmaster this year," she said suddenly. "I'm sorry that you lost your chance because of our…situation."

"Don't be. The protesters are right—it is an antiquated system. And besides—" he slapped the back of a man they were about to pass "—now they can give the title to Roddy here, who will make a fantastic Ringmaster."

Roddy turned and, grinning, cuffed Kieran on the shoulder. "Ringmaster? Yeah, isn't that always the way? I'm always feasting on the pitiful crumbs you leave behind." He turned, apparently belatedly realizing Claire was there, too. "Hi, Claire! Sorry. Didn't mean to sound bitter in front of a lady."

Claire gave Roddy a cautious smile. Kieran had noticed that Claire was even less comfortable around Roddy than she was around the others. Maybe she knew that, as Kieran's best friend, Roddy might have heard the truth about their impulsive wedding.

Kieran took her hand. She had no need to worry about Roddy, who was always spouting nonsense just for fun, but who had never in his life spilled a secret that mattered.

"We just came down to pick up our posters," Kieran said. "We're joining the protesters."

"The hell you are." Roddy shot a quick look at the marching women. "Heyday's economy was built on these ridiculous zebras, and it would collapse without them, whether those ladies know it or not. And if anybody in this town has a personal interest in keeping the economy going, my friend, that somebody would be you. Maybe you'd better go give them a history lesson."

Suddenly Roddy jerked his head to the north in a clear warning. "Uh-oh. Too late. Incoming."

Peggy Waddell, the chairman of the Heyday Little League, had just spotted Kieran and was making her way toward him like a guided missile. Kieran glanced around, looking for somewhere to hide, but it was too late.

She was breathless when she arrived, which made her extravagant praise sound even more overblown.

"Oh, Kieran, I'm so glad you're here. I have to thank you— I can't believe it's true. You've given us the land! We needed it so desperately, and you're—you're magnificent—"

Kieran put out his hand like a cop stopping traffic. "God, Peggy. Don't make a big deal—"

But Roddy clearly loved it. "You may kiss his ring if you like, Peggy." He turned and grinned at Claire. "They worship him around here, you know. We're going to change our name again, and this time we're going to become St. Kierantown."

Kieran wanted to groan. He stole a glance at

Claire, too, but her politely arranged smile was not giving anything away.

"It's true," Peggy started up again. "If it weren't for Kieran—"

"Claire! Claire!" Out of nowhere Erica Gordon came barreling toward them, three black-and-white-striped balloons flying out behind her. She flung herself at Claire, nearly knocking them both down in the process.

"Hi, Claire! I knew you'd come, even though everyone said you wouldn't."

Claire laughed as she righted the little girl. "They did?"

"Yeah. They said well, you do know, Erica, this sort of thing actually isn't Claire Strickland's natural habitat."

Kieran had an overpowering urge to strangle the precocious little brat. Or maybe he should strangle Evelyn Gordon, who probably was the fool who had uttered those snide phrases in the kid's presence. Roddy was scowling at Erica, too, and even Peggy Waddell looked uncomfortable.

Claire, however, seemed completely unfazed. She bent down and smiled at Erica. "Well, they were right. It isn't. But it *is* Kieran McClintock's natural habitat, and, since I'm going to marry Kieran, I wanted to come with him."

Erica looked smug. "That's what I *told* them. But they never listen to me. They think I don't understand what a natural habitat is. As if I haven't had an entire unit on alligators and everything. They think they can talk over my head."

"If they do, they've got another think coming," Kieran said, reaching out to ruffle Erica's hair. "So, kiddo, how come there's no big whomping hello for your old friend Kieran?''

Erica gave him a hug. ''It's just that I see you all the time.'' She turned to Claire again. ''Can you come with me for a minute? I brought my new puppy, even though he's quite likely to disgrace us all. He's really cute, and I want you to meet him.''

Kieran was impressed. Claire didn't even crack a smile. ''I'd love to,'' she said. ''Kieran, I'll meet you a little later?''

''Sure,'' he said. He caught her hand one more time. The engagement ring was cold against his palm. ''Don't forget to come back soon.''

After she left, time seemed to drag. Peggy Waddell wore herself out thanking him for the land, and eventually even Roddy wandered off to get ready for the announcement. Alone for once, Kieran leaned back against the edge of the long, broad stone City Hall sign, which had water cascading prettily over its letters and falling into a cool blue pool.

He scanned the crowd, hoping to catch a glimpse of Claire. But God knew where Erica had dragged her off to. Occasionally he saw Erica's three balloons bobbing along, but Claire wasn't tall enough—he couldn't see her.

He did, after a few minutes, spot Arlington Woodstock, the owner and editor of the *Heyday Herald.* Though Arlington was only a couple of years older than Kieran—and a former Ringmaster himself—the Woodstock family had owned the newspaper here for more than a century. It had begun as *The Moresville Monitor,* a weekly tabloid that was little more than a farmer's almanac.

During Arlington's father's tenure, however, the

Heyday Herald had become one of the best small newspapers in Virginia.

Kieran was surprised to see Arlington here. The Ringmaster Ceremony might be a big deal among the Heyday good old boys, but Arlington didn't cover stories like this himself anymore. He had hired a society columnist and a feature writer to do that.

Besides, he looked pretty grim, not like a man covering a colorful piece of fluff. He caught Kieran's gaze somberly and came loping over toward him, his long limbs moving as if they were made of elastic.

"Hey," Arlington said as he reached the fountain. He put one foot up on the stone coping and pretended to be studying his shoe. "I need to talk to you. Alone."

"Okay. We're alone. What's up?"

"Not here."

Kieran tilted his head. Arlington was a pretty solid guy. He didn't go in for these undercover reporter theatrics. "Why not? What's going on?"

Arlington looked up. His long, bony face was grave under his neatly combed brown hair. "I got a letter to the editor this morning. It's about you."

Kieran narrowed his eyes. "About the wedding?"

But, to Kieran's relief, Arlington shook his head. "The wedding? No, no, I don't run crap like that. No, this is something real."

"Come on, A. Don't talk in code. This isn't Deep Throat stuff, is it? I mean, it's not exactly exposing a national conspiracy, right?"

Arlington chewed on his lower lip. "No. Not a *national* conspiracy."

That was an odd way to respond. Kieran's internal

Geiger counter began to make subtle noises. Something was up. But what?

"Well, what, then? Hell, A, no one can hear us. What is the damn letter about?"

Arlington glanced right, then left.

"It's about a bunch of people getting together to hide the truth about exactly how Steve Strickland really died," he said. "And one of those people is you."

CHAPTER TEN

CLAIRE HAD NO IDEA where the past two weeks had flown.

The time had the unreal quality of a dream. She remembered snippets…colors and phrases and feelings and scents…but she couldn't quite reconstruct the fourteen days as a cohesive whole.

Somewhere during those days she had bought a wedding dress, picked out a bouquet, chosen colors and decorations and music, champagnes and cake and hors d'oeuvres.

But it had been like playing one of Steve's video games. Moving pretend people around in a simulated environment, making choices and taking chances—all of which could be erased with the flick of a button.

Even now, as she stood in her wedding dress, looking down on the final preparations in the exquisite hidden gardens of Aurora's backyard, she felt as if a cloudy gauze had slid between her heart and reality.

Aurora, who had been helping her get ready, had just gone downstairs to check for last-minute glitches. Claire had five minutes alone to think. Which was, she discovered, about five minutes too many.

This strangely distant sadness had swamped her

the minute she found herself alone. Why? The scene below her was gorgeous. And yet, to Claire, the bustling people and the rows of white chairs and the rose-covered trellis looked no more real than so many pretty pixels in a state-of-the-art video screen.

Maybe it was just a self-defense mechanism. Maybe, subconsciously, she was afraid that if it felt too real she wouldn't be able to go through with it.

But she *would* go through with it. She touched Kieran's mother's ring as if it were a talisman, something she'd done more and more frequently as the wedding day approached. She was a mother now, too, and she was learning what Kieran's mother, and her own mother, had learned long ago.

A woman would do anything for her child.

Not that Kieran had asked for much. She knew full well she was the luckiest woman in the world. She could have found herself tied to a dreadful, resentful man who would refuse even to acknowledge his child—or one who tried to use the child to torment her.

Instead, she had Kieran, who had treated her with affection in public and courtesy in private. Kieran, who had allowed her to pick out any bedroom in his mansion, and had made it clear that, for the next few months, she would sleep in that bedroom undisturbed.

Kieran, who would be waiting for her on the other side of that rosy trellis with a bracing smile, his handsome head held high, projecting perfectly the illusion of the oh-so-happy groom.

Only she would know what he really was. A silent martyr paying the final price for his one fatal moment of weakness.

Was that it? Did everything suddenly feel so unbearably sad because she knew how much he hated the idea of this marriage?

Perhaps it was simpler still…just a hormonal flare-up at the worst possible moment.

"Claire, look! Don't you think my dress is pretty?"

Erica marched through the door slowly, as if she were already in a stately processional. Her chin was so high and stiff Claire could barely see her circlet of flowers. The little girl pinched the hem of her blue satin skirt between the thumb and forefinger of each hand, lifting it high enough to show off lacy socks and little white shoes.

"It's beautiful," Claire said. She swept her hands the length of her own simple white satin dress and curtseyed. "Don't you think mine is, too?"

Erica stared, and then her face broke out in a gap-toothed smile. "Oh, I think it's the most beautiful dress in the world! They were right! You are—"

She stopped, clamping her upper teeth down on her lower lip so hard Claire was amazed she didn't draw blood.

"What's wrong?"

"I'm not supposed to do that," Erica said between frozen lips. "I'm not supposed to repeat anything the grown-ups say. I am simply too young to recognize what was never intended for public consumption."

What an adorable child! With a laugh, Claire reached out and gave her an impulsive hug. The whole wedding ceremony was going to feel warmer and easier because little Erica Gordon had agreed to be her flower girl.

"It's okay," Claire said. "You can say whatever you want around me."

Erica struggled another minute, and then she obviously just couldn't stop herself. "Well, okay, they said it's no wonder Kieran got snagged in your web, because it's such a damn attractive web."

She looked at Claire doubtfully. "That's not a bad thing, right? I mean, except for the damn part. My dad always cusses at home. But otherwise, it's a good thing, right? Because he knows you're so pretty. And Kieran knows, too."

Did he? Claire felt a small squeezing sensation around her heart. She would like him to think so.

"Yes," she said, straightening Erica's flowers with an aching tenderness for her innocence and her unique little brand of loyalty. "Yes, it is a very nice thing. Shall we get started?"

"Okay." Erica put her hand in Claire's, ready to walk down to the garden. At the threshold she paused, looking up at Claire with a sober expression.

"Claire." Erica frowned. "I'm a little bit scared to be a flower girl. Are you scared to be a bride?"

And, at that moment, staring down into that serious face, Claire finally understood why she had been feeling so lost and confused.

Yes, she was scared.

In fact, she was terrified.

Because, God help her, this bride was doing the one thing she knew she should never do. She was falling in love with her bridegroom.

SIX HOURS LATER, Kieran poured himself another ginger ale and stared at the library wall, wondering if Claire had changed out of her wedding gown yet.

He put the glass to his forehead and shut his eyes. When she changed, would she come downstairs? What would they do? What would they talk about?

Next door, at Aurora's house, the reception was still in full swing. He could hear the band playing corny songs like "The Way You Look Tonight." Occasional laughter wafted over, sometimes high and musical, like wind chimes, sometimes low and throaty, like doves. If he looked out the window, which he had no intention of doing, he could probably see couples dancing beneath the twinkling lights, stealing kisses under the sourwood tree.

If it hadn't been for Roddy, Claire and Kieran might still be there, too. After the cake, after the champagne, after the opening dance, after a million handshakes and kisses, Roddy had finally sidled up to Kieran under the pretext of handing him a drink.

"Isn't it time you and the bride ducked out, pal? Sticking around looks a little…umm…lukewarm, don't you think?"

Kieran didn't often feel like a complete idiot, but he had felt like one then.

He opened another ginger ale, his third. Where was she? Surely she wouldn't have gone to bed without even saying a word?

Oh, hell. This was impossible.

They should have taken a honeymoon.

Aurora had lobbied hard for Acapulco. Roddy had pulled for the Riviera. But anything of the kind had seemed absurd, given the circumstances of their marriage. Why fly off together into the sunset, only to book separate rooms at the most glamorous hotels? Why waste romantic moonlight and sexy, pounding surf on awkward small talk about the weather?

But now Kieran knew why. Couples didn't take honeymoons, as he'd always thought, just so that they could have two weeks of uninterrupted sex. No, a honeymoon was merely a buffer zone. A safe transition space between the ease of single life and the sudden shock of cohabitation.

He heard a sharp clink against his tumbler, and he jerked up, startled, wondering if he'd broken something. But it was only his wedding ring hitting the glass.

His wedding ring. He stared at his left hand, where the simple gold band now resided, and tried to believe he was married.

"Hi," Claire's voice came from the doorway. "I—I'm a little tired. I thought I might go to bed. I just wanted to say good-night."

He looked up. It was only about ten o'clock. But she was already wearing a simple blue satin nightgown. The wedding dress was gone. She had taken the diamond comb out of her hair, the one that had held her veil in place, and removed the pearls that had circled her tiny throat. She seemed to have washed the makeup from her face. But, even stripped of all the frills, she looked twice as beautiful as when she had walked down that soft green carpet toward him this afternoon.

And at that moment he had already believed she was the most beautiful woman he'd ever seen.

It had been difficult, when the time came, to keep their official kiss short and ceremonial. When she'd lifted her veil and turned her face up to him, he'd felt a violent rush of desire completely unsuited to a public occasion.

He felt it again now, watching her standing there

in that blue nightgown. He forced himself to look away. The desire was just as inappropriate here tonight as it had been out there this afternoon.

But…oh, damn the ridiculous mess it had all become! Why couldn't their story have been different? Why couldn't they have been a normal couple, dating, getting to know each other over pizza and movies and glasses of wine? Why couldn't they have been out in Aurora's garden right now, dancing cleverly toward the shadows so that they could finally steal a kiss?

It might have worked. God knew there had always been sexual chemistry between them. If it hadn't been for Steve's death—

If they'd been given the time they deserved, it might have been fantastic. Eventually, they might even have found their path to that white bridal gown and green velvet carpet the conventional way.

And then this night would have been so very, very different.

"Are you all right?" He forced a smile. He couldn't let his frustration show. It might look to her like anger. "Do you have everything you need?"

"Yes. Everything is lovely. Your housekeeper put all my things away, and she left a pitcher of water, and books. Even flowers."

"Good," he said.

This was a nightmare. Every male instinct—inherited from every McClintock in the family tree, beginning with centuries of warrior Celtic ancestors and flowing all the way down to his own scoundrel father, said, *She's your wife. Go to her.*

But every bit of common sense he possessed was like a metal link, creating a chain of self-imposed chivalry, straining to hold him back. He had taken advantage of her vulnerability once. He could not sink low enough to do it a second time.

Or could he? The devil in him began to whisper again. Look at her! Didn't she seem slightly lost, as if this big house might swallow her up? She didn't even know where all the rooms were, for God's sake. He ought to go to her. He ought to put his arms around her and hold her close, and tell her it was going to be all right.

It didn't have to lead to anything. It didn't have to lead to that big, empty four-poster bed in his room, only two doors down from hers.

But it would. He knew it would, just as well as he knew that the sun would rise tomorrow. Just as well as he knew that the ghost of Steve would always fall between them, no matter how close they tried to get.

"Claire—"

"Kieran. I also wanted to say— I also came down here to thank you."

He set his ginger ale down with a stiff arm. He didn't let go of it, though. He clung to it. It anchored him in this spot.

"Thank me for what?"

"For today."

She took a deep breath. He saw the soft blue fabric lift as her breasts rose. Her breasts were beautiful. He knew—yes, he *knew,* damn it—that her breasts were smoother than any silk or satin. They were velvet warm and full of longing, swelling under his hands. And beneath them her heart could beat like butterfly wings.

He forced his fingers into a fist to dull the ache of remembering. Oh, yes. He had known it all once.

But only once.

She cleared her throat softly. "Kieran, I know today wasn't easy for you. For either of us. I know it wasn't what you had planned for your life."

He gripped the glass again. "Was it what you had planned for yours?"

"Of course not. I would have given anything not to end up here. I had always vowed never to be like my mother. She—"

"Then we're even," he said, more harshly than he had meant to. But her words had stung, if only because he had been indulging in those stupid "what if" dreams. "Because I had sworn never to end up like my father."

"I know," she said. "That's why I wanted to thank you—"

"Stop thanking me, Claire. I'm not doing this for you, any more than you're doing it for me. As we've said a thousand times, we're both doing it for the baby."

She looked very pale. Pulling her robe tightly together at her throat, she nodded.

"I guess we can only hope, then," she said, "that someday the baby will thank us both."

IT RAINED EVERY DAY for a week, and Claire thought she might go stir crazy. One of Kieran's big land deals was about to close, so he was out of the house from early morning until well after dark.

Aurora provided no distractions. She had caught a cold and was under doctor's orders to sleep most of the day.

Claire occupied herself as best she could. She acquainted herself with Kieran's house and tried to make friends with Ilsa, the beautiful housekeeper, who unfortunately spoke primarily Swedish. Claire wished Kieran would give the woman an extended vacation. If Ilsa did everything that needed to be done around the house, how was Claire going to make herself useful?

She worked on her lesson plans for the fall term, but, after the *Hamlet* fiasco, Mrs. Straine had laid down so many laws about curriculum that there wasn't much room for creativity. In two days, Claire had the entire term outlined and ready to go.

Friday started off better, with a dry morning and sunshine squinting weakly through the dirty clouds. But by afternoon the sky was black again, and soon the rain was coming down in torrents.

Claire couldn't stand it any more. She had to get out of the house. She pulled on her coat and grabbed an umbrella from the hall umbrella stand—which in this mansion was a large royal blue vase with a dragon twining around its neck, eerily beautiful and undoubtedly priceless.

Maybe she'd go say hello to Linda, whom she hadn't seen since the reception. They hadn't exchanged more than ten words even then. Linda had been decidedly cool ever since the disastrous wedding-dress expedition.

Maybe she was offended that she hadn't been invited on the follow-up shopping trip. Or maybe she was just moody. Still, Claire sensed that Linda could use a friend. Well, so could Claire. Mending fences between neighbors was as good a way as any to spend a rainy afternoon.

Linda lived only two houses down, but Claire walked slowly, enjoying breathing fresh air in spite of the weather, which really was terrible. The rain pummeled the lawns, digging divots even in this healthy green grass and creating puddles around the flower gardens. The gutters gushed as full as fountains and the sidewalks were a mosaic of green leaves and brown twigs.

As she walked, Claire realized that, seen like this, Riverside Park had a special charm. The patina of age took on a subtle glimmer in the damp. The rain brought out lovely, elegant smells, shaking sweetness from the roses, lifting clean cedar musk from the chips of mulch that floated down the overflowing gutters like fairy boats.

It was so different from East Yarrow Street. This neighborhood had nothing to fear from the storm. No one here dreaded the plop of a new leak in an already patched roof. No one wondered if the low ground would saturate and let water creep over the threshold. No one glanced nervously at the dying oak tree out back, wondering if it could win yet another fight with the wind.

No, on this street the neat lines of square stone-and-brick houses met the elements serenely. They stood shoulder to shoulder, solid and unbowed, as if, in their hundred years together, they'd protected the people inside from all this and more.

Although Claire could see Linda's Porsche in the open garage, and Eddie Mackey's white minivan was in the driveway, no one answered the door at the Tremel house, not even the housekeeper.

Now that she looked more carefully, Claire could see that the left half of Linda's lawn was trimmed, but not the right. Eddie probably had tried to get some lawn work done during the brief dry spell this morning—and found himself caught in the downpour.

Poor kid. He was a hard worker. Kieran used a professional lawn service, but maybe there were odd jobs now and then that he could throw Eddie's way. Claire made a mental note to ask him—next time she was lucky enough to see him.

He'd understand, she was sure of that. He knew that teenagers never had enough money. Claire remembered how hard Steve had worked mowing lawns for his pitiful spending cash. Eddie was probably just about the same age now as Steve had been when he died.

She wandered around the back, tilting her umbrella to ward off the slanting rain. Maybe Eddie would know where Linda was.

She called Linda's name twice, and Eddie's once. But the rain must have smothered the sounds, because the minute she opened the tall wrought-iron gate and turned the corner that led into the backyard, she saw them.

And it was quite clear they thought they were alone.

They sat close together, safely out of the rain, on the shady porch that ran the length of Linda's house. Eddie was perched stiffly on the edge of one of the wicker loungers, his palms on his knees, pressing down on them so tightly the heels of his hands were white.

His face was turned toward Claire, but he had bowed his head and closed his eyes, as if he were in pain. He wore nothing but a pair of red soccer shorts and a pair of muddy cross-trainers.

Linda knelt behind him, leaning over him. She appeared to be massaging his back. Though she was facing Claire, too, she was so absorbed she clearly had no idea anyone had arrived.

But at that moment Eddie's eyes opened, and he looked directly at Claire.

"Oh my God." He jumped up from the lounger, so awkward he looked as if his arms and legs were made of loose springs. "Miss Strickland! I mean, Mrs. McClintock." He swallowed so hard Claire could see his Adam's apple jutting against his throat. "I mean—"

Claire smiled at him reassuringly. She had no idea exactly what had been going on here, but she knew a teenager in pure misery when she saw one. Eddie Mackey's face was flaming as red as his shorts.

Linda, however, didn't seem at all perturbed. She picked up a small towel from the nearest table and began slowly drying off her fingers, as if they'd been covered in something wet, like a lotion or a sunscreen.

Except that there was no sun at all on this miserable monsoon afternoon.

"Hello, Claire," she said. She put down the towel. "Eddie cut his leg with the grass whip. I've just been putting on a bandage."

Claire looked down at Eddie's leg. As if Linda were a puppeteer controlling him with invisible strings, he stuck his leg out so that she could see better. Sure enough, there was a large strip of gauze taped over the center of his shin. Perhaps Linda had even put it there.

But not just now. Her hands had been nowhere near his shin when Claire arrived.

"That's too bad," Claire said. "Does it hurt?"

"It's okay now." He was clearly still in agony, but it wasn't physical. He couldn't make eye contact with either of them. "I'd better be getting home, though. With all this rain, my dad will be wondering where I am."

He reached over and picked up his long, dangerous-looking piece of lawn equipment. The grass whip. He held it in front of him like a defensive weapon.

"I'll finish tomorrow, Mrs. Tremel," he said, still talking to the ground. "If it's not raining."

"Okay, Eddie," Linda said. "Oh, and…happy birthday."

He mumbled something that probably was meant to be *thanks*. And then, as if he had been released from a chute, he darted into the rain, bolted around the corner and disappeared.

Linda stared at Claire. Her eyes flashed defiantly. "Want a Coke?"

Claire shook her head. She climbed slowly up the small set of stairs, lowering and closing her umbrella as she gained the dry ground of the porch.

"Linda," she began. The last thing in the world she wanted was to get into a brawl with Linda Tremel. But this was wrong, Linda knew that. And if she didn't, red-faced, mumbling, mortified Eddie Mackey sure did.

"Linda," she said, trying to sound lighthearted, "that boy is just a kid."

Linda smiled and bent to pick up a small, clear tumbler. She tilted it back, drained it and pocketed an ice cube between her teeth and her cheek.

"Sweetheart, that boy turned eighteen years old today. That boy is a man." She waved a hand toward the table, which was littered with a small bottle of alcohol, a box of gauze strips and tape. "Besides, see? I was just playing Florence Nightingale, not Mrs. Robinson. What's the big deal?"

"It's not a big deal." Claire chose her words carefully. "It's just that, whatever game you were playing, it was making Eddie uncomfortable."

Linda began to suck gently on the ice cube, still smiling. "I suspect that nasty six-inch gash on his shin was making him uncomfortable," she said.

Claire waited.

"And if any of his other body parts were bothering him, well, that's just part of being eighteen." Linda shrugged. "I can't be held responsible for the existence of testosterone, can I?"

"Linda, you can't pretend to think—"

Suddenly Linda's assumed smile dropped. "You know, I'm not sure why I have to answer to you on this anyhow, Claire. I'm pretty damn sure no one appointed you block captain of the Neighborhood Morality Watch. I mean, you've only lived on this block a week, right? Did you think that because you married St. Kieran you became a saint by proxy?"

"Of course not." Claire tried to hold on to her temper.

"That's good, because you don't catch sainthood just because you're sleeping with somebody. And you couldn't catch it from Kieran anyhow, because he doesn't have any. All he has is a cute smile and a boatload of money. Around here, no one can tell the difference between that and real virtue."

Claire couldn't believe how venomous Linda sounded. She remembered the excited young teacher who had helped her set up her classroom that first year. Linda had always had a sarcastic wit, but back then it had been quirky and clever, never mean.

What had happened to that bright, lively young woman?

Austin must have hurt her terribly. Less than three years later, Linda was barely recognizable. She was a bitter divorcée who resorted to anger, alcohol and adolescent boys to make the pain go away.

Claire knew there was no point in staying. Linda wasn't listening. She was ragged with fury, and things would only spiral out of control. Claire picked up her umbrella and put her finger on the trigger, ready to leave.

At the last minute, though, she paused. She turned back one more time.

"Linda, I honestly think you need to talk to someone. A professional. But in the meantime, if there's anything I can do, please remember I'm here for you."

Linda laughed. She dug out another ice cube with her tongue and chewed it with short, sharp bites.

"You?" She laughed again. "What do you know? You're so naive it makes me sick. You know what you are, Claire? You're me three years ago."

Well, at least she had tried. Claire snapped open the umbrella and began to walk carefully down the stairs.

"Yeah, that hurts, doesn't it, Cinderella? You can dish out the truth, but you don't want to hear it."

Claire turned, as Linda had no doubt known she would.

Linda had followed her to the edge of the porch. She had wrapped her arms around the outer column, and raindrops pelted her exposed face. It almost looked as if she were crying.

"Just wait until your prince leaves you, sweetheart. Wait until you're all alone, so damn alone you'd pay the devil just to hold your hand at night. Come see me when that happens, Cinderella. *Then* we'll talk."

CHAPTER ELEVEN

SUNSHINE!

Claire hadn't put on a bathing suit in years, but after this long gloomy spell she couldn't resist the urge to lie out by Kieran's sun-sequined pool and soak up some of the blissful warmth.

So, after Kieran had left for work that beautiful Monday morning, she rushed out and bought a swimsuit at Greenoaks, the local department store. Aurora would have thrown a fit, insisting that Claire shop at some ridiculously overpriced boutique instead, but Aurora was still housebound and couldn't interfere. And as Linda wasn't yet speaking to Claire, she couldn't lobby for some thong bikini the size of a thumbtack, either.

The suit Claire chose was a cheap, conventional one-piece tank, but it was a pleasant shade of turquoise, and it was exactly what she wanted.

When she got back to the mansion, she ignored the soft chaise lounges and spread a towel down at the edge of the pool, where she could trail her fingers in the sparkling blue water. It was heaven. She didn't have her watch, but she must have lain there on her stomach for almost an hour, dozing in and out of a dreamy contentment.

When her shoulders began to sting, as if they

might be starting to burn, she rolled over, groggily feeling for her sunscreen.

But instead she encountered what felt like soft leather. It felt like…a man's shoe. She shaded her eyes with her hand and squinted up.

"Hi, there," Kieran said. He was wearing jeans and a polo shirt. Her pupils were too sun-shocked for her to see his face except as a collection of haloed shadows, but she thought he was smiling. "You're getting pretty pink. Want some help with that sunscreen?"

She was peacefully torpid from sun and sleep, and didn't register her usual tension at his appearance.

She yawned around a smile. "Thanks, but I'm okay," she said. "I was just about to turn over and do the other side anyhow."

But she was too limp to move gracefully. The towel bunched under her as she tried to reposition herself, and the sunscreen rolled away, falling into the pool with a wet plop.

Kieran leaned over her, momentarily blocking the bright sun. He scooped up the bobbing plastic tube, then held on to the edge of her towel, helping her smooth it out.

"Thanks," she said again as he handed her the sunscreen. She sat up on the towel, squeezed a small mound of lotion into her hand and began applying it to her leg.

Kieran took the nearest lounger and stretched out with a sigh. His hair looked so blond out here in the sun. It made him appear as young as a teenager. But now that her vision was clearing, she could see that he might be a little tired. He shut his eyes and let the sun beat down on his face.

"I didn't realize you were already home," she said, lathering the other leg. "Did your deal close early?"

"Yes, thank goodness. We did all the contracts at one sitting. I'm now the proud owner of one hotel, two office buildings and a small horse ranch over near Grupton."

She raised her eyebrows. This was more detail than he'd ever given her about his work before. "What are you going to do with all that?"

He shrugged, still not opening his eyes. "What I always do. Sell them for a profit immediately if I can. Otherwise I'll just collect the rent until the climate changes, and I *can* make a profit. It's not very glamorous."

"Don't you ever keep anything?"

He opened his eyes. "Of course," he said. "My inheritance holdings in Heyday, for instance, will never be liquidated. But these particular properties are pure speculation. Some deals are just moves on a chessboard, merely a way to get from here to there. They aren't ever meant to be permanent."

A flush began burning a path across her face before her conscious mind had even processed the awkward double meaning of his sentences. She glanced at him and saw that his brows had slanted together, as if he had suddenly heard himself.

"Oh, hell," he said, brushing his hair out of his eyes roughly. "You know I didn't mean—"

"It's okay." She poured more sunscreen and concentrated hard on covering her arms. "I know you didn't."

"I would never intentionally say anything—"

She looked up. "Really, Kieran, it's okay. I'm not that sensitive."

She focused again on the sunscreen, addressing her collarbone and shoulders. "After all, it's true, our deal is temporary. So why shouldn't either of us say it? If we have to edit every word we speak, it's going to be a very long summer."

He didn't answer for a minute, but the pause was suddenly tense, a little darker, as if a cloud had drifted over the sun.

She glanced at him again. His posture seemed unnaturally taut. The muscles in his arms were steely hard.

Finally he smiled, but it had a strained quality, too.

"It's going to be a long summer anyhow," he said. "Especially if you are going to lie out here like this, slippery and half-dressed and sexy as hell."

"Sexy?" She glanced down at her suit. "You must be joking. I deliberately bought the most hideous thing Greenoaks had for sale."

He shook his head slowly. "Maybe it was ugly in the store. Out here, on you, it's…" He took a breath. "Not."

She felt as if she couldn't swallow properly. When he looked at her like that her stomach took a small, shocked lurch, the way it did when you almost dropped something and caught it just in time.

She set down the sunscreen, though her chest was only half-oiled. She realized she was clenching her thigh muscles and consciously tried to relax them.

"Well," she said with a forced chuckle, "if you want a decidedly unattractive image to change all that, just picture me six months from now, when I'm so pregnant I can't see my feet."

His fingers tightened on the webbed cushion. He held there a minute, and then, suddenly, he got up and came over to her. He squatted down and put his hands around her upper arms.

"Do you think that helps, Claire?" He was breathing faster, almost as fast as she was. "I don't think you understand. The idea of you like that…pregnant with my baby—"

He seemed to be trying not to finish the sentence, but the words came out anyhow, fierce, hard and strangely thrilling. "It's the most sensual thing I have ever imagined."

She didn't answer. She had no answer, except in her body, which was responding to that ferocity with a rush of hot, sweeping desire.

She wanted him. She wanted his hands on her skin, his lips on her lips.

And would it be so wrong for them to make love? In the most profound way possible, weren't they already one body? They were always connected, physically joined through the secret life inside her, which was growing even now, a tiny bud that would soon flower for everyone to see.

"Claire—"

His voice sounded angry, but his hands had begun to move, and their message was different. Slick with lotion from her skin, his fingers slid across her collarbone, then up her neck. He pressed against her chin, gently tilting her head back.

She closed her eyes. She was ready…so ready. It was as if she had been out here all morning just for this. To warm herself, oil herself, release all tension from mind and muscle. To prepare herself for him.

"Claire." His voice was husky now, all trace of

anger gone. He dipped his head to her shoulder, his soft hair tickling her skin. And then, with a groan, he kissed her throat.

Catching her breath, she rocked back onto the heels of her hands. It was like being kissed by the sun itself. His lips were sure and hard, but gentle and so warm…always moving, gliding with slippery ease across every exposed inch. Down to the curve of her breast, stopped only by the edge of her suit. Then up again, tangling in her hair, which curved behind her earlobe.

Her lips began to tingle. Soon…soon he would find his way to her mouth, and he would breathe the hot sunlight into her…

But, before he reached her lips, a shadow fell across their bodies. Kieran lifted his head. Claire opened her eyes, though she had to squint against the stab of bright sunshine.

"I'm sorry, Mr. McClintock." It was Ilsa, a contrite, half-embarrassed look on her gorgeous face. She was holding one of the cordless phones. "But it is Mr. Woodstock for you. I'm sorry."

Kieran took a deep breath.

"It's okay," he said, smiling at Ilsa to assure her he wasn't annoyed. Claire, who still felt slightly liquid and shivery, had to admire how quickly he had recovered his poise.

Or maybe he hadn't ever completely lost it. Not as she had.

"I told him you and Mrs. McClintock were… swimming." Ilsa blushed as she said it. "But he said it is so important I must come out and get you."

Kieran laughed. "Mr. Woodstock has printer's ink

in his blood, and it makes people pretty pushy.'' He took the phone. ''Isn't that right, Arlington? Doesn't printer's ink make people pushy?''

Ilsa was already halfway back to the house, so well trained that she wouldn't have dreamed of listening in to Kieran's conversation. But Claire, still fighting the last shimmers of sexual confusion, was trying to remember who Arlington Woodstock was.

Oh, that's right. Arlington owned the newspaper.

She looked over at Kieran, wondering what kind of newspaper emergency could have been so important. But to her surprise Kieran's teasing attitude had changed. He seemed to be listening intently.

''Yes,'' he said after a long pause. His voice was low and expressionless. ''Yes.''

He glanced at Claire for the smallest fraction of a second.

And then, ''No. Go ahead.''

Claire's instincts were pricked by the careful monotone. Kieran sounded a little like Steve, who used to become completely guarded and monosyllabic whenever she walked in on the middle of one of his telephone conversations.

But Steve had been a typical teenager, embroiled in small peccadilloes, like hiding bad report cards and bending curfews. And she had been his guardian.

Why would Kieran need to hide anything from her?

''When did it arrive?'' Kieran stood, walked to the chaise and sat on the edge, no longer quite facing Claire, although he didn't turn his back on her completely, either. She noticed his hand was tight around the telephone. ''Read it to me.''

He listened for another minute. As Claire watched,

she realized she was learning to interpret his body language. Whatever he was hearing was not welcome news, not by a long shot.

"That's different." He rested his elbow on his knee and pressed his fingers against his forehead. "They didn't have those details before."

Another pause.

"No one, damn it," he said, finally showing some overt emotion. To Claire's surprise, the emotion seemed to be part irritation, part pure bewilderment. "No one. That's the part I can't figure. No one."

He raked his hand through his hair. "Yeah. I'll be there. Ten minutes."

He clicked off and turned to Claire. "I'm sorry," he said. "I'm going to have to go."

"What's wrong?" She stayed on the towel. His face was controlled, but behind the impassive facade something intense was boiling, and she knew the moment of intimacy had passed them by.

"Nothing, really." He transferred the phone from one hand to the other, then back again. "I just need to go talk to Arlington, straighten a few things out."

"What things?"

"Oh, just—" He paused. "Someone has been writing anonymous letters about me and sending them to the newspaper."

"You must be kidding. Anonymous letters? That's—that's terrible."

"Actually it's not all that unusual. The Mc-Clintocks have been high profile around here for decades. That always makes you a target."

She shook her head. It was difficult to imagine anyone disliking Kieran enough to try to smear him in the paper. As far as she could tell, everyone in town worshipped him.

"But surely they won't—" She frowned. "I thought Arlington Woodstock was your friend."

Kieran shrugged. "He is. But he's the editor first, and he can't suppress any real news just because it doesn't make me look good. He doesn't publish anonymous letters, but he still has to follow up and check into the facts."

"But there are no facts," she said, feeling suddenly indignant. Who did Arlington Woodstock think he was, "checking into" slanderous, nasty, anonymous letters about Kieran? "There couldn't be."

To her surprise, Kieran's only response to her comment was a wry smile. "I'd better get over there," he said, as if she hadn't said a word.

He looked once again as tired as he had when he first came out. She wondered what on earth the letter had said. She wondered if it might be about her. About the baby…

But what difference could all that make to anyone in Heyday? The newspaper was small, but it was respectable. It wasn't a dirty gossip rag.

"Just tell him how absurd it is," she said. If only she were a real wife, so that she could go down there with him and help to set things straight. "He'll believe you. He must know anonymous letter writers are just cowards and liars."

Kieran looked back at her, then. His expression was so odd. He was smiling, but it was full of strange and inexpressible things. Sad, bitter things.

"What is it?" she asked, suddenly frightened.

"Nothing," he said gently. "Just—be careful,

Claire. I wouldn't like to see you start believing in the myth of Saint Kieran McClintock.''

OKAY, STOOGE, Eddie thought as he hung up the phone. *You've really cooked it now.*

Yeah, basically his ass was grass. He'd just told Jeff Metzler that he wasn't going to write an essay on Poe's poetry for him, that he was completely out of the term paper business.

Jeff had not taken it well. Which was to be expected, actually, because, without a term paper, Jeff was going to flunk English big-time. Jeff Metzler's dad might own the local bank, but apparently all that money couldn't buy his kid any brains.

Frankly, Eddie was beginning to wonder whether *he* had any brains, either.

He kept telling himself that Binky Potter would stick by him even if things got a little ugly for a while, socially speaking. But he knew better than that. Only two things could glue Binky Potter down. One was a high cash-factor, and the other was a high cool-factor.

Well, he'd just flushed his cool-factor down the toilet with that phone call to Jeff. And his cash-factor was bottoming out, too, with all the rain they'd been having. Not surprisingly, his customers didn't feel he should get paid for work he didn't do.

So what exactly did he think he could use to keep Binky Potter hanging around?

Well…he could join the football team. That was cool.

Coach McClintock had been trying to talk him into it, but he'd been waffling, not sure he could maintain the grades his father expected, mow enough lawns to keep Binky in jewelry, write extra papers for his "friends" and do well on the team, too.

He'd just about decided to say no for good. Better not to play at all—Coach would go on believing Eddie could have been a star. If he played and turned out to be a dud…

Man, he'd hate that.

But now it looked as if he was going to have a lot of extra time. No papers, no social life, and if he didn't do something quick, probably no Binky, either.

His phone rang. He glanced at the caller ID. It was Binky. *Wow.* Jeff hadn't lost any time pulling out the big guns, had he?

Eddie didn't pick up, and finally the ringing stopped.

She was probably mad. But damn it, he wasn't ready to argue about it. Binky had a way of messing with his mind—and she usually got there by way of his pants. She was especially good at talking dirty on the phone, which of course put her in no risk of having to give out anything but time. If he weren't careful, she'd have him at the computer, typing in the words EDGAR ALLEN POE with one hand and—

His telephone rang again. He leaned his head back, groaning. Binky didn't like "no" as an answer. She'd probably keep calling all night.

He jerked up the receiver. "Look, I can't talk right now, Binky, my dad—"

"Who's Binky?"

The voice on the other end was languid and womanly. A million miles from Binky's choppy, girlish

Valley-talk. Too late, he looked down at the caller ID.

Tremel, Austin, the letters said.

Oh, man. He felt a prickling along his shoulder blades, right where she had massaged them. And then he felt a prickling some other places, too.

"Hello, Mrs. Tremel," he said. "I'm sorry, I thought you were someone else."

"Binky Potter?" She laughed. She had the sexiest laugh he'd ever heard. It sounded as if they shared a secret, something wonderful and a little bit dangerous. "Is she your girlfriend?"

"Ummm—" Eddie didn't quite know how to answer that. When Mrs. Tremel said the word, it sounded lame to have a "girlfriend." It sounded so high school. It sounded like wrestling in the back seat of a car for the chance to cop a feel and then limping home frustrated as hell.

It sounded, in fact, exactly like what it was.

"Yeah," he said. "Kind of."

"That's nice," she said. She wasn't laughing any more on the outside, but Eddie knew she was still laughing on the inside. He must seem so dumb to her. He flushed, remembering how he had jumped up the other day when Mrs. McClintock had appeared out of nowhere. He had been like some idiot in a slapstick comedy, falling all over himself and then running away like he was being swarmed by killer bees.

But the whole thing with Mrs. Tremel was so sketchy.

He couldn't help liking it when she flirted with him. He'd get home and think about it at night, until he was sweating buckets and completely unable to sleep.

But even while it turned him on, it also kind of grossed him out. She was like eight years older than he was. And he knew one thing for damn sure. He knew he didn't want Mrs. McClintock going home and telling Coach that she'd seen Eddie Mackey doing things he shouldn't do with Mrs. Tremel.

"So," Mrs. Tremel said. "I called because I was wondering how your leg is doing."

He touched the bandage. "It's fine," he lied. It still hurt like crazy. "Thanks for fixing it up. It's much better."

"I'm glad," she said. "You're such a great kid, Eddie. I hate to see you going through bad things." She paused. "Do you know what I mean?"

He didn't, really. "You mean my leg?"

"Not just that. I mean I don't think you should be having hard times with anything—or anybody." She paused. "I saw Cullen Overton here the other day. I thought maybe he might be giving you a hard time."

Oh, God. She *had* seen him pass the Tennyson paper. He knew it.

"It wasn't like that," Eddie said. He felt out of his depth. He felt trapped. He reached down and picked at the edge of his bandage. He pulled it a little, just to feel the sting as it tore at the hair on his leg. "Cullen—he's kinda, you know... But he's a friend. He wasn't bothering me."

"I'm not sure," she said. "I'm worried about you, Eddie. I hope you'll believe that I'm your friend. I want you to let me help you."

Mrs. Tremel's voice was very soft, and Eddie felt goose bumps go all through him. Her words were weird, kind of like a promise and a threat at the same time. Like she really did want to help him—but also like she'd be mad if he said no.

"Honestly, Mrs. Tremel. That's really nice, but—"

"I don't want to have to talk to anyone else about it," she said, softer than ever. "You know what I mean. Like your teachers. Or your father."

"No," he said quickly, his upper lip beginning to sweat. He had been holding the phone between his chin and his shoulder, but it started to slip, and he had to grab it with one hand, which also seemed to be sweating. "No, you don't need to do that."

"I hope not. But you're going to have to let me help you. You're going to have to come by and tell me the truth about what's going on."

"Yes." He hardly knew what he was promising. He wasn't even entirely clear what she was asking. But he knew that in order to keep her from telling people about the papers, he was going to have to keep her happy.

"Yes, I'll come by. I was going to come anyhow, to finish your yard."

"Come tomorrow, then," she said, and he could tell she was smiling. "Come to the back door. I think we should be alone when we talk, don't you?"

No, he thought. He didn't think they should *ever* be alone again.

And yet...

He wanted it. He groaned softly and bent over, trying to control how much he wanted it, trying not to think about the way her breasts had felt, pressing into his back while she massaged his shoulders.

His mother and father would hate him if they

found out about this. They'd just think he was a horny little pervert. But they didn't know him anymore. They thought he was still a kid, with nothing on his mind but Nintendo and new sneakers. They had no idea what he went through.

Binky would hate him, too. But she didn't understand, either. From a distance, on the phone, she thought sex was a fun game, a game she always won. In person, when she felt him pushing up against her, she just thought it was disgusting and ugly.

But Mrs. Tremel…

She was a grown woman, a woman who had already been married and wasn't afraid of any part of it. She knew what a man looked like. She wouldn't get angry if he tried to make her touch him. She would like touching him. And she'd know exactly what to do.

"Yes," he said, shutting his eyes and praying his father wasn't listening in on the extension. "I think we probably should be alone."

CHAPTER TWELVE

KIERAN HAD GONE TO BED early. What else was there to do? Claire always went to bed by ten. Sometimes he stayed up, working in the library or his office, but tonight he didn't feel like being the only person awake in a house full of shadows.

As he might have predicted, though, he couldn't sleep. He lay there for half an hour, his window open so he could enjoy the cool summer breeze. The branches of the sourwood tree danced a black, silhouetted waltz with the moonlight across his bedroom wall, and the mantel clock ticked away the minutes. But still he didn't sleep.

At about ten-thirty, he thought he heard a low knock at his door.

He rose onto one elbow, listening. And it came again, a diffident knock, only marginally louder than the beating of his heart. If he hadn't been awake, he never would have heard it.

It had to be Claire. Immediately he thought she must be sick. Badly sick. He knew she wouldn't come to his bedroom door because of a little nausea. He'd seen her coping with that often enough on her own, apparently never thinking to ask him for help.

He got up and was at the door in a flash, pulling it open. "Claire?"

To his surprise, she was fully dressed and, unless the dim hall light was playing tricks, smiling shyly.

"I hope I didn't wake you up," she said. She dropped her gaze to his naked chest, his drawstring sweatpants. "Oh, dear. I did, didn't I? I'm sorry."

"No," he said. He wished he had thought to pull on a shirt. "I was awake. Is everything okay?"

Her smile broadened. "Everything is fantastic," she said. She must have caught his skeptical expression, because she laughed softly. "I know this sounds crazy, but I was lying there in bed, and suddenly I realized that I feel fine. Not queasy, not weak, not shaky, *nothing*. For the first time in a couple of months, I feel completely myself again."

He could feel the waves of relief coming from her whole body. It was his first real hint of how difficult the early stages of her pregnancy must have been.

"That's great," he said. He started to tell her how beautiful she looked, with that smile, and that air of optimism sparkling all around her. But he stopped himself. This wasn't about him, about how her moods, her looks or her health affected him. It was about her return to strength and normalcy.

"So anyhow," she said, holding her hands together in front of her with what appeared to be suppressed excitement, "I was wondering. Does that horse farm you said you bought actually have horses?"

"Yes."

"Do you own the horses, too?"

He smiled. "Of course." Where was this going?

Her eyes were wide, and her smile deepened, growing wide enough that her neat white teeth caught the gleam of the moonlight. "I know this sounds

kind of crazy, but…will you take me out there? Will
you let me ride one?"

He raised his eyebrows. "Now?"

She nodded. "I told you it sounded crazy. It's just
such a beautiful night, and I love to ride, we had
neighbors with horses, and our girls ride at the academy. And now that I'm not sick anymore, I have all
this energy bouncing around inside me." She drew
a breath. "But if it's too la—"

"It doesn't sound crazy at all," he said quickly,
before she could articulate the practical problems, before she could say that it was too late or too dark, or
too impulsive. He didn't want the fire to go out on
this unexpectedly lovely flare of enthusiasm. "Just
give me two minutes to pull on some jeans, and we'll
go."

The ranch was only about half an hour from his
house. Heyday was a small town, and even its out-
lying suburbs, all three of them, gave way to the
wide, unspoiled Shenandoah Valley quickly. Within
minutes they were on open highway, with nothing
but grasslands, oaks and unmarked fencing on either
side. A few more minutes, and they reached the exit
for the ranch.

He had called Oscar, the ranch caretaker, before
they left, to alert him that lights in the stables would
not be cause for pulling out his pellet gun. The man
took his job seriously, and last week he'd shot at a
couple of kids who had come there for a little privacy. He'd missed the girl, but the boy would be
sitting on a pillow for a while, or so the gossip went.

Claire had grown more quiet as they drove, though
Kieran had kept up a chatter of information about the
little ranch, acreage and holdings and assorted odds

and ends about its history. Lazy Gables, it was called, because its main house had been sagging for about eighty years now. Its original owner had died last year, and the heirs had been city kids, eager to sell it off for a song.

"I asked Oscar to get a couple of horses saddled up and ready," Kieran said as he killed the motor near the entrance to the white stables, which also sagged. "He thinks we're crazy, but he agreed. I told him to pick the most docile ones he had."

Claire looked at him. "I'm actually a pretty good rider."

"That's not what I meant. I was thinking about—" He paused. "The baby. If anything happened, if you got thrown…"

She laughed. "I don't think the pregnancy is that fragile. In fact, when I asked the doctor if there was anything I shouldn't do, he said I probably shouldn't go bungee jumping, but not because it was a threat to the baby. Just because it was a damn stupid thing to do."

"I see." Kieran was surprised at what a relief that was. He wished he could have talked to the doctor, too. He had so many questions, and nowhere to take them.

With one last smile, he put his hand on the door. "Then let's go for a ride."

Oscar had tethered their horses to the paddock at the front end of the stable. The two handsome animals waited patiently, moving hardly at all, just an occasional flicker of their ears or light swish of their tails.

The smaller of the two was a pretty Paso Fino trail horse, his glossy brown coat gleaming in the light from the outdoor stable carriage lamps, and the flash on his forehead as white as the moon itself. The second horse, larger by about three hands, was an elegant gray whose black eyes watched them, liquid and peaceful.

Claire touched both the horses gently, stroking their long, graceful necks, murmuring soothing sounds.

She turned to Kieran. Her brown eyes were shining, just like the horses'. "They're perfect," she said. "Have you ever seen anything more beautiful?"

He couldn't answer right away. He had the oddest hitch in his breathing. "No," he said finally. "I don't think I have."

They rode for more than an hour, following the river trail, which was wider and much easier by night than the woodland trails. Occasionally another grassy path would fork off to their left, inviting them into the deep forests of oak and ash and birch. But each time Kieran resisted the shadowy green temptation and chose instead to hug the rim of the river.

This was not the time to go exploring. He had been to this ranch only once before, and he didn't know where its dangers might lurk. He refused to take chances with Claire.

She didn't seem to mind. The river looked enchanted tonight and whispered mysterious things as it tumbled over shining rocks. The nearly full moon rode unusually low in the sky, as if it were tempted to wash its smudged face in the rushing river. Its bright beams turned the water as blue-white as milk.

They didn't talk, but the silence was easy—they might have been old friends. Usually Kieran led, but often the trail was wide enough for them to ride abreast, and he realized that she'd been telling the truth: she was an excellent rider.

She had a good seat. Her balance, rhythm and posture were all inherently graceful. He knew women who'd been taking lessons since childhood who would never handle a horse this well. Had someone taught her? There was so much, he thought, that he didn't know about his own wife.

He took advantage of this quiet time alone to ask a few of the more impersonal questions he'd been storing up. He learned a little about the neighbor who'd had horses and loaned them to Claire and Steve. He learned about the riding lessons at the snooty school where she taught today.

Nothing earth-shattering. But it was a start.

After a few miles they came upon a particularly lovely spot, where a stand of white birches rose at the river's edge and smooth granite stones formed a flat, broad overlook.

She turned to him with those shining eyes. "Let's stop a minute," she said. "We could rest the horses."

The horses accepted being tied to the slim birch trunks as easily as they'd accepted everything else on this unexpected late-night ride. They stood close together, their heads bent to the tall grasses that grew in the spaces between the rocks, and ignored the humans.

Claire and Kieran walked closer to the edge. They stood there for a long minute, staring down at the water, which slid over the rocks softly here, a little out of the way of the current. Just clear cascades, no froth, no chatter, no danger.

They decided, without any words, to sit, propping their backs against the nearest vertical rock as if it were the back of a chair. Behind them, one of the horses whinnied softly, and somewhere in the tree-tops a night bird lifted off, beating the air with slow, whooshing strokes.

"It's very peaceful, isn't it?" Claire sighed. "I feel as if I'm a million miles away from every problem in the world."

Kieran wished that were true. He wished he had some way to make her problems disappear. He wished, at the very least, that he weren't personally responsible for so many of them.

He couldn't make her life perfect, of course. No one could manage such a miracle. But there was something he could do—had already done. Maybe this was the right time to let her know about it.

"I've been meaning to tell you," he said, playing with the grass that tickled at the tips of his fingers. "I asked John Gordon to draw up some documents for me the other day."

She turned toward him. The moonlight lit one cheek, one lovely eye. The branches of the birch tree cast a shadow on the other side of her face, as if she were wearing a dramatic black-and-white mask.

"About the money?" She didn't look upset. She looked rather as if she'd been expecting it.

He remembered how his father had exploded the night, more than two years ago, when Kieran told him he was taking Claire to dinner. "For God's sake don't get involved with a *Yarrow* girl," Anderson had roared, as if *Yarrow* had been a contagious disease instead of a neighborhood. "She'll pick you as clean as a buzzard if you let her."

Kieran wished Anderson had lived long enough to see how wrong he had been. Of course he also wished that Anderson were still alive to learn he was going to have a grandchild.

"Yes, in a way, it is about the money," Kieran said carefully. "I've come to a decision, and I hope you'll agree it was the right thing to do. I've put some money in a trust for the baby."

Her face didn't change, exactly. It merely grew unnaturally still.

"Some money?"

This was the sticky part. She wasn't a fool—she'd probably accept a little help, just to ensure that the baby had a safe and confident life. But he could almost predict how she'd react to this number...

"Yes. Five million. Two and a half million in a trust for the baby, for schools and clothes and health care. And another two and a half million for you. To spend however you see fit."

She surprised him. She didn't turn pale or turn red, or jump up in icy fury. Instead, she smiled. She seemed genuinely amused.

"Very funny. As if there could possibly be any *fit* way to spend two and a half million dollars."

He touched her cheek with the back of his finger. "It's not a joke, Claire. It's true. And it's already done."

She frowned. "Then undo it. It's absurd."

"No, it isn't." He moved a little closer and took both her hands in his. "Please try to understand, Claire. This is my child, too. He deserves to live the way—" Oh, hell, why couldn't he find the words to put this diplomatically? "I mean...he's a Mc-Clintock. Someday everything I own will be his—"

"No, it won't." She was finally getting angry. "You'll have other—" Her eyes glistened suddenly, filling with liquid moonlight. "Other McClintocks. They are the ones who will inherit your money, your lifestyle, your whole ridiculous *town*. Because they'll be the children you planned for. They'll be the children you want."

"Claire." He tightened his hold on her hands. "I want this one."

She shook her head. "You think so now, maybe. Or you think you *should* think so. But as the months go by, you'll come to see him less and less. You'll care less and less. And then, someday, it'll just be too much trouble. You'll stop coming at—"

"No." He brought her hand up to his heart and held it there, even though she tried to wrestle it away. When she subsided, he spoke again, quietly.

"That's not me you're describing, Claire. That's your father."

She stared at him a minute. And then, without a word, she jerked her hand free and clambered to her feet. She went to the very edge of the granite boulder and stared out at the river.

He didn't follow. He knew he'd touched a nerve. It would take a little while for the stinging to ease, and then maybe she could think clearly again.

That was okay. He would give her all the time she needed.

A minute. Three. Then five.

Finally she turned around. She was very pale—but she hadn't shed a single tear. He remembered the shining moonlight in her eyes and wondered how she had willed it to disappear.

He thought, as he watched her stand there, her

back to the cascading river, that perhaps she was the strongest woman he'd ever seen.

"You're right," she said. "I'm projecting my own experience onto this situation, and that's not fair to any of us. I think I can almost understand how you feel about establishing a trust for the baby. Probably you are expecting Ivy League schools and…all the trappings of a McClintock. I could never give him any of that. So if you really feel that you must set aside such a large sum, I—I won't fight you."

He went up to her slowly. "Thank you," he said.

She took a deep breath and held him at arm's length with a fierce, unblinking stare.

"But I won't accept a penny for myself. That's not negotiable, Kieran. I simply will not do it."

He felt her determination, and he yielded to it. He had, for the moment, no choice.

Someday, somehow, perhaps he could change her mind, but not tonight. Tonight she was immutable, like a force of nature. The current of pride that ran through her was stronger than the river below them, a river that had cut chasms into mountainsides rather than be deflected.

It was awesome…and strangely exciting. The weakness he'd seen in her the night she told him about the baby was gone. Now she was filled with a power that was brave and fierce and sexual all at the same time.

He touched her face with his fingers, and when she didn't pull away he let them slide into her hair. Soon her small, elegant head, tilted with desperate resolve and yet trembling with vulnerability, was held in his hungry hands.

"Kieran," she said in a tight voice. "Please don't kiss me."

"Why not?"

"Because we agreed from the beginning that this would be a mistake. Because we know it will just complicate things."

"Claire—"

"And because I don't want to think that I have to let you. I don't want to feel that you've bought the right to touch me with your two and a half million dollars."

Stung, he started to pull away. But he looked at her again, at her glimmering eyes and her full, frightened lips. And he knew everything she said was, quite simply, a lie. She didn't mean a word of that senseless gibberish. She'd drawn it out of air, like an imaginary shield, and she was holding it up between them, hoping he'd believe it was real.

"Then *you* kiss *me,* Claire," he said, pulling her close again. "Not because of the baby, and not because of the money. Kiss me because it's always been like this between us, *always.* Kiss me because you want to."

For a split second, he saw surrender in her eyes. He saw her melting toward him, into him…. Then she blinked, and it was gone.

"I'm sorry," she said. "I can't do that."

CHAPTER THIRTEEN

THE DAY OF THE Ringmaster Parade it rained again, and Eddie, along with the entire town of Heyday, held his breath. He had a big date tonight with Binky, and not just any date. He *needed* to see her. To talk to her.

If the rain canceled the parade…

But by sunset the clouds had cleared away, and the freshly washed sky was as fancy as a big top, painted in gawdy stripes of cotton-candy pink and snow-cone blue.

The parade began at sundown. Standing under the streetlight at the corner by the fire station, Eddie watched the first few floats go by and then checked his watch again.

Binky was late.

But just a few minutes late—no big deal. He tried to still the little voice inside his head that whispered incessantly. *Wake up, you dork,* it said. *She's not coming.*

But the voice was made of pure panic and insecurity. She'd promised she would come, just as soon as she got finished preparing the cheerleaders' float. She'd even agreed not to ride on it this year—which had left Eddie speechless. Binky loved being the center of attention. If she would give up that float she must really care, no matter what anyone said.

Including that know-it-all voice in his head.

He thought back on last week, when they'd gone to the park, the morning after the fiasco with Jeff's Edgar Allen Poe paper. Binky had kissed Eddie right there in front of at least six people. She had sworn she didn't care about Cullen or Jeff or any of them. She loved Eddie.

He had been so relieved he almost cried, which would have been the most pathetic thing any guy on this entire planet ever did. In his gratitude, he had given her the lariat earrings, even though it had just about cleaned him out to redeem them from the lay-away contract.

He felt around in his pocket now. He hoped she wasn't hungry tonight. If he included his dimes and nickels, he had almost enough money left for the two of them to split a hot dog.

"Hi, Eddie."

He turned around, pathetically eager, a grin on his face. But it was just Mrs. McClintock, not Binky. He tried not to look disappointed. Mrs. McClintock was really nice. And she obviously hadn't ever told anyone what she saw that day at Mrs. Tremel's house.

At the thought of Mrs. Tremel, Eddie's conscience wriggled uncomfortably. When he found out Binky wasn't going to dump him, he had decided not to go to Mrs. Tremel's house after all. But he hadn't ever called to cancel. He knew that was crappy, and he felt kind of bad about it.

And he also knew that, by standing her up, he might have made Mrs. Tremel mad. Maybe even mad enough to tell somebody what she'd seen.

But he'd rationalized that away, too. What, after all, *had* she seen? Eddie had handed something to

Cullen, that's all. It could have been anything. If she told anyone, he could always deny it.

Still, the whole thing didn't feel right. Tomorrow, after he was completely, one hundred percent sure about Binky, he'd fix it. Tomorrow he'd go over there, finish Mrs. Tremel's lawn and explain that she must have misunderstood what she saw. Then everything would be cool.

"Eddie, are you okay?" Mrs. McClintock was looking at him intently, and he realized he'd been lost in his thoughts a long time.

"Yeah," he said. "I'm fine. Everything is fine."

"Have you seen Coach McClintock?" She tilted her watch. "We were supposed to meet here in time to see the Ringmaster float go by."

It was a good sign, Eddie thought, that even Coach McClintock could be a few minutes late. If he could lose track of time, then obviously scatty Binky Potter could, too.

"No, I haven't seen him yet tonight." Eddie looked at her awkwardly. "You know, Mrs. McClintock, I've been wanting to tell you how sorry I was about…you know. What happened to Steve."

She looked completely surprised. Which made sense, as he'd pretty much pulled that one smack out of left field, hadn't he? *Smooth,* Mackey. He mentally knocked himself upside the head. *Real smooth.*

"That's very nice, Eddie." She paused. "Did you know Steve?"

"Not really. He was older than I was, and he was really popular and all, but he was really nice to me. Well, he was really nice to everybody. Everybody liked him a lot."

God, he sounded like an idiot talking moongobble. But he couldn't bring himself to be more specific. He couldn't tell her that Steve had single-handedly lifted him up out of social oblivion by inviting him to play a pickup touch football game after school one day.

It had been such an offhand, Steve-like thing to do. Eddie, just a freshman, had been hanging back, afraid to push his way in. He still remembered the flush of pleasure that had washed through him when Steve called out, "Hey, Mackey, catch!" and tossed him the football.

Luckily, Mrs. McClintock didn't seem confused. It was as if she heard what he meant, rather than what he said. Suddenly he liked her even more.

She really was Steve's sister, that was for sure.

"Thanks, Eddie," she said, her eyes looking kind of misty. "That means a lot to me. I like to think that people around here remember him."

"Oh, heck, yeah, we all do. Steve was the best."

Mrs. McClintock touched his shoulder—not in that unsettling way Mrs. Tremel did, but in a gentle way, almost like his mom.

They stood together silently after that, watching the parade. Five or ten minutes went by. He saw just about everyone he knew—everybody but Binky. His heart was like a balloon losing air. It kept sinking toward his kneecaps.

Another minute, and then Coach McClintock appeared, apologizing for being late. He leaned in and kissed his wife on the cheek, just a little peck, but she smiled that special way and seemed to blush, as if she really liked it.

Coach gave Eddie a smile, and then he took Mrs. McClintock's hand. They were probably waiting for the Ringmaster float. Coach knew Ms. Ginger, the nice lady who owned the restaurant downtown. She was the Ringmistress this year. And Mr. Hartland, who was the Ringmaster this year, was a good friend of Coach McClintock's, so they probably wanted to laugh and holler and generally make a big fuss about it.

Eddie couldn't care less who was Ringmaster. He didn't care about the whole stupid parade. He didn't care about anything but Binky.

A couple of minutes later, when the Heyday High Cheerleading Squad float came rolling by, Eddie was really glad the McClintocks were too wrapped up in each other to pay much attention to him. He knew his shock must be written all over his face, and he wouldn't have wanted anyone to see how pathetic he looked.

A dozen good-looking girls dressed in sexy, pleated miniskirts and tight tank tops held little whips, with which they pretended to control wild "beasts" inside fake circus cages. The animals wore face makeup and costumes, but Eddie knew who they were. They were the coolest of the cool football players.

Cullen and Jeff and Joe and Carter and Mark.

And there, right next to Cullen the gorilla, her silver lariat necklace and earrings sparkling as they passed under the streetlights, stood beautiful, bitchy Binky Potter, not even caring that she was breaking his heart.

CLAIRE HADN'T HAD this much fun at the Ringmaster Parade since she was five years old.

Her father had taken her here that year. It was his

last visit to Heyday—the last bubble of innocence Claire could remember in her whole life. The very next day, their little apartment had erupted in shouting and tears when her mother announced that she was going to have another baby.

After saying a few things so terrible even a five-year-old could understand, things like ''I don't believe for a minute it's mine'' and ''you're not getting one more penny,'' Claire's father had stormed off.

She never saw him again.

Almost a year later, when Stevie was cutting his first tooth, her mother had pulled Claire onto her lap, saying, ''I know you heard your father say some bad things, and I just want you to know they weren't true.'' She had shown Claire a bunch of important-looking papers, one that supposedly proved that her daddy was Stevie's daddy, too, and another that said he had to send them a check every month for pretty clothes and going out to McDonald's and stuff.

Claire had nodded and pretended she understood, but she hadn't. Her father never sent the checks anyhow, so what good was that paper? And she didn't see what difference it made who your dad was if he never came to see you. If you belonged to someone, you didn't need a piece of paper to prove it.

But every year after that—until tonight—it had always made her kind of sad to go to the Ringmaster Parade. She couldn't look at the Ferris wheel without remembering the way her father had swung his feet and made the car rock, filling her with laughter and terror.

''So where are you right now?'' Kieran nudged her shoulder as they walked through the noisy little carnival. ''You seem a million miles away.''

"I was." She smiled over at him, suddenly so glad that he was Kieran McClintock, a man so different from her father there simply was no comparison. Maybe, she thought, she hadn't really repeated her mother's mistakes after all.

"I was remembering how much I used to like this when I was a little girl."

"Yeah? What did you like best?"

She widened her eyes dramatically. "The Scrambler."

He laughed out loud. "You're pushing your luck a little bit, aren't you? Just a week ago you couldn't hold down a cup of broth, and tonight you've had a nasty veggie hoagie, a candy apple and the last bite of my hot dog. Now you want to ride the Scrambler?"

She grinned. "Yes, sir, I do."

He gave in, of course, and even stood in the long line without complaining. He was the most gracious, good-humored man she'd ever met. Ever since that midnight ride at the Lazy Gable Ranch, when she had refused to admit how much she wanted to kiss him, she had been expecting some kind of retaliation. A sulk, perhaps, or the cold shoulder. Maybe even outright anger.

But Kieran had offered her none of those things. His immediate reaction had been a tense withdrawal. That was only human—both of them had clearly been physically edgy, struggling against the desire that always flared when they were alone. But he had rallied quickly, and by the time they were halfway home he was himself again, solicitous and warm.

It had almost made her feel guilty for resisting him. But she had to protect herself. That sun-dazed afternoon by the pool, when he had kissed her practically senseless, had shown her how vulnerable her defenses really were.

As they boarded the ride, she caught a glimpse of Erica Gordon in the next Scrambler car over. The two of them exchanged a laughing thumbs-up sign as the big, yellow-spider machine began to clank and turn. And then suddenly everything was flashing past her in a mad kaleidoscope of swirling color. Centrifugal force shoved her up against Kieran's side. He put his arm around her, and, with a low squeal, she buried her face in his shoulder.

When the ride stopped, her insides kept strangely spinning. She had to take Kieran's hand just to hold her balance as she stepped down.

"Oh, dear," she said, putting her hand on her forehead. She shot a sheepish look his way. The world wouldn't slow down.

He shook his head, chuckling. "I hate to say it, but I told you so."

"No, I'm okay," she said, but then her head began to swim in earnest. "Oh, dear," she said again.

He put his arm around her and began leading her away from the Scrambler. She followed blindly, squeezing her eyes shut, fighting the disagreeable echo of Portobello mushroom, stringy sprouts and green peppers.

"Kieran, I think I need—"

"It's right here," he said. She opened her eyes and saw that he had led her to the small city hall building, which had been opened tonight in order to provide extra rest rooms. She felt a rush of gratitude for his cleverness. This was the cleanest, brightest venue in the area for someone in her condition.

"Thanks," she said as quickly as she could. And then she rushed in, praying there wouldn't be a line. There wasn't. Most people probably didn't even know this building was open.

By the time she felt fit to return to the carnival, at least ten minutes had passed. She opened up a paper towel, ran cold water over it, and then used it to pat down her face.

At the mirror next to hers, a pretty teenage girl was applying lipstick as red and thick and sticky as a candy apple. She wedged the tube into her ultra-tight jeans and then spent several seconds arranging her shining blond hair so that it dangled seductively over one eye.

Claire, watching from around the damp paper towel, almost spoke to her. She almost said, *Slow down. You don't want to end up like me...*

But of course she couldn't do it. The girl wouldn't have listened. She was clearly on the prowl. She probably thought the carnival would be a terrible disappointment if she didn't end up in the arms of whatever eager boy was out there waiting for her right now.

The girl left, but Claire waited a little longer. Outside, she could hear the sound of children screaming with that same delighted terror she remembered from her long-ago Ferris wheel ride. She smelled onion rings and corn dogs and wondered briefly if she might have to duck back into one of the stalls.

But apparently her stomach had settled. Finally she threw the paper towel in the trash, gave her hair one last swipe and returned to the place where she'd left Kieran, almost ten minutes ago.

He was still there. But Aurora York was with him.

The two of them looked up at Claire's arrival with that sudden jerk into silence that undoubtedly meant they'd been talking about her.

"Hello, dear," Aurora said with an air of extreme solicitude. She reached out and brushed Claire's damp hair from her forehead. "Are you all right now, dear?"

"I'm fine," Claire said evenly. "How about you, Aurora? The cold hasn't come back, has it?"

"Oh, no, I'm as healthy as a dragon. You're the one we need to be thinking about. I've told Kieran to take you home and make sure you put your feet up."

Claire glanced at Kieran, who gave her a stare of wide-eyed innocence. "I told her you probably wouldn't stand for that," he said. "I mean, we haven't been on the Twister yet. And you did say something about wanting some fries."

Claire fought down a twisting sensation of her own and smiled at Kieran. "I could probably be persuaded to call it a night," she said.

"Yes, you do that, dear," Aurora interjected. She put her hand on Kieran's arm. "I'll come and see you tomorrow," she said in a conspiratorial tone. "We'll talk more then. And I'm sorry for what I said. I'm just a batty old lady, you know. I get ridiculous ideas."

With that cryptic parting statement, Aurora hugged them both and made her way back to the carnival. When Aurora was safely out of earshot, Claire gave Kieran a straight look.

"What exactly was that all about?"

Kieran smiled. "She guessed, that's all. About the baby. Apparently she's suspected all along—you must have been pretty green around the gills those mornings when you were staying at her house.''

"I was. But she never said a word.'' Claire thought it through. "That doesn't account for that last statement, though—that apology for whatever she said earlier.''

Kieran looked momentarily uncomfortable. "Oh, that was nothing. You know how she is.''

Claire knew a dodge when she heard one. "No, I don't. Maybe you should tell me.''

"Oh, it's just the usual nasty gossip, the kind we knew we'd get. She was afraid I didn't know.'' He shrugged, as if it were all meaningless...which told Claire that it wasn't meaningless at all. "Apparently someone had told her that you were going to have a baby, but that it was... You know. It wasn't mine.''

Claire stiffened. Aurora, the woman Claire had thought was her one real friend in Heyday, had actually repeated a statement like that?

Claire felt hard, icy bits forming around her heart. She knew exactly why the Heyday elite found that story so easy to believe. All of them, even Aurora, judged a person's character by the size of his stock portfolio. Claire Strickland was poor, ergo Claire Strickland might well be a tramp and a liar.

She lifted her chin. "And what exactly did you tell her?''

He put his hand over his heart. "I told her I was shocked to the tips of my toes. I told her that I had rescued you from a harem, but you had sworn that you were unsullied. I told her that I was so dumbstruck at the prospect of having the Sheik's illegitimate baby foisted on me that I felt quite faint.''

He grinned, and slowly she felt the little chips of

ice inside her begin to melt. He had, of course, said nothing of the kind.

"Right. But what did you *really* say?"

He touched her cheek. "What do you think? I said I was the happiest father-to-be on the face of the earth."

Of course she knew he hadn't said that, either. But it was sweet of him to pretend. It was his way of telling her that he, at least, didn't judge her by the Snob Standard.

In the end, his opinion was the only one that mattered.

She was suddenly very tired. He seemed to understand that, and began walking toward the car without being prompted. He helped her in, as if she were something very expensive and breakable.

Though the drive was short, she dozed a little as he chauffeured her back to the mansion, away from the blinking colored lights and synthesized music of the tiny carnival.

When they finally arrived, she opened her eyes, sensing groggily that something was different. She stirred, and at that moment she realized exactly what it was.

Even though they were alone, and none of their usual playacting was required, all the way home her husband had been holding her hand.

CHAPTER FOURTEEN

KIERAN HATED TO LEAVE the house so early the next morning. He would have liked to wait until Claire woke up. He would have liked to be sure she felt okay after last night's foolishness at the carnival. He felt responsible. He should never have let her go on those wild rides.

But John Gordon called at 7:30 a.m. with surprising news. Bryce McClintock was in Heyday. He had just made an appointment to stop by Gordon's law firm to pick up some documents pertaining to the inheritance.

Bryce would be there any minute, and he'd made it clear he didn't plan to stick around. If Kieran wanted to see his black-sheep brother, John had said, he'd better get his butt over right now.

Kieran made it in twelve minutes. Bryce might not be keen to see him, but it didn't seem right to let another fourteen years go by without at least trying to extend an olive branch. Surely now that they were both grown men, they could let go of the sibling rivalry that had tormented their youth.

But the minute Bryce, one bold eyebrow cocked quizzically, looked up from the paperwork he was reading, Kieran knew nothing had changed. Bryce had inherited his mother's dark good looks, but he'd inherited Anderson's sardonic arrogance, too. The combination was lethal, granting Bryce the ability to break female hearts and crush male egos without breaking a sweat.

"Good morning, baby brother," Bryce said as if they'd seen each other yesterday. He had been alone in the office. John Gordon must be out copying documents or checking files.

"What brings you here?" Bryce lazily held out the legal-size papers he'd been reading. "Want to buy a barn? A pet store? An abandoned fraternity house? I seem suddenly to possess all manner of real estate debris."

Once, back when Kieran was a vulnerable teenager, that smile, that drawl would have made him flush with a sense of rejected inferiority. But the intervening years had leveled the playing field. The sarcasm that would have wounded the boy bounced harmlessly off the man.

"Hi, Bryce," Kieran said, determined to be pleasant. John's luxurious office had two leather chairs for clients. Bryce was already in one, so Kieran took the other. "It's good to see you. It's been a very long time."

Bryce smiled. "Yes," he agreed. "But it really would have been awkward to come back while the old man was still here. He did say if I ever set foot in Heyday again he'd have me arrested. Or was that drawn and quartered? Something unpleasant, I remember."

Kieran remembered, too. What a wild summer that had been. "Tarred and feathered, I think," he corrected. "But you know he didn't mean it. Dad never stayed mad at anyone for long."

Bryce had returned to studying his document.

"No," he said musingly. "It was always difficult for Dad to maintain any emotion, wasn't it? Love, for instance, seemed to come and go at a particularly rapid pace."

For a minute Kieran wondered why the hell he'd bothered coming here. Bryce hated Anderson McClintock—his mother, Sophia, bitter at having been discarded, had seen to that. But Sophia had died five years ago, and now Anderson was gone, too. Surely it was safe to put down the swords and wage peace for a change.

"Bryce, look. Obviously he forgave you. He left you an equal share of everything. And we are brothers, you know, so we might—"

An odd rustling noise emanated from somewhere nearby. Kieran broke off and looked down curiously.

Bryce tilted his head toward the desk. "I think Mr. Gordon may have mice," he said. "Very big mice."

At that moment, Erica Gordon popped her head out. She'd been hiding in the kneehole.

"I'm not a mouse," she said. "I'm a real person."

"Oh, a *real* person." Bryce's smile was surprisingly warm. "Nice to meet you, real person. Do you live under the desk?"

Erica stood up, brushing down her crumpled shirt and jeans. "Of course not," she said. "I just hide there when I want to listen to stuff. You don't need to tell my dad, though."

Bryce seemed to consider that. "No," he agreed. "I don't believe I do."

"Thanks." Erica studied him curiously. "My mom told me that you didn't look anything like Kieran, even though you're his brother. She was right. She says it's because your father was a tomcat. I

don't think she meant that exactly. I think it's a metaphor. Look up metaphor in the dictionary, you'll see
what I mean.''

"A tomcat. Let's see." Bryce's face was absolutely sober, but his eyes twinkled slightly. "Actually," he said, "I think it's a euphemism."

Erica's brows knit together. "I don't know euphemism. I'm only in second grade."

"Bryce is just kidding you, Erica," Kieran broke
in. "Where's your dad?"

"I don't know." She frowned at Kieran. "Do you
want me to go get him? You're just trying to get rid
of me, aren't you? Where's Claire? Is she okay? Dad
said she puked her guts up last night. I'll bet that's
a hyperbole. Look it up in the dictionary, you'll
see—"

"Erica, shut up." Kieran couldn't help laughing.
"Go get your dad, would you?"

Lifting her chin, Erica retreated in an indignant
silence.

Shaking his head, Kieran grinned over at Bryce.
"Erica," he said, "is one of a kind. Thank God."

Bryce chuckled. "I don't know. Spunk can be a
valuable asset." He put down the document suddenly. "So who's Claire?"

Illogically, Kieran felt a sudden sense of discomfort. He could take Bryce's jabs and taunts, but he
didn't feel like exposing Claire—or their fragile marriage—to all of that. It was too new, too vulnerable.
Too private. And the details were so strange—he realized he did not want to mention the unwanted pregnancy. It was too...

Too like Anderson.

"Claire is my wife."

Bryce's eyebrow went up again. "Really. That was brave."

Kieran felt himself stiffening. "What was?"

"Oh, you know. Taking the long, pointless walk to the altar. Making vows that you know you'll never be able to keep."

God, he went straight for the jugular, didn't he? It was hot in this room. Kieran stood up. "And why wouldn't I be able to keep them?"

Bryce laughed. "You are a McClintock. You did warn the poor bride that you come from tomcat stock, I hope."

Kieran's jaw was clenched so tightly it ached. "You really are a bastard, aren't you, Bryce? No wonder Dad always said you—"

Just then John came back into the office. He looked from Bryce to Kieran carefully, as if he smelled the tension in the air.

"Hi," he ventured quietly. "Everything okay?"

Kieran couldn't quite bring himself to answer. He was glad he'd been interrupted. He had been about to say things he'd regret.

Bryce stood, still smiling. He dropped the file he'd been reading onto John's desk.

"Everything's fine," Bryce said. "But, in fact, I was just leaving. I'll have my lawyer give you a call in a few days to sort out the details."

"But you *are* a lawyer." John looked confused. "And you said you wanted to—"

"Well, you know what they say about lawyers who represent themselves." Bryce shrugged. "Besides, I've got urgent business waiting for me in the Bahamas. I think her name is Leanne."

He turned to Kieran. "Sorry I haven't got time to

meet your wife," he said. "But that's okay. I'll drop by again someday, and then I can meet the next one."

CLAIRE SLEPT WELL AND LONG. When she woke she knew it was late. Sunshine must have been streaming onto the bed for hours. When she put out her hand, the sheets were as warm as if another living body had been lying next to her.

It was a pleasant sensation, and she shut her eyes, rubbing her hand up and down the soft white linen. But then, just as she was dozing off again, she heard a muted thump and felt a small vibration.

She opened her eyes and looked up. Sunlight had mingled with the crystal prisms in the overhead fixture to create tiny rainbowed bars of light. As the thump sounded again, the rainbows jiggled slightly.

She sat up, staring at the ceiling. Someone was upstairs, in the empty bedroom just above her.

She felt a stir of curiosity. No one used that room. This was Ilsa's day off, and Kieran was usually out of the house by this time. Could he still be here? Had he slept late too?

Claire grabbed her robe and went upstairs to investigate.

The door to the third-floor bedroom was pulled to, but not completely shut. She could easily hear the banging around inside, and the muffled curse as something fell.

"God damn it, what *is* all this crap?"

It was Kieran, all right. Claire opened the door, smiling.

"Everything okay?"

Clearly, it wasn't. Kieran had every drawer in the

room open. Clothes and shoes and purses and books and boxes—and some things even Claire couldn't identify—spilled out from every direction.

"Good heavens," she said, unconsciously echoing Kieran's cry. "What *is* all this stuff? I thought this room was unused."

Kieran glared at the mess. "Me, too. I knew Dad kept a few things from the Final Three in here, but I had no idea it was so—" He cast his eye around the room, obviously at a loss for words. "So insane."

Claire came in, touching some of the cascading fabrics and tumbled accessories as she passed. It definitely was madness, and there seemed to be no method to it. Plastic flip-flops from the drugstore lay on top of exquisite beaded organza gowns. Dog-eared paperbacks appeared to be bookmarked with braided-gold bracelets.

She looked at Kieran quizzically. "Who on earth are the Final Three? A trio of crazed shopaholics?"

He picked up a red-and-black lacy teddy, the kind of undergarment even Linda Tremel would blush to wear. He grimaced and tossed it aside.

"Sort of. The Final Three is what I always called my dad's last three wives. Wendy, Stephanie and Cindy. He went through marriages pretty fast there for a while."

Claire laughed. "Did he know you called them that?"

"Oh, that was the clean version," he said, kicking a feather boa out of his way, releasing dozens of fluffy pink dust motes into the air. "Roddy and I had a private name for them, too, based on their initials."

"And it was?"

"The Witch, The Snitch and The Silicone Bitch." He wrinkled his nose sheepishly. "I was only fourteen at the time, remember. I thought silicone was spelled with a *c*."

She couldn't help it. She laughed, even though for a minute she could almost see him, fourteen and defiant, trying to pretend he didn't care, trying to make a joke out of the wreckage of his home life.

"How many wives did your father have all together?"

"Five. He got started late. He didn't marry at all until he was almost forty. But he made up for lost time. Sophia was his first wife. She's Bryce's mother. Bryce is—" He broke off, his face suddenly darker.

The subject of Bryce was clearly still a sore one. Claire didn't know Bryce well, but she had heard about him. Everyone in Heyday, even down in Yarrow Estates, had heard about Bryce McClintock, though he'd visited his father only in the summers.

If Kieran was the family saint, then Bryce McClintock was definitely the sinner.

"And then Dad married my mother," Kieran went on. "Her name was Colleen. But that didn't last long. She died during an emergency C-section."

"Yes, I knew—Aurora has been filling me in. How tragic that was! Aurora says Anderson loved your mother very much. She contends that if Colleen had lived, there never would have been any more marriages."

"That's what my father always said, too. But I guess we'll never know." Kieran shrugged casually, as if he were tossing off a cobweb that had brushed his shoulder. "Anyhow, after that there were the Final Three."

She shook her head. "Five wives…"

"Six serious relationships, if you add in Charlotte Balfour," Kieran said. "He never married her, but apparently he should have. They had a son together. Talk about a bombshell. We'd never even heard of Tyler Balfour until the will was read, and now a third of Heyday belongs to him."

Claire was silent for a moment, trying to digest it all. She'd heard about Tyler from Aurora, too. An illegitimate son, revealed only after Anderson's death.

No wonder it had shocked Kieran to discover he, too, was about to have an illegitimate child. At first, the news of her pregnancy had sounded to Claire like the snap of a steel lock closing, trapping her, delivering her to her tragic destiny, where she would be forced to relive the sins of the past.

It probably had sounded exactly the same to Kieran.

She picked up a black stole studded with art-deco silver rectangles and pretended to study it. "Do you mind? That a stranger gets a third of everything?"

"No." Kieran looked at her somberly, and she knew that the answer was true. "The only thing I mind is that he *is* a stranger. I understood that my father was far from perfect, but I never thought he was capable of abandoning one of his own children, however he might have felt about the mother."

Instantly the awkwardness was back. Everything, it seemed, kept bringing them back to their own uncomfortable situation.

To avoid taking the subject further, she began to sift through the contents of a drawer in a beautiful maple highboy. It was filled with lace and bits of cloth cut into pieces, but not yet sewn together.

She held up one of the scraps. "Which of your stepmothers liked to sew?"

To her surprise, Kieran came over and looked at the fabric carefully.

"I assume these must have belonged to my mother," he said. "In fact, that's why I'm in here. I'm hunting for something of hers. Aurora tells me that, before my birth, my mother hand-embroidered a christening gown. I thought that, if we could find it, then maybe when the baby is born—"

He broke off. "Of course if it doesn't appeal to you, feel free to say so. I know that, considering that you'll be a McClintock such a short time, you might not want to make a big deal of the McClintock heirlooms."

She put the pieces back in the drawer and turned to face him squarely. "Of course I'd like to use it," she said. "It's true, I won't be a McClintock for long. But our child is not a McClintock by marriage. He's one by birth. And he'll be one forever."

Kieran started to speak, but then he seemed to change his mind. He looked at her a long moment, and then, slowly, he nodded.

They both got focused on the search, then, though they kept the conversation deliberately light, laughing occasionally at some outrageous acquisition from the Final Three, who obviously had been avaricious women with short attention spans. But the christening gown never surfaced. Maybe Anderson had decided it shouldn't even share storage space with all this tasteless greed.

Claire was rummaging in the closet when she

came across a box of things that couldn't have belonged to any of the wives. It had a distinctly manly look—no lace, no pastels, no feathers.

She brought it out. "Look, Kieran—I think it must be some of your old things."

He gave the box a quick glance. "No kidding," he said. "Well, maybe you should double-check, just in case the gown somehow found its way in there."

She put the box on the bed, which, in this unused room, had been stripped down to the bare, quilted satin of the mattress. She unfolded the flaps and began to pull things out.

"Your high-school diploma. Your SAT scores. A plaque that says you were the MVP of the Little League All-Stars. A box of old baseball cards, probably worth a fortune by now." She cocked a smile in his direction. "Not that you need it."

"Good grief, why did the old man keep that stuff?"

"Apparently," she said, "he was more sentimental than you realized."

She kept digging, fascinated by this glimpse into Kieran's past. The years were all mixed together, giving everything equal weight. The picture of Kieran at ten, in the traditional Little League pose, bat over his shoulder and cap tilted back, must have been just as real, just as alive, to old Anderson McClintock as the picture from last year, when Kieran had been roasted at the annual chamber of commerce banquet.

Finally, at the bottom, she felt something odd. Leathery, slightly squishy, rounded… She extricated it curiously. It was a football.

A football signed by Steve Strickland.

If she had been thinking, she would have guarded herself better. But she hadn't been expecting anything like this, and the small gasp escaped her lips before she could stop it. Kieran put down the armload of baby shirts and sweaters he'd been sorting and looked over at her.

"What is it? Did you find something?"

She would have given anything to be able to whisk the football behind her back or under the bed, or safely into the box. But it was too big to hide, and he had already seen it, anyhow.

Besides, it wasn't hers to hide. It belonged to Kieran. Two years ago, after an exciting 22/21 victory over the Grupton High Bucks, her brother had given it to him.

Kieran crossed the room, and she held the football out numbly, extending it in both hands without a word. What was there to say? The inscription said it all.

He took it from her with one hand, palming it with an unconscious authority, like a man who had tossed, kicked, served, batted and putted all kinds of game balls since infancy. The inscription had rotated toward the bottom, so he flipped it gracefully, just an inch above his fingers, like a master chef tossing an omelet in the pan.

Then he looked at the bold, black letters, written in permanent marker. In her mind, Claire read along. The words came to her clearly, in Steve's light, sassy voice.

To Coach, it said in Steve's awkward chicken-scratch that passed for cursive. Steve had never mastered the art of graceful handwriting. *With thanks. Because this is just the beginning!*

And then the date.

For the longest time, Kieran stood there, staring at it. He must have been reading it over a hundred times, or maybe he wasn't reading it at all. Perhaps he didn't need to. The words might already be burned into his mind, as they now were into Claire's.

This is just the beginning. No one needed to point out the terrible irony of that phrase. When Steve wrote it, he had only a few days left to live.

But how happy the words looked, with their excited, bold letter-strokes and the naive optimism of that exclamation point. Steve had been happy by nature, but that night had been special. When Steve had come home, still damp from his after-game shower. he had picked Claire up and twirled her around as if she were a rag doll. He had laughed, recounting every play, every risk taken, every yard gained, all the way up to the last-minute two-point conversion that had given them the win.

She looked at the football now, waiting for the usual reaction, waiting to be battered like a buoy at sea by waves of agony and anger. Waiting to be pierced by the lightning-sharp awareness of all that Kieran had taken from her.

But none of that came. Instead she heard, deep in her heart, only this lovely echo of Steve's pure, unadulterated joy.

She raised her eyes from the football and looked at Kieran. She wanted to tell him. But she saw instantly that, though she had been spared this time, Kieran had not. A terrible pain, barely held in check, contorted his features. His breath came at a cost, inhaled in small, ragged increments with an audible struggle.

He placed the football carefully back into the box. And then, without looking at Claire even once, he went to the window. He shoved the sash pane up roughly and leaned his hands on the sill, his forehead against the upper glass. It was as if he couldn't get enough air.

"It's all right," she said. That wasn't very eloquent, but it was only thing she could think of. Words weren't much good at a moment like this— she had learned that two years ago, when everyone had tried to make her feel better by serving up comforting phrases and earnest, well-intentioned prayers.

No, words wouldn't help at all. She wished, instead, that she could reach inside her mind and touch the memory of Steve's laughing face. She would pluck that memory, like a flower, and hand it to Kieran now. She would rub it across his aching heart like a balm.

"That was a good night," she said, though her voice sounded rusty, as if she hadn't spoken in a long time. She hadn't spoken of these things, anyhow— not in two lonely years. She suddenly realized she should have. It was like letting a gunshot wound heal over with the bullet still inside. It might look repaired, but the poison just kept building, unseen and unchecked.

She cleared her throat and went on. "He was so excited. I honestly don't think I ever saw Steve any happier than he was that night, when you won that game."

"I didn't win it. Steve did." Kieran hadn't turned around. He was still staring out the window. There were long pauses between his sentences.

"He was good, Claire. I know you never wanted him to play, but he was just so damn good."

She inhaled. "I know."

"And yet, I'd go back if I could. I'd tell him no. I'd refuse to let him on the team. If it meant he'd be alive today, I'd go back and—"

She couldn't bear to hear him blaming himself. Wasn't that ironic, after how hard she'd tried to force that blame like a hair shirt over his shoulders? For the first time, she realized that bringing Kieran pain didn't lessen her own pain even one ounce. Apparently the pit of grief, once entered, was bottomless.

"Don't you think I would do that, too? I've told myself a thousand times that, if I could just go back to that morning, I would tie him up and lock him in his room and burn his car to ashes before I'd let him get behind that wheel."

He didn't answer. Slowly, without a deliberate decision, she found herself walking over to the window. When she reached him, she stopped and took a deep breath.

"But we can't go back, Kieran," she said. "That morning is gone forever."

"Yes," he said. "Forever." On his lips, that word was the blackest, deadest word in the English language.

But somehow she found the courage to ignore the word. She reached out, and, though her fingers hesitated at the last minute, she touched him. She slipped her hands up under his arms, moving in as close as she could, until their bodies were aligned from shoulder to knee.

He stiffened. But she ignored that, too. She lay her

palms against his hard, rippled chest. Under her left hand, his heart was hammering wildly.

She rested her cheek against his upper back and let the warmth of her body seep into his cold, unyielding muscles.

"Don't you see, Kieran?" She turned her head and kissed the curve of his shoulder blade. "For Steve's sake, and for our own, all we can do now is try to find a way forward."

CHAPTER FIFTEEN

KIERAN DIDN'T DARE TO TURN AROUND. In his mind he kept seeing the windshield of Steve's car as it was being winched onto the tow truck. The impact had shattered the glass into a million pieces, but some skinlike safety feature still held the crazy, opaque mosaic in place. Not a single shard had spilled onto the muddy ground.

Kieran felt like that now—broken on the inside, but held up, held together, by something he only half understood. So he couldn't look at Claire. He was afraid that, if he did, he might finally fall apart.

"Kieran, talk to me."

"What is there to say?" He didn't want to be cruel, but it was time to be honest. "Do you want me to say it's all my fault? *It's all my fault.* Do you want me to say I'm sorry? *I'm sorry.* But it still won't bring Steve back, will it?"

"No, it won't." Her hands tightened. "Don't talk to me, then. Hold me." Her voice sank to a whisper. "Please just turn around and hold me."

Did she want to comfort him? Did she really believe that he was strong enough to take her comfort—and not take everything else, too? He squeezed shut his eyes, dimly recognizing as a hint of moisture dampened his lower lashes that he must, just moments ago, have been close to tears.

It was unendurable. It was wrong. What kind of man could stand here, simultaneously wracked with grief for a dead boy and tormented with a driving lust for the dead boy's beautiful sister?

"Claire, I can't." He tried to still her hands. But she slipped out from under his weak grip and continued to move her fingers across his muscles, rubbing. Could she be unaware that she was spreading fire? She traced his rib cage, behind which his heart was alternately pounding and stumbling, then pounding again.

As she found the less-protected vulnerability of his stomach, he gripped the windowsill, breathing so hard he left a circle of condensation on the glass. She lingered there only a second, and then she moved lower, running her hands slowly down, past his belt. And further...

A stab of lightning galvanized him as her fingers connected with the perfect center of his need. He groaned without meaning to, backing up, feeling the warm thrust of her breasts against his shoulder blades.

"Claire." God help him, she wasn't comforting him anymore. She was seducing him.

And he was already lost. He felt her touch as keenly as if he were naked, as though the denim of his jeans were nothing more than a coat of paint. Deep, unseen muscles began to pulse and burn.

He turned then, with another low groan, and took her face between his hands. She met his gaze with eyes dazed by the same hunger that was tearing him apart.

It was going to happen. After weeks of tortured awareness—weeks of imagining he could hear the soft beat of her heart as he tried in vain to sleep, weeks of sweating dreams in which she appeared at the edge of his bed, naked and bathed in starlight.

After forcing himself to accept that it was hopeless. After all that, it was finally going to happen.

He didn't hold back. He couldn't. He pulled her up to him, and he kissed her, opening her mouth roughly, staking his claim, posing his demands. Warning her that this time it was going to be different.

The last time they made love, she had been limp, numb inside her cocoon of grief, clearly desiring release but passive, unable to participate. She had been like a wax statue, spread out naked on her carpet, permitting him to use her quiescent beauty to pleasure himself. Because he'd been insane with desire, he had made love to her in spite of all that, and his climax had been shattering and true. But he had been haunted by the prickling half shame of it ever since.

This time, she had come to him. She had deliberately broken through his defenses, and he was not going to settle for a repeat of that one-sided torture. This time they would both be exposed and helpless, both quivering and aching and blind.

But she didn't even try to hold back. She tilted her head, spread her lips and invited him to take as much as he wanted. She was thrillingly alive, sweet-hot with hunger.

Their mouths still locked, their fingers began to fumble against each other, opening buttons, unlocking zippers, removing clothes, gown and jeans and shirt and anything else that stood in their way.

Somehow they remembered, at the last minute, that they still stood in front of the window. They stumbled toward the bed, unwilling to let go of each other. He reached it first and fell sideways onto the bare mattress, his head pillowed by a stray piece of blue velvet, his arms tangling in black silk scarves, the edge of the mattress catching him behind the knees.

He reached for her, trying to carry her with him, but she murmured a soft denial and wriggled free. Before he could even register what was happening, before he could do more than lift up onto his elbows, she was kneeling beside the bed, her hands splayed on the inside of his thighs, pressing them apart.

"Claire, wait—"

But her face was intent and focused. She didn't even seem to hear him. He watched, helpless, as she slowly absorbed him into the rhythmic heat of her soft, enveloping mouth.

And he couldn't stop watching. Even when his arms began to liquefy and tremble, he couldn't take his gaze away from the sight of her brown hair falling across him.

Only superhuman control made it last even two fiery minutes. He had spent the past month on the edge of torment, only one careless thought, one unguarded dream, away from losing control. And now—

Now nothing stood between him and the release he had longed for. Except his determination that they would know this miracle together.

He reached down and, putting his hands on either side of her head, urged her up toward him, up over him. He slid back, all the way onto the mattress, and took her with him. Their bodies joined with a gentle, shuddering perfection, and he gritted his teeth, fighting back every instinct he possessed.

Bright sunlight from the window kissed her breast, and then, as she bent over him, he kissed it, too. He tucked her soft hair behind her ear, so that he could see her face more clearly.

"Go slowly," he said. "I can wait."

And at first, she did. But she caught up with him quickly, and soon she began to move faster, and still faster, panting softly, her hands clenching and unclenching against his chest.

In the last, intolerable seconds, he simply stopped breathing, and closed his eyes. It was the only way. The fuse had burned down to the bomb, and, if she didn't join him now, there was nothing he could do.

But, just when he thought it was too late, he heard her cry out. He felt her pulse and shudder, and he opened his eyes just in time to see her double over, jerking softly and gasping for air. With a hard groan of grateful release, he surrendered, too, and let the glowing explosion consume him.

When it was over, she lay on top of him, a featherlight weight of slippery skin and ragged breath. He had no sheet to pull over her, so he found the velvet cloak that had been his pillow and draped it across her naked back.

A red stiletto high heel grazed his elbow. He had almost forgotten where they were. But as he glanced around, he saw a dozen strange bits and pieces of forgotten treasures that had tumbled toward them on the bed.

This was never how he had expected it to happen.

But maybe, he thought as he stroked the curve of her back, quieting her breathing slowly, this room was the perfect setting. It somehow seemed right that, in this place of broken dreams, one dream, at least, had finally come true.

WHEN CLAIRE WOKE UP, the room was very quiet, and the peach-colored sun told her they'd been lying here for several hours. Kieran was still sound asleep. She watched him for as long as she dared, drinking in the beauty of his naked body, the strangely young, innocent elegance of his relaxed face. He was so perfect, physically. She didn't ever want to forget how he looked right now.

She was surprised at how strong the urge was to wake him…to ask him to make love to her again. She wondered if this was part of the hormonal take-over of pregnancy. She could gladly have stayed in this room with him for days, getting to know his body, getting to know her own, discovering all the complicated, breathtaking paths that led to this plateau of physical bliss.

She wondered, too, how much today's decision would hurt her, later on. It seemed reckless to indulge even once in something this addictive. When they parted, less than a month from now, she would have no way to satisfy a craving for his body.

On the other hand, if this month was her only chance to know such joy, it seemed a sin to throw it away.

Suddenly she realized that the utter silence had been broken. She listened, and heard a distant, muffled pounding. It was someone at the front door. She eased down from the bed, careful not to knock over any of the debris that lay cluttered around Kieran's body. She picked up her gown, pulled it over her head and went to the window.

Aurora stood just outside the portico, glaring up at the house, as if she knew they were in there and didn't much like being ignored.

Aurora, who had a key.

Kieran breathed deeply and turned on his side. The slanting sunlight gilded his lean hip, his small, tight buttock. There were no sheets....

Aurora must not come up here and find them like this.

Claire grabbed her robe and let herself out the bedroom door. She took the stairs swiftly, her hand gliding along the polished banister. She made it to the front door just as Aurora was opening it.

"Hi," Claire said, trying to hide her breathlessness. "I'm sorry. I was taking a nap, and I didn't hear you knocking."

Aurora was casually dressed, and her hat was made of straw, but she still had her trademark feather, a long peacock feather this time, with its purple eye quivering with avid curiosity.

"Claire! You're still in your night clothes! Are you all right? It's four in the afternoon. You must have been napping all day, because the courier left me these when he couldn't rouse anyone over here." She held out two large envelopes and shook them for emphasis.

"I'm fine," Claire said. "I'm just— Well, I know Kieran told you about the baby, and I—"

"Yes, of course. Women do sleep a lot in the early months, I hear. Although you want to stay as active as you can. I never understood the women in my day, who wanted to be treated like china dolls when they were pregnant. Having a baby is a perfectly natural phenomenon.''

''Yes,'' Claire said meekly. ''My doctor said the same thing. He said to carry on normally.''

''That's absolutely correct,'' Aurora said, as if the doctor needed her approval before he could give orders. ''But where's Kieran? He doesn't have the excuse of being pregnant. Surely he hasn't been lying in bed like a slug all day.''

''And what will you do if you find that he has been?''

At the sound of the low, amused voice, both women turned toward the staircase, where Kieran had just come into view. Claire flushed at the sight of him—that was how far gone she was, God help her. Just the sound of his voice made her heart beat faster, as if it carried the echo of her soft whimpers and moans.

But he showed no signs of having spent the afternoon making love. He was neatly dressed in jeans, unwrinkled broadcloth shirt and sneakers. His hair was brushed, and his face looked fresh and wide-awake.

Aurora frowned, but Claire could tell the older woman's mood had lifted at the sight of him.

''I'll tell him McClintocks don't fritter away perfectly good afternoons, that's what I'll do,'' Aurora said. ''I'll remind him that he's got to give a speech at the Tri-County Club tonight.''

Kieran patted his pocket with a smile. ''It's already written.''

''And I'll tell him he promised to talk to Mallory Rackham, who needs to arrange for some repairs to her building.''

"We have a meeting set for Monday morning."

Aurora sniffed, and her peacock feather shivered, as if sharing her irritation that they couldn't find anything to legitimately disapprove of.

"Well, then I guess I'd just tell him to answer his door. I don't need to be acting as his personal postmistress." She held out the two letters stiffly. Claire, who was standing closer, took them with a polite smile.

Kieran trotted down the rest of the steps. He went over to the door, kissed Claire softly on the cheek and gave Aurora a grin.

"Come on," he said. He put his arm around the older woman. "You don't care about Mallory Rackham or the Tri-County Club. What's really got your feathers all starched up today?"

She turned her head away, clearly planning to give him the cold shoulder. Claire, who had put her fingers up to trace the lovely after-tingles of Kieran's casual kiss, knew the huff wouldn't last long. Aurora adored Kieran and was, for all her blustering, completely wrapped around his little finger.

"Come on, Aurora," he said, his voice coaxing and low. Claire bit her lower lip as the tones thrummed against something hidden deep in her midsection. "What's the problem?"

Aurora tilted her chin up. "Well, I don't want to bother you, of course, but you did say that you'd check on my hot water heater. I suppose a busy man like you can't remember little insignificant things like that, but—"

"I was just on my way over," he said. He picked up a small bag of tools that was sitting on one of the beautiful foyer chairs. "See?"

Aurora looked slightly mollified. "Well, if you're sure—"

"I'm sure." Kieran smiled over at Claire. "Want to go out and get some dinner when I get back? I have that speech tonight, but we could squeeze in something quick. We've—got a lot to talk about."

"I'll say you do," Aurora interjected. "I haven't heard any of the details about all this. I don't know when the baby is due, or what you'll name it, or which room you've picked out for the nursery. That third-floor spare room has a nice sunny feel, and I've always thought it would be perfect for—"

"Aurora," Kieran broke in. "The hot water heater?"

But Claire heard Aurora babbling all the way out the door and down the steps. Obviously that was what had been bothering the good-hearted old busybody—she felt left out. Claire was glad that Kieran would be the one to walk that particular tightrope, deflecting awkward questions while assuring Aurora she was getting all the interesting details.

Claire sat down on one of the foyer chairs, the one next to the bust of a veil-draped woman with flowers at her breast. She ought to go get ready for that early dinner. But being completely dressed seemed to eliminate all chance of finding herself back in bed with him…

She shut her eyes against a shiver of remembrance. Oh, she had been right to worry, hadn't she? She was already addicted to him.

Sighing, she looked at the two envelopes Aurora had handed her, both special deliveries requiring someone's signature, which must be why the courier had refused to leave them at the unanswered McClintock door.

One of them was addressed to Kieran from the firm of Gordon and Gordon, Esquires. Maybe information about the trust? She lay that one aside and turned to the other. Odd. It had Claire's name on the front, but listed no return address.

Curious, she ran her finger under the flap and opened it. Two things fell out. The first was a carefully cut clipping from the *Heyday Herald*— a short article that Claire still knew by heart. It had run in the bottom left-hand corner of the front page the day after Steve's death.

HHS Quarterback Dies on Way To Practice

And a subhead—*Slick roads, speeding blamed for tragic accident.*

Claire barely glanced at it. She didn't want to see the small, black-and-white photograph of Steve, smiling boyishly, so cocky and full of life. She had torn up her own copy of that picture, which the newspaper had returned to her, apparently unaware that it was forever poisoned now.

The second thing that fell out was a note addressed simply to "Mrs. McClintock." It was handwritten, but employed an awkward, artificial lettering that was obviously designed to keep the author anonymous.

If the newspaper continues to ignore my letters, the note began, *I'll have to expose the truth myself. You think your husband is such a saint. But why don't you ask him about the conspiracy he cooked up to protect his precious football team?*

And the final, blood-chilling line.

Why don't you ask him how your brother really died?

THE MOST BORING PLACE ON EARTH was Eddie Mackey's house on a weekend afternoon. You couldn't have friends over—even if Eddie still had any friends—because his mom was always dusting and doing laundry and stuff, and she said she couldn't bear for people to see the place looking such a mess.

His father sat in front of the television all day long, hypnotized by one news show after another. His mom had always explained to Eddie that "Dad needs time to unwind," as if being a dentist were as stressful as international espionage.

To Eddie, it looked more like a power issue. Eddie's dad sat there on his Barcalounger throne, pointing his remote control at the TV like some kind of magic scepter. No one, not even Eddie's mom, was allowed to talk in the room except during the commercial breaks. So if you had something to say, you had to carve it up into three-minute sections.

Mostly Eddie avoided being home on the weekends. That was one advantage of mowing lawns, at least. But today his lawn mower was in the shop until five o'clock, which, combined with the recent lousy weather, pretty much meant he was screwed.

After buying Binky those earrings, he didn't even have money to get his mower out of hock. He was going to have to ask his dad for a loan. Frankly, he'd rather eat the contents of his mom's vacuum cleaner bag with a spoon.

His dad was a news junkie, and he was flicking through eighteen different news channels as fast as the remote control could go. If he didn't settle on something, Eddie didn't see how he was ever going to *get* a commercial break.

But finally, with a grunt of annoyance, his father settled for a stock market report. Eddie waited patiently, and the minute a car ad came on, he jumped right in.

"So, Dad, I was wondering. Is there any chance you could advance me some money? I had to have the clutch replaced on the mower, and it's kind of expensive."

His father muted the television. Not a good sign. He looked at Eddie, frowning. "Why haven't you put any money aside for situations like this? Every businessman knows equipment needs to be repaired occasionally. If I had to ask for a loan every time I needed a new X-ray machine—"

"It's the weather," Eddie said. "It's rained practically every day for three weeks. I haven't been able to cut grass for ages."

"Well, that, too, could have been predicted, couldn't it? That's a pretty typical summer in Heyday. I can't say I'm impressed with your financial planning, Ed. Where has all your money gone?"

Eddie willed himself not to look guilty. His dad had told him from the very beginning that Binky Potter was playing him for a sucker. If he found out about four hundred dollars' worth of silver jewelry, not to mention the other little rings and hair-thingies and little fancy boxes and figurines and...

His mother came in, her arms full of cleaning supplies. "He's a teenager, Ted. It's expensive being a kid these days. And he doesn't get an allowance anymore—"

"It would be a lot less expensive if he hadn't chosen that decorative little bloodsucker for a girlfriend."

"Ted." Eddie's mom looked almost angry. "Don't say things like that. Binky is a sweet girl. Eddie really likes her."

"Yeah, well, I like Jaguar XKEs with camel-colored leather seats, too, but I can't afford them, so you may notice I don't have one."

That pretty much was the trump card. Eddie's dad worked very hard, and he found it annoying that he couldn't have exotic cars and boats and stuff like most doctors and dentists did. He always said that was the price of practicing in a Podunk town like Heyday, but Eddie's mom had family here, so they couldn't really move.

Eddie's mom should have known better than to say anything else. But apparently she was pretty mad. She squeezed the bottle of Tilex so hard her fingertips were white and a hint of lemony scent wafted into the room.

"He isn't asking for a Jaguar, Ted. He's asking for a loan. Don't you think you could help him out?"

"No, I don't." Eddie's dad's mouth set in a tight, straight line, and he didn't look at either of them. He stared at the soundless television, on which a happy family frolicked around a pool, laughing and hugging and drinking name-brand sodas. "He's not a kid anymore. He can vote and sign contracts and choose his own associates, whether we like them or not. It's about time he learned how to solve his own problems."

And then he hit the mute button one more time, just as the newscaster started talking about the NASDAQ. The king had spoken, and that was the end of the matter.

Except for Eddie, who still needed seventy-five dollars by five o'clock.

His mother looked as if she might be struggling with an impulse to throw the Tilex bottle at the television. Instead, as usual, she took a deep breath and turned to Eddie.

"Oh, Eddie, I forgot. You got a call earlier, while you were taking in the mower."

Eddie's father punched the button to raise the volume—his signal that conversation in the room was annoying him. But Eddie and his mom seemed to have entered into a mini-rebellion.

Eddie smiled at her. It wouldn't change anything, but it helped to know someone cared. And his heart leapt up irrationally, hoping against hope that it might have been Binky.

"Yeah? Who was it?"

"Let me think. Oh, that's right. It was Mrs. Tremel."

CHAPTER SIXTEEN

WHEN KIERAN CAME HOME, less than an hour later, Claire was dressed and sitting in the library, her hands folded in her lap over the anonymous letter. She knew she must look like a stiff, unpleasant mannequin, but she just couldn't seem to relax.

Not until he told her that this hideous letter was just a collection of lies. Not until he assured her that no one had kept secrets from her about the details of Steve's death.

Kieran seemed to sense instantly that something was wrong. He entered the library smiling, but the smile dropped as he registered her posture and the unmistakable chill in the room.

He tightened then, too. "Sorry to take so long," he said, obviously testing to see if that might be the problem.

As if she might resent the time he devoted to helping Aurora. As if Claire were one of those spoiled, bitchy women who hated to be kept waiting. How wrong could he be? Apparently having sex with someone really didn't give you any insight into their true character.

Something she'd be smart to keep in mind herself.

"It's no problem," she said. "It's just…the mail Aurora brought over—yours was some correspondence from the lawyers. It's on your desk."

He looked relieved. "Oh. That's probably just the paperwork on the trust." He strode over to the large desk and slit open the packet, apparently eager to show her that he had no secrets.

He leafed through the document quickly. "Yes, that's all, it's just the trust. And—" He seemed surprised by the papers at the end of the stack. "Oh, good grief. What is this? Damn all, Gordon. I shouldn't ever have told you—"

He seemed to be talking to himself. She wondered what could cause such emphatic annoyance. "What did John Gordon do?"

Kieran tossed the papers onto his desk. "I told him about the baby last night, after I realized Aurora had found out. I thought it would be best, because Aurora was bound to blab it all over town anyhow. Well, it appears he's drawn up tentative agreements to lay out what we'd do about custody in the event of—"

He looked uncomfortable. "You know. Hell, it's so typical, so like a lawyer to go racing around protecting my interests whether I ask him to or not."

"Protecting your interests?" Something cold slithered down her spinal cord. She had been such a fool. Such an amazing fool. She tightened her hands. "Is that what you call the baby? Your *interests?*"

He shook his head impatiently. "You know what I mean. That's how lawyers think."

"And protecting them from what? From me?"

He tilted his head and narrowed his eyes, as if trying to figure out where her flat, distant tone had come from. With a low curse, he came over and knelt beside her chair. "Claire, what the hell is going on here? What's wrong? If you're angry about what happened upstairs—''

"No," she said. "It's not that."

"Are you sure? Have you decided that you're sorry it happened?"

She couldn't look at him. "No, I'm well aware that I instigated it."

He chuckled softly. "*Instigated?* You're not taking vocabulary lessons from John Gordon, are you?"

"I mean, I chose to…to make love. I don't regret my choice."

"Neither do I," he said. He touched her hands. "So what is it, then? Surely you can't be upset about Gordon being an overzealous fool. You know him. He pushed for a prenup, and now, because I told him our plans, that you'd agreed only to a short-term marriage, he's pushing to formalize the custody arrangements. Lawyers just aren't capable of leaving things alone—''

"It's not John," she said. She forced her lungs to expand enough to draw the breath she needed. Moving her hands, she exposed the letter beneath. "It's this."

He looked confused, but he reached out and picked up the letter. The clipping drifted to the floor. Looking down at it, a dirty beige slash against the rich pink Oriental carpet, he made an angry sound.

"Oh, my God," he said. "No."

She stared at him, blood draining from her face as if someone had opened a plug. "You know what it is," she said. "You've seen one of these before."

"Yes," he said. "The goddamn cowards. Yes."

She had been so very afraid of this. Sometime during the past forty-five minutes, as she sat here waiting for him to come home, she had remembered the

other anonymous letters he'd mentioned that afternoon by the pool.

Hate letters about Kieran. Anonymous accusations
that had been sent to Arlington Woodstock at the
Heyday Herald. She felt stupid now, that she hadn't
connected the two events immediately.

"Well?" She was amazed at how calm her voice
sounded, considering her heart was in a free fall. "Is
it true? Was there some kind of conspiracy?"

He stood, the letter still open in his hands.

"Yes," he said. His face completely blank. "I
suppose technically there was. Although a conspiracy
usually implies intent to harm, doesn't it? And our
motives were exactly the opposite. In a way, we simply conspired to protect."

"And that makes it right?"

"We thought it did," he said quietly. "But maybe
it would be better if I just tell you the whole story,
from the beginning."

She nodded. "I'm listening."

But even now that he had decided to tell her, he
couldn't seem to settle down. He started to dump the
letter into the trash can, but stopped himself. As if
acknowledging her rights, he handed the letter sol-
emnly back to her. Then he moved to the desk, and
then to the window. And then, finally, he stood behind the chair next to hers.

"The day Steve died, after they took you home, I
went back to the scene of the accident. Steve's car
was still there, though he… They had already taken
his body away. Bill Johnson…" He paused. "You
remember Bill?"

"Yes." She would never forget the young policeman who had stood there, crying, and tried to tell

her Steve was dead. Poor Bill, only about twenty-one himself. He hadn't yet mastered the vocabulary of tragedy. She wondered if the world had changed for him that day, too.

"Good." Kieran gripped the back of the chair. "Bill came up to me, because he knew Steve and I had been close. He said he needed to confess to someone that he had removed something from the scene of the accident."

"Something? Something like what?"

"A couple of bottles of beer, one of them open and half empty. Bill said he grabbed them without thinking. He said he didn't want people maligning Steve, implying that he'd run into that tree because he'd been drinking."

Bottles of beer? She couldn't quite take it in. But it was strange, Claire thought, irrelevantly, that cold blood trickling icily through your veins could keep a heart beating so very, very fast.

"Of course he wasn't drinking," she said. "The beer probably wasn't even his. He had a lot of friends, they were always riding around together, it could have been anyone."

"But it wasn't, Claire." Kieran looked sad but un-flinching. Now that he had decided to unburden his conscience, apparently he was going to plow through to the end. "It wasn't one of the other boys. It was Steve."

Steve drinking—and driving? Oh, wouldn't Kieran like that? It would shift the blame away from the arrogant coach who ran his team like boot camp, forcing his players to race through murky streets to mandatory predawn practices. Instead it would place the blame on Steve himself.

It was a dirty, self-serving lie. She wanted to slap him. She half rose from her chair, intending to do so. Then she caught a glimpse of his face, which already looked as tormented as any man's could be, and she slowly sank back down.

"You can't prove that bottle was Steve's," she repeated dully.

"Yes, I can. Dr. Tremel, the medical examiner, found alcohol in his blood. Steve wasn't far over the limit, just a fraction of a point. But legally he was drunk when he got in the car that morning."

Oh, Steve, no... She wanted to cry the words out loud, as if she could make her brother hear her, two years too late. *Not after what happened to Mom...*

But she didn't let a single sound escape. She refused to show weakness now. And besides...

"That's not possible. Someone would have told me. It would have been listed on the death certificate...."

But again, as she saw the look on Kieran's face, she let her words trail off. "So this is the conspiracy. You and Bill Johnson and Dr. Tremel conspired to keep the blood alcohol levels from showing up on Steve's death certificate?"

"Yes." Kieran ran his hand through his hair roughly. "Technically, Sam Tremel decided by himself. He came to Bill and me later and asked us to corroborate what he'd already recorded. We agreed to keep silent. So, if there was a conspiracy, in the end we were every bit as guilty as Tremel."

It was surreal. Was it possible that, while she had been lying in the dark, mourning the loss of her laughing young brother, the only family she had left in the world, these men had been behind closed doors, deciding what version of the tragedy she would ultimately be forced to live with?

"But you said you were trying to protect someone...." The letter had accused him of protecting his precious football team. But maybe that wasn't the whole answer. To her horror, she heard herself, even now trying to help Kieran find excuses. "Were you trying to protect Steve?"

Kieran shook his head. "Steve was beyond needing our protection."

She lifted her chin. "I hope you aren't going to contend that you were trying to protect *me*."

"I— We—" He hesitated. "It was very complicated, Claire."

"Tell me anyhow."

Kieran ran his hand over his face, as if he were very tired. "Tremel, I think, was trying to protect me—and the Heyday High football program. We were on a roll, we were set to be the state champions. A lot of the good old boys around here are big boosters in the alumni program. If it had come out that these underage players were drinking, were even coming to practice under the influence..."

"Yes, I see. Quite a scandal. St. Kieran might not have survived it."

Kieran didn't seem to hear her sarcasm. He was looking out the window. "Bill Johnson, I think, really was trying to protect Steve's reputation. He was very young. He idolized Steve because he was so gifted on the football field."

She braided her fingers. "And you? What is your excuse?"

"I'm not sure. I guess, in the end, I didn't see how revealing the information could do anything but harm. To Steve, to the program, to you—and, of course, to me.''

"Ah, yes. To you.''

His hands tightened on the chair back.

"You don't need to work so hard at blaming me, Claire,'' Kieran said, with the first flare of anger she'd seen in the entire conversation. "I'm not trying to spare myself. I have known all along that I'm guiltier for Steve's death than anyone realizes, even the author of those disgusting letters.''

"And why is that? Because you started your practices so early? Because you rode the boys so hard?''

"Much more than that. I'm responsible because I knew there was the possibility Steve was drinking. I'd already caught him at it once.''

She sat upright. "What do you mean?''

"Just what I said. I had caught him drinking a few weeks before, after one of the football games.''

She could hardly sort through all the implications of this revelation. "Why didn't you tell me?''

"I know, Claire.'' His voice was black. "I thought I could handle it, though I see now that was foolish—''

"Not foolish,'' she said, her voice harsh and bitter. "Arrogant. Criminally arrogant.''

"Yes, all right. Arrogant. I thought he respected my judgment. I read him the riot act, and he promised me it would never happen again. I believed him.''

She was suddenly so angry her vision was cloudy and tinged with red.

"But damn you, Kieran, it wasn't your decision. I was his *sister,* his guardian, his best friend. I needed to know. I could have stopped him. I could have forced him to get help. I could have—''

''I know,'' he said again. ''But he begged me not to tell you. He said you had enough to worry about. I agreed that I wouldn't, not as long as he stayed clean. I told him that if I ever caught him again, he'd pay for it big-time—''

She heard a small, wounded sound, but she wasn't sure whether it had come from Kieran—or from her own open mouth.

Kieran looked at her with dead eyes. ''I never dreamed that he'd pay for it with his life.''

BY THE TIME IT GREW completely dark, Claire had driven up and down the streets of Heyday for more than two hours, trying to get her emotions under control. After a while, she'd parked the car and walked aimlessly. She'd spent the last hour of blue twilight sitting on a park bench, watching a father and his son race remote control boats in the pond, terrifying the ducks.

But nothing she did really seemed to help. Her mind was a gnarled ball of shock, anger, disappointment and fear. No matter where she pulled, trying to unknot the mess, it just seemed to draw the tangle tighter. She never could lay the feelings out separately and get a clear look at them.

Two boys jogged by, one a little younger than Steve, both of them wearing T-shirts stamped with the distinctive striped logo of Heyday High School. She watched them until they disappeared into the leafy shadows of the tree-lined sidewalk. One of them was much shorter than Steve, but had his smooth running style. The other was heavier, but he had Steve's shining brown hair.

She felt, once again, on the edge of tears, and wiped the moisture away so roughly her skin burned. This was why she'd fled from Heyday in the first place. No one really existed here, except in relation to Steve.

She stood, then, shakily, and walked toward her car. She ought to go back to Kieran's house and get the key to her apartment in Richmond. She needed some time alone.

The park was in the center of downtown, and a dozen businesses looked out over it, including the hotel, the movie theater, and the Black and White Lounge. As Claire reached the long line of cars that always ringed the periphery of the park on a Saturday night, she saw a woman just up ahead who looked familiar.

It was Linda Tremel. She stood beside her own car, but she had slumped over it, her head down on the hood as if she were sick, or crying. As Claire watched, Linda raised her head slowly. Looking down, she tried to unlock her car door, but she clearly pushed the wrong button on her keyless entry pad. The car's lights flashed, and a small horn-beep sounded, indicating that she had locked it instead, but Linda, apparently unable to process the signals properly, jerked and tugged at the door.

She seemed irritated out of proportion to the situation. She let go of the door and knocked her keys against the window. Then she sank her head onto the hood again and cursed loud enough for Claire to hear it three cars back.

Clearly, Linda was very drunk.

But Linda was the last person Claire wanted to talk to tonight. So now what?

Claire's fury hadn't blinded her to the one inescapable coincidence of the whole anonymous letter farce. The medical examiner who had decided to leave the blood alcohol levels off Steve's death certificate had been Dr. Sam Tremel, father of Austin Tremel, father-in-law of Linda Tremel. Claire didn't know exactly how Linda had learned of the conspiracy, but she didn't doubt for a minute that she had.

Or that she had now decided to use her knowledge to cause trouble. Falsifying a death certificate was undoubtedly illegal, but Dr. Sam Tremel had died last year, so he wasn't her target. Maybe Linda hoped to embarrass her ex-husband, Austin—but Austin didn't even live in Heyday anymore, and he was a lawyer, not a doctor, so his father's sins couldn't really hurt him much, either.

No, it wasn't that simple. Looking at the other woman now, disheveled and tearful and uncoordinated, Claire thought she knew which bull's-eye Linda had been intending to hit. It wasn't really a person—it was a marriage. Linda, embittered by Austin's rejection, forced to turn to teenage boys for comfort, couldn't bear to see Claire make a success of her marriage to Kieran. She obviously would stop at nothing to sabotage it.

If only Linda knew how unnecessary any such campaign had been. Claire's pretense of a marriage had been destined to implode in less than thirty days anyhow, as surely as if a time bomb had been planted inside its foundation.

For one terrible second, Claire toyed with the idea

of just getting into her car and driving away, leaving the wretched woman to fend for herself.

But, in the end, she couldn't do it. Even if she had no interest in saving Linda from her own recklessness, what about the other innocent drivers who might stumble into her destructive path? Not all drunk drivers ran into trees, hurting only themselves.

She squared her shoulders and forced herself to close the distance between them. Linda's face was turned away from her, still resting on the hood of the car. Her right hand dangled limply, and from her fingers hung the car keys, swaying, apparently half-forgotten.

Claire locked her fingers around the cool metal and slipped the keys easily out of Linda's slack fingers.

"Hey!" Linda's head came up and whipped around. "What do you think you're doing?"

"You seemed to be having trouble with the lock," Claire said. "I thought maybe I could help."

Linda's face was streaked with tears and dust from the hood of her car, but as she realized who Claire was, she smiled anyhow. It wasn't a pleasant sight.

"Why, if it isn't Mrs. Saint. How exactly do you think you can help me, Claire? I would have thought you might have enough problems of your own to deal with today."

If Claire had harbored any last doubts about who had sent the letters, they were gone now. But she wasn't going to tangle with a drunken woman in the middle of the street. The important thing right now was to get Linda home safely so that she could sleep it off.

"I can help by driving you home," Claire said. "You could pick up your car tomorrow."

"I'm not going home. Why should I go home? There's nobody there. There's never anybody there."

"Where *are* you going?"

"I'm going to a party." Linda's eyebrows went up in a way that she probably meant to be haughty. "You wouldn't know these people, not anymore. Now that you're Mrs. Saint, you don't visit people on the wrong side of the river anymore, do you?"

"Don't be silly, Linda. What's the address? I'll drop you off."

Linda leaned forward, and Claire got a good whiff of the alcohol on her breath. She must have been drinking since dawn.

"I don't know the address," Linda said belligerently. "I just know the house. It's the Snowdens. Near the high school. You take a left off...oh, yeah. You take a left off Poplar Hill."

Although the unhealthy pleasure with which Linda had spoken those words made her feel slightly ill, Claire struggled to remain poker-faced. She must not have been successful.

"See? You can't take me to the party, little Claire. You don't have the guts to drive on Poplar Hill. Too many ghosts on Poplar Hill."

"Linda—"

Linda stepped back, her eyes glittering in the light from the street lamp. "So why don't you stop pretending you're Miss Perfect, so damn well-balanced and *together?* Why don't you admit you're every bit as messed up as I am? And give me back my goddamn keys."

Claire tightened her fist around the keys, in case Linda might decide to lunge for them. She didn't know quite how she was going to handle this, but she knew she wasn't going to let the woman drive. Linda was a little bit mad tonight, both from liquor and from the exhaustion of a long-term emotional overload.

Luckily, at that moment, a taxi meandered by, the driver hopefully eyeballing the Black and White Lounge. Apparently on a Saturday night he expected to find a few wobbly customers needing to buy a safe ride home.

Claire moved into the street and waved her hand. The taxi swerved obediently to the park side of the street.

Linda stiffened. "You think I can't drive myself?"

"I just don't want you to run any risks," Claire said. She wasn't even angry with Linda anymore. She just felt sorry for her. "You know the truth about Steve's death, obviously. Well, I don't want you to end up like Steve. You don't want that, either."

"No, because there wouldn't be anybody who would mourn for me, the way you have for Steve." Linda's eyes suddenly filled with tears. She lifted her beautifully manicured hand and touched Claire's cheek. The booze must have reached the maudlin stage. "No one would miss me."

"I'd miss you," Claire said. "We were good friends once, you know. We could be again, if you'd just—"

"Yeah, I guess so." Linda's mouth fell. "But Austin wouldn't miss me. He wouldn't miss me one bit."

"Maybe not." Claire put her hand on Linda's shoulder and shook her slightly. "But Austin isn't the only man in the world, Linda. You need to move on. There are people who will help you, if you'll let them.''

That was as close as she dared come to suggesting therapy. She hadn't forgotten how furious Linda had been the last time Claire had said such a thing.

Linda looked uncertain, and Claire took advantage of her momentary quiescence to open the cab door.

"There you go," she said. "Tell the man where your friends live, okay?"

To her relief, Linda climbed in without protest. But when Claire shut the door, Linda rolled down the window and thrust out her hand with a sudden air of desperation.

Claire reached out and took it. Linda's eyes were glistening with tears again.

"What is it, Linda?"

"I just wanted to—" Linda frowned, and one tear fell down each of her hollow cheeks. "You said I didn't want to end up like Steve. And you're right— I don't. But listen to me, Claire, I'm serious. Get out of Heyday. Because you definitely don't want to end up like me."

Claire put the car keys in Linda's hand, confident that the woman no longer felt the need to drive, or indeed even had the energy to argue the issue. She watched the taxi until it was out of sight. Then, realizing that her own hands were as shaky as if she, too, had been drinking, she got into her car and turned the ignition.

Was Linda right? Was this sappy, needy love she had developed for Kieran going to turn her into another Linda? Would she grow bitter and ugly and vengeful?

Surely not.

And yet, already she lay awake at night, listening for his footsteps. Already, she dreamed that he might come to her and tell her he wanted to make this a real marriage. To forget the divorce. To keep her, to love her.

To love their child.

It was more than wishful thinking. It was self-destructive lunacy. She should go back to Richmond. Just for a while. Just long enough to clear her head and think this through...

Her mind racing, she pulled out of her parking space, into the deserted street. And into a sudden jolt of screeching tires and buckling metal.

Her neck jerked sideways, her wrist twisted. Then her car skidded, and stopped just short of hitting Linda Tremel's abandoned sedan.

She heard somebody yelling. But it took her many shocked seconds to figure out what on earth had happened. The empty street hadn't been empty after all. Another car had been coming around the corner, around the edge of the park. She had pulled right out into its path, and its nose had crumpled the front left fender of her car.

"Hey! Are you all right?"

A man was rapping at her window, and, realizing that her left hand hurt too much to use, she reached across the steering wheel and rolled down the window with her right hand.

"Yes," she said. "I'm fine. Are you?"

The man nodded. "Yeah, I'm okay. My car isn't even hurt too bad. Your fender took most of the hit. I'm sorry about that."

"No, it was my fault. I was distracted." Claire put her hand on her stomach and said a little grateful prayer. "I'm a fool, but I'm a lucky fool. And I won't let it happen again."

CHAPTER SEVENTEEN

WHEN CLAIRE HADN'T COME HOME by eleven o'clock, Kieran was going crazy, no more than thirty seconds from calling the police. John Gordon, who had stopped by after the Tri-County Club meeting to have a long, let's-get-this-straight-once-and-for-all talk about that goddamn custody document, had hung around, clearly aware that something was wrong.

"You probably put your foot in it," John said when he finally wormed it out of Kieran that Claire was overdue.

"What?" Kieran was pacing, occasionally stopping to look out the window at the dark street, where only tree shadows moved. He couldn't imagine what John was talking about.

"Yeah, you probably said some dumb little thing that upset her. Women like to pull the disappearing act when they're mad. They like to see how worried you get. It makes them feel needed. Evelyn does it at least once a month."

Kieran didn't bother to set him straight. He didn't bother to remind him that Claire wasn't like most women, their marriage wasn't like most marriages, and he knew exactly what he'd said to upset her, and it wasn't any "dumb little thing."

Let John continue babbling, Kieran thought. Maybe the background noise would keep him from going completely insane.

But where *was* she?

He had jogged upstairs an hour ago, just to be sure she hadn't packed her clothes. She hadn't. He had even fingered through the items on her dresser— something he'd never done before—to be sure she had left behind her key to the Richmond apartment. She had.

So obviously she was coming back.

Wasn't she?

"And she is pregnant, right?" John whistled and shook his head. "Well, let me tell you, that makes them absolutely go whacko. I mean, a sane, intelligent woman will suddenly come after you with a butter knife because you didn't bring home sprinkled donuts, which, by the way, she's never wanted before in her whole entire life."

Kieran let the curtain drop back into place. "I'm going to call the hotel. Maybe she decided to check in for the night."

"Wait a minute here, my friend." John put his hand over the telephone. "The *hotel?* What exactly did you say to this lady? I mean, was it really bad? *Fatal?* Do we need to worry that she's bolted, and you're going to end up with zilch custody of a kid you can't even find?"

"Damn it, John. Stop obsessing about the custody document. That doesn't matter right now."

"The hell it doesn't. You told me this marriage was all about the kid. Well, so is the custody agreement. You think you two can agree amicably, but I've seen enough of these things to know how quickly it all goes south. Look at tonight. Already you're having problems. Oh, yeah, it matters, believe me. It matters.''

Kieran moved John's hand firmly and picked up the cordless handset. He dialed the number for information service.

"What matters," he said, "is making sure she's all right."

He was jotting down the number for the hotel when he heard Claire's key in the door. He put the phone down, his heart suddenly doing a disagreeable yo-yo loop in his chest. He hadn't heard her car come into the driveway, which must mean she parked in the street.

Which must mean…

He went to the library doorway on leaden feet. He watched silently as she came in, observing that her pace was slow, too, and her head was bowed.

John was right behind him, breathing heavily.

Claire looked up at the two of them. She didn't look very surprised to see John there.

"Sorry, I didn't mean to interrupt," she said in a strangely flat tone. "I just came back to pick up a few things and get the key to my apartment."

Kieran knew then that his instincts had been right. Whether she went to a hotel or to Richmond, or simply vanished into the night—it all amounted to the same thing. It was over. Nothing they had built in these few short weeks had been strong enough to survive what had happened here this afternoon.

Even that amazing morning of lovemaking hadn't made any difference. Their relationship was as fragile as a house of cards, and, as he'd known it would, the truth had toppled it.

"You're leaving? You're going back to Richmond?"

"Yes," she said evenly. "For a little while, anyhow. I have some things to—sort out."

John was suddenly at his shoulder, murmuring. "Kieran, if she's booking, you really should settle this issue now, before she—"

Unfortunately, his murmur was hardly subtle. Kieran saw the shuttering of Claire's face as she processed John's thoughtless words. Kieran turned his head slightly, just enough to speak over his shoulder.

"Shut up, John."

He turned back to Claire. If he thought begging would help, he'd be on his knees. They needed more time to sort this through. But he could tell that nothing he said, even if he wrote it in blood, would make a dent in that iron composure.

"If you'll stay, just a day or two, I think maybe we can work this out—"

"No," she said. "I'm sorry."

John's breath was hot against his neck. "Kieran, for heaven's sake. If she leaves without signing the custody—"

Claire leveled her gaze just behind Kieran's left ear, probably at the exact spot where John was leaning in, whispering.

"I'm sorry to disappoint you, John, but I'm not going to sign anything right now," she said coldly. "When I get to Richmond, I'll be retaining my own attorney. I'll tell him to call you. The two of you can battle it out."

John subsided, but Kieran could tell he still wasn't happy about it. Too damn bad. No one in this room was happy about anything right now. The air practically hummed with emotional stress.

"Claire, please don't overreact." Kieran walked into the foyer, though he didn't get close enough to touch her. She stood directly beneath the chandelier, and the light poured over her as if she were inside a protected bubble. It would have been easier to coax a compromise out of that marble lady in the corner.

"I know things look difficult right now. But we really need to talk."

She shook her head. "We've already talked. Now I need to think."

"If you'd let me, I really believe I could—"

She put out one hand. Her face was tight and pale.

"Don't try to make me stay, Kieran. I can't think here. This town holds too many memories for me. It holds too much pain. It doesn't leave enough room in my mind for answers."

He looked at her. When she put it that way, when she asked for release from pain, how could he tell her no?

He tilted his head and settled for saying the only thing he could.

"Maybe the answers aren't in your mind, Claire. Maybe they're in your heart."

"I hope not," she said. "Because I buried my heart two years ago, under a tree on Poplar Hill."

THE NEXT NIGHT, Sunday night, Eddie stood in front of his bathroom mirror, holding his bottle of Armani Mania and wondering if most sophisticated grown men wore cologne. His dad didn't—he just slapped on some aftershave that smelled like fruit. But his dad had been married about fifty years. Maybe younger men, men who were still trying to impress women, did.

Eddie compromised by wearing just a little bit. Maybe Mrs. Tremel would just assume he smelled nice. Heck, she'd probably be so glad he didn't stink of grass clippings and gasoline she wouldn't even notice the cologne.

He put on khakis and a polo shirt, the kind of thing his parents made him wear out to a family dinner. He knew he looked pretty good, because his mom smiled when he came down the stairs. She put her hand against his cheek and said, "Well, cutie pie, I hope Miss Potter knows what a lucky girl she is."

But then his mom always thought he looked great. It made him feel bad, looking at her adoring smile and realizing how many secrets he was keeping from her. Maybe, in a way, it would have been easier to tell the truth if she didn't always think he was so perfect. Maybe then it wouldn't seem like such a shock.

But naturally he didn't tell her anything. He just shrugged and smiled and headed out to his car. He deliberately let her go on believing he was taking Binky Potter out to the movies, when actually Jeff Metzler was probably the horny moron sucking popcorn from her fingers tonight.

He'd thought the idea would really upset him. But actually, picturing Binky and Jeff together helped. It made him feel a little less squeamish about what he was going to do.

Binky Potter might think she was the sexiest little thing in Heyday, but tonight Eddie wouldn't have to settle for sucking the tips of anybody's fingers. Tonight he was going to be with a real woman.

If he didn't puke out of sheer terror first.

He got to Mrs. Tremel's house much faster than he'd expected to. He was at least ten minutes early, so he turned off his engine and waited a couple of houses down. He thought about driving around the block a few times, but that seemed just too darn lame. It was bad enough that he had to be home by one.

The night was pretty romantic looking, he thought, with all those stars and a breeze that smelled especially nice here in the expensive part of town. Maybe they would do it outdoors, by the pool....

He put his head down suddenly, banging it into the steering wheel with a groan. Who was he kidding, trying to sound all smooth and debonair? By the pool, in the bed, it didn't matter, because he wasn't up to this. He knew about women. Guys talked. They said that real women liked a guy who could last forever, because for them things took a little longer.

How much longer, he wondered? He wasn't sure he could hold off for like hours or anything. Because he was such a stupid, inexperienced kid, he was already walking around with a fire in his pants.

He should have stolen the bottle of scotch from his parents' bar. They never drank. It would be months before they'd notice it was gone. But he hadn't been sure whether liquor was a good idea or not. Some guys said it really helped, and others said it pretty much made you worthless.

He wished he could have asked his dad about some of this. It was frustrating to have to get your information from ''guys,'' who probably didn't know much more about it than you did. But the idea

of talking to his dad about anything this tricky was
totally whacked.

Anyway, how could he have fit his questions into
the three-minute commercial breaks?

At least he knew enough to buy some condoms.
He had driven all the way over to Grupton to get
them. He hoped Mrs. Tremel didn't think that was
insulting, like he thought *she* was dirty or anything.
Maybe she'd be glad. Maybe she thought he was
dirty, the kind of kid who would sell fake term papers to his friends and plan secret meetings with
older women.

Man, he was making himself crazy. He looked at
his watch and realized he'd been out here dithering
so long he was now almost ten minutes late.

He turned his car back on and slowly turned into
Mrs. Tremel's driveway. She had told him to pull
right into the garage, and sure enough she'd left it
open. He had been glad she thought of that, because
he didn't want Coach McClintock, who lived only a
few houses down, to look out and see his car here.

He glanced over at the McClintock house, which
seemed to be completely dark. He thought of what
he'd heard today—that Mrs. McClintock and Coach
had argued, and Mrs. McClintock had gone back
home to Richmond. Eddie didn't believe that. If she
was gone, he figured it was just because she had an
appointment or something. He'd seen them holding
hands at the parade, and they didn't look at all like
people who were about to split up.

But then, he figured, he probably didn't look like
a kid about to sneak into a divorced lady's house
and, with any kind of luck, lose his long-despised
virginity.

He got out of the car, and he heard her voice float out of the depths of the dank, black, chilly garage. It made the hair on the back of his neck stand up straight.

"You're late, Eddie," Mrs. Tremel said with that voice that was part laughter, part come-and-get-it. "Didn't you really want to come?"

He shivered and tried to see in the semidarkness. Where was she? But she must have pushed a button somewhere, because suddenly the air got even blacker. He heard the groaning descent of a large garage door, locking them in together.

"Oh, man…"

Had he said that out loud? He heard footsteps.

Oh, man. Oh, man.

And suddenly he forgot to worry about how long he would last or how good he would be. As he waited for her to come toward him in the darkness, he went back to his original question.

What were the odds he'd make it through this night without puking?

CHAPTER EIGHTEEN

At 2:00 A.M., Kieran's telephone rang. He hadn't been sleeping, so he answered it on the first ring. Maybe Claire had changed her mind.

But he must have been sleeping, after all. He'd obviously been dreaming to come up with such a ridiculously optimistic idea.

It was not Claire, of course. It was Ted Mackey, Eddie's father.

Kieran listened a few moments to the poor guy, who was almost inarticulate with worry. Apparently Eddie hadn't come home for his usual 1:00 a.m. curfew. Because he was usually so punctual, Dr. Mackey had begun making calls immediately. On his first try, he had discovered that Eddie wasn't out, as he'd assumed, with his girlfriend Binky Potter. In fact, Dr. Mackey and his wife had been shocked to learn that Binky Potter no longer *was* Eddie's girl. Binky had apparently sounded bored by the whole thing. She had no idea where Eddie might be.

From there they'd called his closest friends, who had all seemed to express the same lazy indifference. After that, they'd called the cops, who had said they'd keep an eye out, but speculated that Eddie would probably be home before long with his tail between his legs.

Then, in desperation, Mrs. Mackey had thought of

calling Kieran. "He seems to think a lot of you," Dr. Mackey said stiffly. "If something were bothering him, he might not think he could tell Janey and me...."

Kieran could imagine how difficult that had been to admit.

"I'm sure he's okay," Kieran said, "but I'll make a few calls. I know some of their hangouts. I'll have a look around."

Dr. Mackey seemed pitifully grateful and asked for Kieran's cell number so that he could stay in constant touch. Kieran gave it to him, even though he agreed privately with the police. Pushing curfew for an hour or so was fairly standard for an eighteen-year-old boy eager to make the most of his waning summer vacation.

Still, there was something odd about the reaction of Eddie's friends. Kieran knew those kids. That's just how they'd act if they were feeling guilty about something.

He decided to make a few calls of his own. When he was finished, he actually was a little unsettled. It sounded as if Eddie Mackey had been more or less ostracized from his entire social set. That would be hurtful for anyone, but it could completely crush an insecure, hormonal teenager.

He called Bill Johnson at the police department and gave him the background. Bill agreed to check it out, and Kieran knew he would be thorough. Bill was turning into a damn fine police officer.

Still, Kieran was wide awake now, and with everything he had on his mind he wasn't going to get back to sleep. He might as well prowl around and see what he could turn up. He pulled on his jeans

and a T-shirt, crammed his shoes into some old
sneakers and headed out into the night.

He checked all the usual places—the dead-end
road that was an unofficial Lover's Lane, the spot by
the river that was perfect for skinny-dipping, the con-
venience store just outside the city limits that was
rumored to be half-blind when it came to spotting
fake IDs.

He came up empty. No kids on the loose, no white
minivans parked in suspicious places and definitely
no Eddie. It was, all in all, a pretty tame Sunday
night in Heyday.

In the end, he just got lucky. His cell phone rang,
and it was Andy Giff, the security guard who made
the nightly circuit of the elementary, middle and high
schools for the county. Andy was a Heyday High
alum, a football season-ticket holder, and, ever since
they won the state championship, one of Kieran's
biggest fans.

Apparently Andy just wanted to give Kieran a
heads up, because he'd seen a teenage boy horsing
around in the middle of the football field, acting
weird.

"He's throwing a ball to nobody," Andy said. "I
told him to get along home, but he said he wasn't
budging, he wasn't hurting anything, which was true,
strictly speaking. I guess I'm gonna have to call Bill
Johnson, but I thought I'd tell you first, in case he's
one of your boys. If you can get him to head home,
maybe we don't have to bring Bill into it, you
know?"

Kieran agreed, his car already in a U-turn. He was
only about a mile from the school. "Thanks, Andy,"
he said. "Tell you what. Ask Bill to call Dr. Mackey

and tell him we think we've found Eddie. But ask him to give me half an hour to see what I can do, okay?''

The electric lights on the football field were out, naturally—it was almost three in the morning. But a clear, starry night shed plenty of light onto the long green rectangle surrounded by rows of empty concrete bleachers.

Even without the proof of the white minivan parked by the front entrance, Kieran could tell that the boy churning down the sidelines, as if the entire Green Bay Packer defense was hot on his heels, was Eddie.

Eddie was a natural runner, and he tucked that football so neatly under his arm it would have been impossible for even the best tackle to strip it. If he decided to try out, he would be a real asset to the team.

And the team just might be a real asset to him— especially if what Kieran had heard from Cullen Overton and Jeff Metzler tonight was true.

But first Kieran had to find out why the kid was out here in the middle of the night, talking trash to the security guard, which was a much dumber move than he'd ever seen Eddie Mackey make.

''Hey,'' he called as Eddie dove over the goal line and rolled to a pretend touchdown. ''What's the score?''

Eddie looked up, his scowl bordering on hostility. When he recognized Kieran, his expression lightened a little, but it never exactly became friendly.

''It's a friggin' shutout, man,'' he said, his voice as sour as his face. He took the football and spiked it into the ground, something he'd never be allowed to do in a real game. "Eddie Mackey puts a big fat doughnut on the scoreboard. Social life, home life, sex life—*zero.*"

That sounded pretty melodramatic. Kieran scrutinized Eddie as carefully as he could without being obvious. He was looking for the telltale signs of alcohol—slack facial muscles, unfocused or bloodshot eyes, uncoordinated movement, slurring…

Eddie looked stone cold sober. But Kieran had learned the hard way you couldn't take anything like that for granted.

"You haven't been drinking, have you?"

Eddie laughed. In the cool silence of the huge, empty field, the harsh tones echoed eerily. "Hell, no. I'm a loser, man. I've got no fake ID, and I've got no friends. Where would I get booze?"

"You're a smart kid. You might think of something."

"Maybe I'm not as smart as everybody thinks I am. Maybe, when you get right down to it, I'm pretty damn dumb."

"That would surprise me."

"Well, ask around. Ask anybody. Ask Binky Potter."

"You sure her opinion is the one we're looking for here?" Kieran smiled. "She's still a kid in a lot of ways. You may run a little deep for her."

"Oh, yeah, I'm deep, all right. Binky Potter was too immature for me, a cool stud like me needed a *real* woman." Eddie kicked the dirt viciously and banged his head once against the goalpost. "Man, did I feed myself a load of crap or what?"

For the first time, Eddie seemed to have dropped his fierce belligerence. His voice, on that last line, had sounded deeply wounded, almost plaintive. Kieran's instincts told him they might finally have reached the heart of the matter.

"So…" Kieran tried to sound casual. "Does that mean you did get yourself a real woman?"

Eddie didn't lift his forehead, but he cut his eyes sideways to glance at Kieran. He closed his eyes again immediately, but not before Kieran saw that they were full of misery.

"Yeah. Yeah, I got myself a woman. I think you could say I got myself more woman than I could handle."

Oh, boy. Kieran braced himself for whatever sordid story might be coming. He had a feeling that, if he kept a nonjudgmental silence, Eddie would just start spilling his guts. Whatever this kid was holding inside was eating him alive.

Eddie let himself slide down onto the ground. The dirt around the goalposts was damp with dew, just this side of muddy. But he didn't seem to notice.

"The whole thing was such a disaster. She's a lot older than I am. It wouldn't ever have crossed my mind that she might, you know, like me. But she knew about the term papers—I mean, she knew about something I did that could get me into a lot of trouble. And it seemed like she was trying to say that if I'd just come over and if we could just—"

He drew his knees up to his chest and dangled his arms over them limply. He looked at Kieran, his gaze clearly asking for help getting through this part of the story.

Kieran decided to treat it matter-of-factly, at least until he could get the important details laid out. "If you'd have sex with her, then she wouldn't turn you in?''

Eddie sighed, as if relieved that the word had been spoken.

''Yeah, that's what it seemed like she meant, only she never came right out and said it, you know? So I was like guessing, but... Anyhow, it wasn't like something I wouldn't want, I mean she's really hot and everything. And Binky never...''

He stopped again. God, Kieran thought, this was like pulling teeth. These kids obsessed about sex 24/7, but they were even terrified of the terminology. They were obviously unprepared for the intricate complications of a love life.

Again Kieran stepped in with the common-sense approach. ''Binky is a virgin, so this older woman was pretty tempting.''

Eddie looked up, nodding. ''Yeah, exactly. Because she's been married and everything, she's divorced, so she would know all about it, right?''

''Umm...theoretically.''

Even as he gave that calm answer, Kieran almost laughed out loud. As if anyone ever knew *all about it*. Look at Kieran himself. He'd had sex just once since his wedding four weeks ago, and that one encounter had tied his emotions into so many knots he was afraid he might never get them sorted out.

But this wasn't the moment to start worrying about his own problems. He needed to stay focused on Eddie.

It sounded like a twisted mix of seduction and blackmail. Kieran was angry, angry as hell at whoever had taken advantage of this kid's raging hormones and rotten judgment.

With a sudden insight, he knew who it was. Though Eddie hadn't given the woman a name, in Kieran's mind she already had a face. He could see Linda Tremel at the Senior Send-off, smiling like the Cheshire cat and observing that Eddie Mackey had "bedroom eyes."

But he needed to stay calm. If he let his fury toward Linda take over his thoughts, Eddie might sense them and read them as anger toward Eddie himself.

"Okay," Kieran said as neutrally as he could, "so what happened?"

Eddie was picking at the cuff of his khakis, which were black with mud. He didn't look at Kieran at all.

"Nothing. Not a damn thing. I'm like this pathetic, terrified kid. She's looking all gorgeous and ready to go and I'm—" He groaned and leaned his head back against the goalpost. The light wasn't quite strong enough to be sure, but Kieran thought he saw a glistening in the corners of Eddie's eyes. "I'm nothing, man, nothing. I can't do a thing."

The relief that washed through Kieran was so intense it surprised him. He hadn't realized just how creepy he had found the idea of Linda Tremel blackmailing this kid into being her unwilling replacement for Austin. Kieran liked Eddie Mackey. He thought the kid had guts and brains—and kindness, too, which was something you didn't see all that often in teenage boys anymore.

He damn sure didn't want Eddie's first experience with sex to be as Linda Tremel's coldly manipulated boy toy.

But he knew that, at least right now, Eddie didn't share his relief. So he hid it as best he could.

"Nothing, huh? Actually, that's not terribly surprising," Kieran said. "Given the circumstances."

Eddie opened his eyes. "What does that mean?"

"Well, you probably didn't feel completely right about going there in the first place. I mean, it was a little like blackmail, wasn't it? And she's older than you, so probably it wasn't a relationship that meant anything special to you."

"It wasn't a relationship at all," Eddie said. "I just work for her. It was just supposed to be, you know, just sex. Except I couldn't even manage that."

Here's where it got tricky. Kieran was hardly a child psychologist, but he figured that the two of them needed to be at the same level for this part of the discussion.

He took a seat next to Eddie on the mud and joined him in staring at the green-black field that stretched away before them. A mist had rolled in, giving the whole place an unreal quality. That helped, a little. It took the edge off.

"Look, your body's not some kind of machine, with an on button and an off button," Kieran said lightly. "Believe it or not, it's connected to your brain. If your brain doesn't feel good about a situation, it's very possible your body won't feel good about it, either. It's quite likely to go on strike, to say heck no, forget this, pal, I'm not interested."

Kieran was glad to hear a small chuckle from Eddie's side of the goalpost. He looked over, and saw that Eddie was actually smiling. "Kind of like when protesters stage a sit-down," Eddie suggested.

"Yeah." Kieran grinned back. "Kind of like that."'

For a long minute, Eddie was silent. Then Kieran

heard him take in a deep breath and let it out in a sigh.

"So I guess I'm going to have to tell you about the other thing, too."

Kieran hesitated. "The blackmail thing?"

"Yeah."

He shrugged. "You don't have to tell me. But you do have to tell somebody. That's the only way to make stuff like this come right. You have to tell the people who can help you fix it."

"Like my parents?"

Kieran nodded. Eddie was going to be doing a lot of talking tonight—and soon. Kieran had spotted Bill Johnson over at the west entrance, with Dr. and Mrs. Mackey in tow, but Bill was cleverly holding his ground until Kieran gave him the high sign.

He didn't think Eddie had seen them yet, which was a good thing. He needed to get this off his conscience, and sometimes it was easier to start by telling an impartial third party.

Eddie blew out a breath through his lips noisily, like an irritated horse.

"Okay, whatever," he said. "I'll tell anyone you say I have to tell. But first…first I want to tell you." He gave Kieran a one-sided smile. "That okay with you? I mean, I know it's really late. Mrs. McClintock won't be mad, will she?"

Kieran felt the funny little twist in his gut at the sound of that name. Mrs. McClintock. She wasn't Claire Strickland anymore. She was Mrs. McClintock.

At least for another few months.

"No," Kieran said, and even he heard the wistful note in the word. He wondered where Claire was right now. He wondered if she was able to sleep. He wondered if she'd approve of the way he'd handled this mess with Eddie.

"Mrs. McClintock won't mind a bit."

CLAIRE HAD BEEN IN Richmond a week, and she'd been trying very hard to turn her apartment into something that resembled a home. She'd bought paint and curtains and a crib, all of which were supposed to transform the spare bedroom into a nursery.

But she hadn't yet had the heart to start work. When she looked at the little pile of purchases, they looked like such puny, ineffectual weapons with which to ward off sorrow and darkness.

So she bought more things. Baby clothes, and stuffed toys and cloth books and even a big plastic tub that was on sale at the baby boutique. None of that helped, either.

The only time she felt really happy was when, on her second day back, she went to the doctor and listened to the baby's heartbeat and watched the small wiggling lines on the ultrasound. Maybe happiness, she thought, required the cooperation of another person, even if that person was only a thump on the microphone and a squiggle on the monitor.

Maybe happiness simply couldn't be experienced unless it was shared.

But that was ridiculous. It was far more likely that happiness couldn't coexist with lingering resentment and bitterness. In her heart, she knew that her only real problem was her refusal to let go of the anger she felt toward Kieran.

She knew it wasn't entirely his fault. She had to accept some of the blame, too, for not being a better surrogate mother, for not policing Steve's behavior more strictly. But Kieran's silence felt like treason. It felt like a personal betrayal of Claire's budding trust. If the anonymous letters hadn't spilled the secret, he probably never would have told her the truth.

Somehow, for her child's sake, she had to find a way to move on. But how? She felt the anger like a physical weight, like a stone, much, much heavier than the baby, who was still just a promise floating deep inside her body.

She couldn't think about it anymore.

She decided to tackle some of the unopened boxes that had come with her from Heyday two years ago. She had never found the energy—or the courage— to go through them, because she knew they were filled with mementos of Steve.

Maybe that would be one way of clearing out the ghosts. And maybe, after these two years of healing, she would find that it didn't hurt as much as she had feared.

After all, she had expected the sight of Kieran's football to fill her with agony, and instead it had brought only a lovely memory of a very happy night.

But it wasn't wise to think back on the day they'd found the football. The ball itself might not hold bitter memories, but the long morning of amazing love-making that had followed was going to be difficult to forget. If she let herself remember the scent of him, the taste of him, even for one piercing second, she wouldn't be able to go on.

So she forced it out of her mind, brought a paring knife out of the kitchen and opened the first box.

Most of the contents were easy enough to handle. A couple of Steve's old shirts. She set them aside for the donation bin. A few of his school books, not much of Steve there—he'd hardly ever picked up the things. Some of her own old clothes, also for the donation bin. Some bills she'd long ago forgotten, the final electricity statement for the house on Yarrow Street, the cancellation notice for a CD club Steve had joined without telling her.

And then she pulled up a crumpled piece of paper that she almost threw away as trash. Some instinct made her unfold it, though, and she realized that it was Steve's eleventh-grade fall progress report. He'd tried to hide it from her by balling it up and stuffing it under his mattress.

It was terrible. Three Ds, two Cs and a lone B, in art.

She had discovered it one morning while making his bed. Steve had been singing in the shower, getting ready for football practice. She had gone storming into the bathroom, waving the progress report in her hand, forgetting that, at seventeen, Steve would be horrified at the thought of his sister glimpsing him undressed.

He had refused to open the shower curtain until she threw him a towel. But she had waited, fussing and fuming, refusing to let him off the hook until he came out, dripping and sheepish, and explained how on earth he could have let his grades slip so badly.

Oh, she had been so angry! The steam in the bathroom had moistened the progress report, so that the letters had begun to run. But she kept waving it around, so disappointed in him, so furious…

And suddenly, staring down at that smeared piece of paper, Claire realized that she felt the same way right this minute.

She was very, very angry.

Not at Kieran. Not at herself.

At Steve.

Steve, who had lied to her. Steve, who had been drinking and driving, the one thing they had, after their mother's death, sworn they would never, never do. Steve, who had been so sunny and talented and special, but who had thrown it all away.

She sat down, trembling. This was it, then. This was the anger she'd been carrying around for two years, unable to put it down because she didn't even know exactly what it was. She hadn't dared to let herself know. How could she possibly be angry with her lost and broken little baby brother?

But she was. She was so angry it practically tore her heart to bits. Instead, she put her hands together and ripped the progress report to shreds, saying his name, over and over, with a harsh, blistered cry.

Oh, Stevie, Stevie, how could you?

Steve, who had been her only family. Her only laughter, her only confidante, her only reason for living.

Steve, who hadn't given a damn about any of that and had done this stupid, stupid thing.

Steve, who had let himself die, and had left her all alone.

CHAPTER NINETEEN

AT HEYDAY HIGH, the first week of the school year was always one big party, culminating in a student-teacher exhibition football game on Friday night. Ordinarily, Kieran, who coached the student team, loved the festive, slightly nutty event as much as anybody. But this year it was just an obligation he had to get through.

This year he had bigger things on his mind.

The minute the final score was posted, and the fans began storming the field, he intended to jump in his car and head for Richmond, where he was going to do his damnedest to make Claire forgive him and come back home.

He'd tried to be patient. She'd asked for time to think, and he'd given her almost two weeks. At first he'd found his heart twisting every time a petite brunette woman walked by. Lurching every time the telephone rang. But finally he realized that this wasn't going to be that easy. She wasn't just going to decide to come waltzing back into his life as if nothing had happened.

He was going to have to go and get her. He was going to have to grovel, beg, make promises, make a scene. He was going to have to expose how he really felt, without any assurance that she gave a damn. If she didn't, he was going to have to try something else. He was going to have to pull out all the stops, appeal to her love for their unborn child, her dreams of giving that child a happy life.

To heck with being a patient saint.

It was time to be a man.

Claire Strickland was not only the mother of his child. She was also the love of his life. With her, he could create the stability and permanence he'd always dreamed of. Without her, he'd fall apart. He wouldn't turn to a series of bimbo wives, as his father had, but only because he knew firsthand how wretched that was for the child. Instead, he'd just become the loneliest man on the planet.

"Coach, I think Principal Vogler must have nosed around in our playbook." Eddie Mackey, suited up for the first time in the striped uniform of the Heyday High Fighting Zebras, was bouncing with nervous energy. "See? They're lining up for the Snubnose Slide!"

Kieran looked, pretending to care. Compared to the rest of his life, what did this football game matter? But the students had their hearts set on stomping the teachers, and they were counting on Kieran to show them how. He tried to focus.

"No, that's not the slide," he told Eddie. "It's similar, but see how they've got both wide ends tucked in close?"

Eddie studied the field, his eyes intent over the black slashes of kohl the boys used to fight the glare from the klieg lights. Eddie had done nothing but study the playbook for almost two weeks now— partly because he wanted desperately to make a good showing, and partly because, considering he was grounded and on an academic warning, he didn't have much else to do.

He almost hadn't been able to join the team at all. Principal Vogler had been adamant at first, and Eddie's dad had required a lot of convincing, too. It didn't help that Eddie had refused to fork over the names of the students who had submitted his term papers as their own. But Kieran had backed him up in that, proud that the kid had been unwilling to lighten his own punishment by sloughing some of it off onto the shoulders of the other boys. A pettier person might have welcomed the chance for payback.

Besides, Kieran had a pretty good idea who the culprits were, and, as they were all on his team, he had his own ideas about how to make them pay for their sins.

In the end, both Vogler and Dr. Mackey had agreed, though they insisted on assigning Eddie a hundred hours of community service. He'd be tutoring elementary school kids who were having trouble reading. Between the tutoring and the football practice, he was too busy to get in trouble.

The whole, sordid Linda Tremel story they'd kept to themselves, as much to keep from humiliating Linda as anything else. Poor Linda. Kieran had confronted her immediately. It had been a struggle, but he had eventually talked her into getting some help. She'd even agreed to start Alcoholics Anonymous. He believed she would follow through—though she was defiant on the surface, she had seemed oddly relieved that someone had intervened. Even so, he planned to stay in close touch, just in case.

"Oh, yeah, I see," Eddie said finally. "The play they're running is kind of a cross between the Snubnose Slide and the Cherry Picker.'' He tilted his head, frowning. "How is *that* going to work?"

Kieran chuckled. "It isn't. Now go tell Overton I want to see him. These guys are going out on downs, and then I'm putting you in."

Eddie looked blank. "You are?"

"I am. If you have a hope in hell of being ready to play by the season opener, you're going to have to spend some time on the field. An exhibition game against a bunch of middle-aged pencil pushers seems as good a place as any to dirty up that uniform, don't you think?"

"Yes." Eddie shoved on his helmet. Even in the shadows, his eyes were round and gleaming. "I mean, yes, Coach."

Eddie trotted off obediently, and Kieran turned back to the game, smiling. He liked the kid's attitude. The other boys obviously hadn't forgiven Eddie yet, but they would, once they saw him throw a couple of touchdowns. Nothing succeeded like success. He only hoped that Eddie would be too smart to take Binky Potter back when she came sashaying over, as she undoubtedly would, shaking her pompoms and apologizing prettily.

The game seemed to go on forever. And, maybe because Kieran wasn't focusing as sharply as usual, the score was uncharacteristically tight. The teachers might be middle-aged pencil pushers, but they seemed to have an irritating ability to advance the ball down the field.

The lead seesawed. Jeff Metzler let Principal Vogler slip through a tackle—Jeff would be a long time living that one down—and Eddie's first pass was an interception. The teachers went ahead by seven.

But finally Eddie found his rhythm. He went long to Mark, who then ran it thirty yards to tie the game. At that point Kieran pulled Eddie out. One touchdown was enough to establish his credentials. And in the end the kid was still too green to count on. Kieran went back to Cullen, but he noticed that Cullen gave Eddie a congratulatory pat on the shoulder pad as the two of them passed on the field.

That was a start. That was enough for now.

In the end, the students got it together. They went ahead by two touchdowns, and from then on the teachers seemed to be discouraged. When the final whistle blew, the kids had won by twenty-one points.

You'd think they'd just clinched the Super Bowl. They came screaming up to Kieran, dumped a whole cooler of ice water over his head and swept him onto their shoulders.

He laughed as expected and allowed the nonsense to go on, but in the back of his mind a wry voice was suggesting that he probably should have let them lose. Now that he was soaking wet, he'd have to stop by the house and change before he could hit the road.

He mentally calculated the time. It was after ten o'clock now. If he went home right now, changed, then drove the speed limit the entire way, he still wouldn't get to Richmond before three.

Was that too late? Hell, no. When your heart was on the line, uptight Miss Manners prohibitions against middle-of-the-night visits didn't mean squat.

From his throne on the shoulders of his players, who were now marching him in front of the bleachers so that he could accept the cheers of his fans, Kieran had a bird's-eye view of the crowd.

For a minute, as they passed midfield, his heart

stopped. He thought he saw Claire. But he'd been having these hallucinations for two weeks now. Every tiny, graceful woman he glimpsed seemed to have her hair, her walk....

He leaned forward, almost off-balancing the boys who held him up. Yes, he saw her everywhere. But this woman...

This woman really was Claire.

She stood by the fence, and she was looking right at him. God, she was beautiful. She was the most beautiful woman in the world.

And, best of all, she was smiling. He tried to maintain eye contact, but the jostling, chanting march was so bumpy he could hardly manage it. As they drew closer, he thought he saw her holding something up in her hand, as if she wanted him to see it.

He squinted around the drops of cold water that still dripped from his hair. She was definitely holding something. She was shaking it a little, teasingly. And finally he realized what it was. It was a small plush toy shaped like a football.

He cocked his head, silently posing a half question. But she merely continued to smile.

At that moment, the football players noticed her, too.

"Hey, look! It's Mrs. McClintock," Eddie Mackey called out. "This way!"

The ridiculous parade swung sharply in Claire's direction, nearly knocking Kieran to the ground. They carried him closer, and finally, ceremoniously, they set him down in front of his wife.

He was suddenly out of breath and speechless. He felt as if he'd been running, not riding the shoulders of those laughing, chanting boys. But what was the point of saying a single word, anyhow? He just wanted to take her in his arms and hold her so tightly she could never disappear again.

But he couldn't. Too many things remained unresolved between them.

"Hi," he said. *Wonderful beginning.* He had a mental script the size of *War and Peace* prepared, like a lawyer who had been preparing for his great Supreme Court summation. He had a list of all the reasons why she should give him another chance. He had all the promises lined up, all the ways in which he was going to make it up to her for everything, for Steve, for the stupid lawyers, for the unwanted baby, for *everything*.

But he hadn't expected to deliver it here, soaking wet and in front of about two thousand people, many of whom had heard gossip about their separation and couldn't wait to see whether she was going to kiss him or slap him.

He took her arm and led her off to the edge of the bleachers, the only spot with even a hint of privacy. And then, taking a deep breath, he settled for saying the first honest, simple thing that occurred to him.

"I've missed you," he said. "I missed you so much I thought I'd go crazy."

She smiled softly, as if maybe she sensed that the statement was merely the tip of the emotional iceberg.

"I've missed you, too," she said. "It's been a very...difficult two weeks."

That was good. Not that he wanted her to suffer, but it would have killed him to think she hadn't minded their separation at all.

"I'm sorry," he said impulsively. "I'm just so

damn sorry, Claire. I've made so many mistakes, and I don't know how to fix any of them."

"I know," she said.

"I was coming to Richmond tonight, to tell you that. I can't bring Steve back, but if you'll just come home to me, I'll spend the rest of my life making it up to you the best I can. Let me try to make you happy, Claire. Whatever you want, I'll try to give it to you."

"You don't have to make anything up to me," she said. "That's why I came here today, to tell you that."

"But I do," he said.

"No, Kieran. Listen." She lifted her chin, in that way she had. It always meant she was trying to access a little extra courage. "I have finally realized that you aren't responsible for what happened to Steve. I've been focusing my anger on you because I couldn't bear to be angry with the person who was really responsible. I couldn't bear to be angry with Steve."

He just looked at her, stunned. Her voice was so steady, and her eyes, though still sad, were unclouded. Was it possible she actually meant this?

"I am responsible," he said. "At least partly. I should have told you the minute I discovered what he was up to."

"Yes, and I should have watched him more carefully. There's plenty of blame to go around. But Steve had the ultimate responsibility to make good decisions, and he simply didn't do it. I wanted you to know that I've finally come to terms with that."

She looked around the football field. "This is the first time I've been back here since he died, did you know that? I came to Heyday early today, and I've made a visit to each of the places that have frightened me for so long. I went to Poplar Hill." She closed her eyes. "I even put flowers on his grave."

"Oh, God, Claire—"

She touched his arm. "It's okay. I'm okay. I think I'm finally ready to put the past behind me and start thinking about the future."

He held his breath. The future. How did she see that now? Had anything changed? Was he going to be allowed to play any part in it?

"Claire, wait. Don't talk about the future yet. Not until I say something important, something I should have said a long time ago. I've made a lot of mistakes in all this, but the biggest one was not ever telling you how much I love you."

She began to speak, but he reached out and touched her cheek, her satin-warm, beautiful cheek, and stilled the words.

"I think I have loved you for years," he said. "Only I was such a fool I didn't see it. How could I believe I could be so lucky? How could I find a wife, a family, a lover, a friend—and every dream I ever dreamed—all in one woman?"

Her eyes sparkled in the bright field lights, as if she might be on the edge of tears. All around them people were laughing and shoving and waving Fighting Zebra flags, but Kieran and Claire seemed to exist in a small cocoon of silence. Everything else slid out of focus as he waited for her response.

"You don't have to say all this." She reached up and shakily wiped away a glistening drop from her cheek. "I have come back, and I'll stay if you want me to. We can make it work. We can make a family. You don't have to—"

"Yes, I do. I have to say it because I'll burn up inside if I don't. I love you. I love you." He reached out and took her in his arms. "I love you."

She held back just an instant. Her gaze searched every inch of his face.

"I love you, too," she whispered, finally.

She came to him easily, as if she belonged there, as if all the terrors of the past two weeks had been no more than a long, absurd nightmare. She rested her head on his shoulder, as if she didn't even notice that he was soaking wet. He tightened his arms, and kissed his wife's soft hair.

His wife.

His one and only wife.

He smiled, and, ducking his head, found the delicate shell of her ear, and he kissed that, too. She nestled closer, murmuring with a sound that made him think of naked skin and hungry bodies threaded together in beams of sunlight.

"Take me home, Claire," he said. "Take me home and make love to me again."

She lifted her face, laughing. "Soon," she said. "Don't you want the present I brought you?"

She held up the little football and shook it. A small, sweet chime inside it rang. It sounded like wedding bells.

"What is it?"

"It's for the baby," she said, still smiling. "If you're going to raise a star quarterback, I hear you have to plant the love of football early."

"A star—" He inhaled sharply. "Does this mean

you've had the ultrasound? Does this mean you know—''

She slid the football down between them, slipping it into the palm of his hand. It was so small, he thought numbly. So tiny, for a tiny baby.

''The test—'' He was suddenly too overcome to talk intelligently. ''You've found out? It's going to be a boy?''

She shook her head with a tolerant affection.

''Good heavens, Coach McClintock. When did you get to be such a chauvinist?'' She took hold of his other hand and brought it in to rest against the almost imperceptible swell of her stomach. ''I'd like you to meet the next star McClintock quarterback, who is very much a girl.''

*Turn the page for an excerpt from THE
SINNER, The second book in* THE
HEROES OF HEYDAY *trilogy by
Kathleen O'Brien.*

*THE SINNER (Harlequin Superromance
#1249) is available in January 2005.*

CHAPTER ONE

"No KIDDING, that's...your job? You get *paid* to guard Lara Lynmore's body?"

Bryce McClintock flicked a look at the name tag of the stammering young man next to him. Ted Barnes, Assistant Event Manager, Eldorado Hotels. Ted was a just-barely twenty-something kid whose silver, European-cut suit said he wanted to be all Hollywood glamour, but whose freckled face said he'd just stepped off the bus from Iowa.

The way the kid's mouth hung open as he looked at Lara Lynmore gave him away, too. Real Hollywood types took celebrities for granted. And Lara Lynmore wasn't even technically a "star" yet. Although ever since her first leading role, as Bess, the doomed black-eyed beauty in the high-budget movie version of "The Highwayman," had premiered this summer, she was getting pretty close.

Close enough to have attracted about a million innocent, panting fans, like this guy.

And one stalker, an obsessed former stuntman named Kenny Boggs.

Kenny wasn't just annoying. He was dangerous. Bryce had seen the irrational, increasingly hostile letters the stuntman had sent to Lara Lynmore after she rejected him. He'd heard the threats on her telephone recorder. Kenny meant business.

Which was why Bryce who had just taken early retirement from the FBI so that he could bum around in the Bahamas, parasailing and beating the house at blackjack, found himself in the idiotic position of working as a bodyguard for America's Sweetheart.

However, Ted wasn't to blame for Bryce's career problems. Ted was just a sweet sap who was going to break his corn-fed heart trying to Be Somebody, and then slink home to marry the patient girl who would never guess that every time her sensible husband made love to her, he'd be thinking of Lara Lynmore.

So instead of telling him to buzz off, as he had planned, Bryce just nodded. "Yeah. I'm her bodyguard. But it's no big deal. It's just a job."

A sighing silence. Though Bryce didn't want to take his eyes off the crowd for long, he glanced over at the kid one more time. Was that drool he saw shining at the edge of his open mouth? *God.*

"Movie stars are people, Ted. They're pretty, but they're just people."

Ted didn't even blink. "Not Lara," he whispered. "Lara Lynmore isn't just people. Look at her."

Bryce didn't have to look at Lara to know what Ted was talking about, but he did. And he saw what he'd seen every day, every night, for the past six weeks. A twenty-six-year-old brunette with the long-legged, ripe-breasted body of a wet-dream goddess and the sweet, wide-eyed face of the girl you'd loved and lost in high school.

It was that off-kilter combination that got you. Bryce was tough—he prided himself on it—but even he wasn't so tough he didn't feel it. It was like a one-two punch, sharp and below the belt.

Today Lara was giving a speech to the ladies of the Breast Cancer Awareness luncheon, so she wasn't wearing her usual party-girl getup—no dagger-cut necklines, no sequins, no peekaboo lace.

Which wasn't to say *no sex*. She looked sexy as hell in a feminine rendition of the riding clothes seen in *The Highwayman*. A pair of tight-fitting white breeches, a cardinal-red jacket, a white ruffled kerchief at her throat pinned by a simple sparkling diamond. A red ribbon gathered her long, dark hair at her neck and let it spill down her back all the way to her fantastic butt.

Bryce shifted and tightened his jaw. Ted from Iowa might be right. Lara Lynmore really wasn't just an ordinary person. She was dangerously potent, the female equivalent of heroin. People who ventured too close could get addicted, get crazy, get hurt.

Bryce wondered what Ted would think if he knew that, just last night, Bryce had taken a willing Lara Lynmore down to her lacy under-nothings, right there on her living-room sofa—and had chosen to stop there. To walk away empty-handed.

He'd think Bryce was nuts; that's what he'd think. Bryce half thought so himself. He still wasn't sure what had stopped him. God knew this job had teased every one of his hormones into a raging fury. It was like some kind of torture, standing within inches of this high-octane beauty 24/7 trying to keep those hormones on a leash. No wonder they'd ended up panty-dancing on the sofa last night.

Maybe what had stopped him was the thought of Darryl, Lara's lawyer. Darryl, who had roped Bryce into this bodyguarding gig by playing on an old law-school friendship. *Just for a few days.* Darryl had begged, until California's best professional bodyguard was free and could take over.

You're the only one I can trust to control this until the professional can take over. It's serious, Bryce. This nut wants to kill her.

A few days, like hell. That had been six weeks ago. Finally, last night, just in the nick of time, just before the panties came off, the new bodyguard had called to say he could start tomorrow.

Which meant Bryce only had to get through today, and then he was home free.

And, thankfully, today looked like a piece of cake. He'd already vetted the help, everything from the waiters and chefs to good old Ted here. He'd made the setup crew change the position of Lara's podium—they'd put it in the center of the dais, but he needed it closer to the wings where he'd be stationed.

And then, making himself truly popular, he'd made them remove the first row of tables, which was much too close to the dais.

That had improved the situation, though even now, things were a little too tight to be ideal. But when he looked out and saw the hundreds of pink hats and light blue, yellow and pink party frocks in the audience, he felt better. The Breast Cancer Awareness luncheon was an ocean of estrogen punctuated by a few slim, white-clad waiters circulating gracefully among the tables.

A corky muscle-man like Kenny Boggs would stand out in this crowd like a circus clown in a cemetery.

"And, in conclusion—" Lara's voice sounded good over the microphone, which accentuated its throaty undertones. "I'd like to thank all of you for—"

Bryce had seen a copy of her speech. Three more sentences, and they were out of here.

Suddenly, without reason, his heartbeat quickened, instinct sending a jolt of adrenaline through his system. Something was wrong.

His eyes narrowed, scanning rapidly over the smiling crowd. Damn it. Every instinct he owned was telling him something was wrong. *What was it?*

It was... Scanning... Scanning...

It was that waiter. That waiter in front, the one who was just a little broader in the shoulders than the others. The one who had a tray in his hand, but was walking between tables instead of slowly rotating around just one, as all the other waiters were doing, picking up uneaten fruit tarts.

Bryce edged forward for a better look. What in hell was the guy doing? His serpentine movements were bringing him ever closer to the dais. Still, it wasn't Kenny. Kenny Boggs had blond hair, and this guy was...

Shit. Bryce came out from behind the dais just as the waiter looked up. It *was* Kenny, what a fool, what a maniac, here of all places, even with dyed hair and a uniform he should have known—

Their eyes met for one broken edge of a second, but it was enough to warn the muscle-bound psycho that he'd been made.

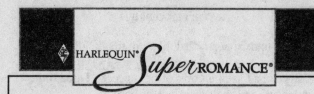

Seattle after Midnight
by C.J. Carmichael
(Superromance #1240)
On sale November 2004

"Hello, Seattle. Welcome to 'Georgia after
Midnight,' the show for lonely hearts
and lovers...."

P.I. Pierce Harding can't resist listening to
Georgia Lamont's late-night radio show.
Something about her sultry voice calls to him.
But Georgia has also attracted an unwanted
listener, one who crosses the line between fan
and fanatic. When the danger escalates,
Pierce knows that he will do anything to keep
Georgia safe. Even risk his heart...

Available wherever Harlequin books are sold

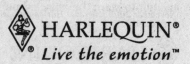

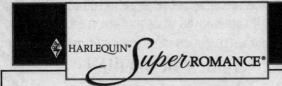

A Family Christmas
by Carrie Alexander

(Harlequin Superromance #1239)

All Rose Robbin ever wanted was a family
Christmas—just like the ones she'd seen on TV—but
being a Robbin (one of those Robbins) pretty much
guaranteed she'd never get one. Especially after
circumstances had her living "down" to
everyone else's expectations.

After a long absence, Rose is back in Alouette,
primarily to help out her impossible-to-please mother,
but also to keep tabs on the child she wasn't allowed
to keep. Working hard, helping her mother and trying
to steal glimpses of her child seem to be all that's in
Wild Rose's future—until the day single father
Evan Grant catches her in the act.

NORTH COUNTRY
Stories

Alouette, Michigan.
Located high on the Upper
Peninsula—home to strong
men, stalwart women and
lots and lots of trees.

Available in November 2004 wherever Harlequin books are sold

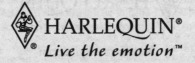

HARLEQUIN®
Live the emotion™

If you enjoyed what you just read,
then we've got an offer you can't resist!

Take 2 bestselling love stories FREE!

Plus get a FREE surprise gift!

Clip this page and mail it to Harlequin Reader Service®

IN U.S.A.
3010 Walden Ave.
P.O. Box 1867
Buffalo, N.Y. 14240-1867

IN CANADA
P.O. Box 609
Fort Erie, Ontario
L2A 5X3

YES! Please send me 2 free Harlequin Superromance® novels and my free surprise gift. After receiving them, if I don't wish to receive anymore, I can return the shipping statement marked cancel. If I don't cancel, I will receive 6 brand-new novels every month, before they're available in stores. In the U.S.A., bill me at the bargain price of $4.69 plus 25¢ shipping and handling per book and applicable sales tax, if any*. In Canada, bill me at the bargain price of $5.24 plus 25¢ shipping and handling per book and applicable taxes**. That's the complete price, and a savings of at least 10% off the cover prices—what a great deal! I understand that accepting the 2 free books and gift places me under no obligation ever to buy any books. I can always return a shipment and cancel at any time. Even if I never buy another book from Harlequin, the 2 free books and gift are mine to keep forever.

135 HDN DZ7W
336 HDN DZ7X

Name	(PLEASE PRINT)	
Address	Apt.#	
City	State/Prov.	Zip/Postal Code

Not valid to current Harlequin Superromance® subscribers.

Want to try two free books from another series?
Call 1-800-873-8635 or visit www.morefreebooks.com.

* Terms and prices subject to change without notice. Sales tax applicable in N.Y.
** Canadian residents will be charged applicable provincial taxes and GST.
All orders subject to approval. Offer limited to one per household.
® are registered trademarks owned and used by the trademark owner and its licensee.

SUP04R

©2004 Harlequin Enterprises Limited

Christmas comes to

HARLEQUIN ROMANCE®

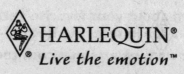

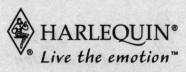

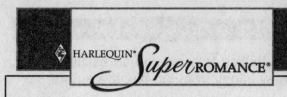

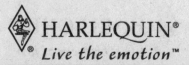